CROOKED PARADISE #4

EVA CHANCE
& HARLOW KING

Lethal Empress

Book 4 in the Crooked Paradise series

All rights reserved. This book or any portion thereof may not be reproduced or used in any manner without the express written permission of the author, except for the use of brief quotations in a book review.

This is a work of fiction. Any resemblance to actual persons, living or dead, or actual events is purely coincidental.

First Digital Edition, 2021

Copyright © 2021 Eva Chance & Harlow King

Cover design: Jodielocks Designs

Ebook ISBN: 978-1-990338-15-1

Paperback ISBN: 978-1-990338-24-3

Mercy

I woke up gasping, images of my men dropping like flies around me flashing through my mind. Someone had attacked us—we'd been hit by darts—and then everything had gone dark.

My eyes popped open, and the world swam for a moment. My head was throbbing, and there was a pinch of pain on the side of my neck where the needle had hit me. My body burned to move, to defend myself and the guys if they were still with me, but I was too dizzy to orient myself... Where the hell *was* I?

As my vision cleared, everything around me came into sharper focus. I was lying on my back in a large room. The air was warm, and a soft glow washed over me from a crystalline fixture encased in an elaborate molding on the high ceiling. My head rested on a silky pillow. I managed to sit up and found that the rest of me had been lying on a thick Persian carpet.

Whoever had brought me here had taken a whole lot more care in my comfort than I'd have expected. I'd have assumed it'd been Xavier or someone else with the Storm behind the attack, but they'd never treated me anywhere near this gently before.

Not just me—us. My men were spread out on the rug around me, each with their own pillow under their heads. If I hadn't known better, I'd have thought they were having a good night's sleep.

I scooted toward Rowan, who was nearest to me, and gripped his shoulder. "Rowan," I said urgently, giving him a shake. "Wake up." When he didn't respond, I slapped him lightly on his cheeks.

His eyes opened, and he blinked up at me as if trying to place me. His voice came out creaky. "Mercy?" Then all at once, he tried to sit up—too fast. His body swayed with what I guessed was the same dizziness I'd been hit with when I first woke up.

"Careful," I said. "Somebody sedated us. It takes its time wearing off."

Rowan tensed, his gaze flicking around the room as he ran his hand over his short blond hair. "Who grabbed us? What the hell is going on?"

"I don't know. I didn't see anyone when it happened, and no one's been around since I woke up."

At my other side, Wylder groaned and rubbed his forehead, swiping away the auburn strands that had fallen rumpled across it. Gideon and Kaige were stirring as well. At least they all appeared to be *alive*. These days, with everything we'd been through, I'd count that as a blessing.

Wylder looked at me, concern darkening his bright green eyes. "Are you okay?"

I stretched my arms and rolled my head experimentally. The dizziness was gone, and the pain in my neck had already faded. "I'm fine," I said. "For now."

With a jolt of fear, my hands dropped to my sides. I was still wearing the same clothes as I remembered, but my weapons—my gun and my knife—were gone. So was my phone. Shit. It wasn't surprising, but the loss still made me feel uncomfortably naked.

Kaige was frowning as he checked himself over. His massive brawn flexed beneath his fitted tee. "My gun's been taken too. Who the fuck is messing with us?"

Gideon winced when he came up with nothing as well. I wouldn't be surprised if he was more bothered by his missing phone than his lack of weaponry. With his tongue flicking over his lip ring, he peered around the posh room with its old-fashioned stylings and knit his brow. "This is very strange. They obviously could have killed us, but they didn't. So they must want something from us other than our lives."

Wylder arched an eyebrow. "Which means we can assume it wasn't Xavier, right? That fucker *definitely* wanted to mount all of our heads on pikes."

"Yeah," I said, pushing myself to my feet taking in the rest of the space. A long, polished oak table stood at the other end of the room with five matching chairs on either side. A few pieces of what looked like expensive artwork hung on the walls. "But who else would have wanted to take us captive? And why leave us here like this? They haven't even restrained us."

"They figure we don't stand a chance of escaping even without tying us up," Wylder muttered, looking offended by the implication.

Kaige focused on the door. He got up, wobbling for a second, and marched over to try the curved handle. It jarred in his hand, locked. He growled at it. "We need to get the fuck out of here."

"Easier said than done," Rowan murmured as he stood.

There was a huge bay window, but it was locked too, with iron bars running over the panes so even breaking the glass wouldn't get us far. Wylder walked past it along the length of the room. I peered at the daylight showing through the window. It was impossible to tell how many hours had passed since we'd been taken or even whether it was still the same day, and I found it jarring to not have any sense of the actual time.

"How *long* have we been here?" Wylder said abruptly. "Did I miss Roland's funeral? If these assholes stopped me from being there for my brother... Damn it!" He slammed his fist into the wall.

"Wylder," I said, going to him and placing a hand on his shoulder.

He stiffened, guilt etched all over his face. "It was the least I could do for him, Mercy. His last send-off. He deserved it."

"He does, and you'll be there when it happens." I didn't know if that was true, but I had no idea how else to console him. I hadn't gotten to have a last send-off for my family either. At some point, when I didn't have a psycho breathing down my neck, I could go pick up the ashes from the coroner... Maybe I could have some kind of ceremony then.

As that thought passed through my mind, a key clicked in the lock on the other side of the door. We all froze.

Before we had a chance to come up with any kind of plan, the door flew open and two men and a woman strode into the room. They were dressed in collared shirts and dress pants as if they were here for a business meeting and not a kidnapping, but I could make out the outline of a holster at each of their hips. They were armed. One of the men rested his hand on his weapon without taking it out—just a reminder that he could if he needed to.

We all eyed them warily, but the woman simply gave us a mild smile. "We'd appreciate it if you'd please sit down at the table. Our boss will be with you shortly."

"Your boss?" Wylder demanded. "Who the fuck is that, and where the hell are we?"

The woman didn't flinch at his hostile tone. She motioned toward the table. "Please, just sit, and he'll explain everything."

I exchanged a glance with the guys. This was all very weird, but we *did* want an explanation, and it didn't look like we were getting out of here easily anyway. We were probably better off finding out what we were up against.

We nodded in mutual understanding and turned toward the table, but Wylder hesitated. "What time is it?" he asked the woman. "How long have we been here?

"It's just past noon," she said without needing to check. "You arrived about an hour ago."

His shoulders came down an inch. The funeral had been scheduled for four o'clock, if I remembered right. He'd still have a chance to get there... if this "boss" had any intention of letting us leave after he'd given his explanation.

We walked over to the table and by unspoken agreement sat in the chairs facing the door. I'd rather have a wall at my back, and I'd bet the guys felt the same way. The three figures who'd ordered us to sit there sauntered over but stayed standing at the edges of the room.

I shifted on my seat, itching for answers. Thankfully, I didn't have to wait long. The door opened again, and a silver-haired man stepped into the room, flanked by two other men who looked like bodyguards.

The man in the middle was obviously the guy in charge. He wasn't all that tall, but his broad shoulders filled out his expensive suit, and he gave off an aura of power that quivered over my skin even from across the room. His slate gray hair was slicked close to his knobby skull, which made his thick eyebrows stand out even more over his penetrating eyes. As he walked over to the table with even but unhurried strides, I placed him in his mid to late fifties.

He was a total stranger. I'd have remembered that face if I'd seen it before. The guys' expressions showed the same confusion I felt.

The man sat in the seat in the center, opposite Wylder. His bodyguards stayed standing behind the chairs on either side of him. He considered Wylder, then me, then the other guys, his gaze returning to the Noble heir after a moment.

"Wylder Noble," he said in a smooth conversational tone, and tipped his head to me as well. "And Mercy Katz. The heirs to two of the most powerful gangs in Paradise Bend, even if that's not saying much."

I bristled automatically. "Who the hell are *you?*"

He showed no sign that my tone affected him. "I'm the man who really owns everything you believe is yours."

Wylder's hands clenched where they were resting on the tabletop. "I thought you were going to explain why you dragged us here. All I'm hearing so far is cryptic bullshit."

A hint of a smile tugged at the corners of the man's lips over his narrow, jutting chin. "Cryptic, maybe, but not bullshit at all. There's a lot you don't know about how the world works, Mr. Noble. But I know a lot about all of you already." His gaze flicked along the table. "Kaige Maddon, the enforcer with an anger problem. Rowan Finlay, the negotiator and peacekeeper. And Gideon Whitlock, the brains locked in a body that betrays him."

Gideon's back went rigid. "Anyone could have known that," he said in a low voice as cool as his dyed blue hair.

"I'm only scraping the surface." The man folded his hands in front of him and gave us a real smile, and just like that, I was sure he meant everything he said. A chill ran down my back.

"I'd still like your explanation," I said.

"Of course you would. It'll just be difficult for you to wrap your heads around it." He drew in a breath. "Let me start by apologizing for the abrupt way I had you brought to me. Time was of the essence, and I didn't want to risk any complications in securing your cooperation. I've done you no harm, and I'll let you go once you've heard my proposal. I've been watching the situation in Paradise Bend for some time now, and it's become clear that you could be valuable allies there."

"Allies in what?" Wylder said. "What proposal? Why should we listen to a damn thing you say?"

The man fixed his gaze on the Noble heir. "Because I really do own every inch of ground and every brick on every property you consider your own. Did you honestly believe that the Nobles were the highest level of power a criminal organization could reach? You have lesser gangs paying tribute to you, and in turn those above you take their cut."

Wylder frowned. "We don't pay tithe to anyone."

"Oh, but you do. Those of us higher up simply have more subtle ways of collecting our dues." The man cocked his head. "Haven't you wondered about the recent surge in conflict in your county? Where all these unexpected intruders are coming from and why?"

"Are you responsible for that?" Kaige burst out, looking ready to jump over the table and throttle the guy if he said yes.

The man chuckled darkly. "No, I'm trying to put a stop to it. It's actually very simple. I'm part of a group of thirteen who call ourselves the Devil's Dozen. We each have a code name: I go by 'the Long Night.'

Between us, we control all the illicit and underground businesses throughout the world. Each of us has holdings on various continents, our own territories that we rule over from behind the scenes and benefit from. Every criminal who rises at all above the level of petty pickpocket answers to us, whether they know it or not. And Paradise Bend is part of my domain."

"I've never heard anyone mention the Long Night or the Devil's Dozen," Gideon said.

"Which speaks to our expertise in secrecy." The man who called himself the Long Night smiled thinly. "Most who get far enough to find out that much about us are either working directly for us or don't live to tell the tale elsewhere. You can consider yourselves a lucky exception—for now."

I wasn't sure if I bought his story, but *he* sure seemed to believe it. Another shiver ran down my back. "Are you going to tell us why you're making an exception?"

The Long Night gave a vague wave of his hand. "There's always jockeying for power between the Devil's Dozen members. It's hard to avoid it among master criminals, as I'm sure you can imagine. I've been distracted by other concerns recently, and the Nobles' continuing expansion throughout the state—with excellent financial results—caught the eye of a couple of my rivals. They set their sights on Paradise Bend and decided they'd grab it and everything associated with the organizations there out from under me before I realized what was happening."

He shook his head, apparently at the folly of those

rivals, and something clicked in my head. This tall tale suddenly made a sickening sort of sense.

"The Storm," I said, my voice coming out in a hush. "And the Red Shark. That's who you're talking about—they're in the Devil's Dozen too, with the same kind of crazy code names."

And this was why we'd never heard of them before, hadn't had any idea where they'd come from. We'd been caught in the middle of a territory war involving gangs bigger than any of us could have dreamed existed before this meeting.

"Aren't you a clever little thing?" the Long Night said with apparent amusement. I hated the patronizing note in his tone. Maybe this superiority complex came automatically with the knowledge that you reigned supreme over vast territories and millions of people, but that didn't mean I had to like it.

"What is up with the weird names anyway?" Kaige asked, looking bewildered.

"They're connected to traditional labels for the full moons, which are important to us for reasons you don't need to know," the Long Night said, and turned his attention back to me and Wylder. "Let's focus on where you come in."

Wylder's jaw had hardened. "Yeah, I'm still waiting to hear about that. If you're so all-powerful, why don't you get rid of the idiots who're trashing our home? Why're you sitting back and letting us take all the blows?"

"At this moment, I have other, rather pressing responsibilities," the Long Night said. "I've seen what you can do even with your meager resources, and it's rather impressive. The Red Shark has backed off, but the Storm's forces remain. Before I expend energy and manpower I'd prefer stayed elsewhere, I'd like to give you a chance to clean up the mess for me."

"You want us to do your dirty work, possibly because you see us as expendable," Rowan said evenly. "Why would we help you?"

The Long Night leaned forward on the table, his hands clasped in front of him. "I intend to protect what's mine and keep my reputation intact. I need this conflict to end soon if I'm going to ensure that none of the others in the Devil's Dozen get ideas about my territories being vulnerable."

"That doesn't answer his question," Gideon said evenly.

The older man gave him a baleful look. "I was getting to that. I'll offer you support in the form of information about the Storm's operations and a certain amount of supplies. If you can run the Storm's people out of Paradise Bend for good within a week, I'll support both Mr. Noble and Miss Katz in running your respective organizations as you see fit. Besides that, I have other business opportunities to offer you in the long run once you're done with the Storm."

"Within a week?" I repeated. "That hardly gives us any time at all."

The Long Night looked at me with his hollowed eyes. "That's all I can afford before the risk to my status becomes too great. You're lucky I'm offering you any opportunity at all. If you don't come through, I'll have to crack down on the fighting with everything I have—and that'll mean a total clearing of the board. There won't be anything left for you to call home, and none of you will be around to mourn that loss. I'll knock down the Nobles and the Claws and everyone else with a stake in the underground businesses of the county and set up people who answer directly to me to run things."

The Long Night's gaze slid across us as we all took in that statement. His smile turned grim. "So, what do you say? Will you take the deal, or would you rather die?"

Mercy

WITH THE LONG NIGHT'S LAST WORDS RINGING IN my ears, I blanched. "You're not serious. You'd slaughter *everyone* in all the gangs—?"

The Long Night raised an eyebrow. "I wouldn't say it if I wasn't serious. I need it to be clear to everyone watching that I'm in control. It's up to you whether the law is laid down by you two in my stead or whether I have to rain down hellfire myself to get it done. If you aren't an asset to me, then you're a liability I can't afford to keep around."

Beside me, Wylder shook his head vehemently. "I don't understand. All we need is more time—"

"My colleagues have left me no choice," the older man said. "If things continue the way they are, extreme measures will be necessary. I can't have my authority challenged elsewhere over this squabble here." He spoke as if this was nothing more than business to him, as if he wasn't talking about destroying hundreds of lives. And maybe he *didn't* care.

I glanced at Wylder, whose jaw was clenched, his fists bunched at his sides. The stakes were so high, and if we failed, we'd lose everything.

Gideon gave the Long Night a narrow look. "I wonder if you're setting us up for failure. Using us to thin your enemy's ranks so there's less for you to clean up when you do have to sweep in."

"I trust your capabilities." The Long Night studied Gideon and then Wylder. "Maybe you don't feel the same."

I couldn't keep quiet. "The Storm has a massive presence in the Bend already. If you actually want to give us a chance, make it a real one."

"Unfortunately, Miss Katz, not everything is about you. Time is slipping away from us, and every moment you waste here arguing with me about it is another precious second lost that threatens my empire. And if you think that what you've seen so far is even a quarter of the actual size of Storm's army, you're very, very wrong."

Fear coiled in my gut. He didn't seem like it on the surface, but the Long Night was just as terrible as the Storm or the Red Shark. There was clearly a reason this group that called themselves the Devil's Dozen had been able to maintain control from the shadows over the decades. They were ruthless.

I knew without a doubt that the Long Night would make good on his promise to sweep through the county and kill anyone who stood in the way of his power. In my mind's eyes, I already saw the destruction. My ears echoed with the imagined screams as a massacre of everyone who'd ever associated with any of the gangs in Paradise Bend—Nobles, Claws, Steel Knights, or the many other smaller outfits—raged through the streets.

I cleared my throat and glanced at Wylder before turning back to the Long Night. We couldn't make a decision this huge and horrible with the man insisting on it breathing down our necks. "If you don't mind," I said, "I think we should take a few minutes to discuss this in private, just between the five of us."

"Very well," the Long Night said. "I respect that you want to take your time before making any commitments. Just remember that the clock starts ticking soon. I hope to hear a positive response from your side."

He rose from his chair and signaled to his people. Both the bodyguards who'd arrived with him and the three figures who'd entered ahead of him pulled in around him and walked with him out of the room. They closed the door behind them until it was only the five of us.

The second we were alone, Gideon's gaze darted along the molded details of the ceiling. "I'm not sure how 'private' this conversation really is. I find it hard to believe that a man in his position wouldn't have cameras on us."

Rowan sighed. "Well, there's nothing we can do about *that*. He's going to find out what we decide anyway."

Wylder pulled his chair back and to the side so he

could face me better. "Did you have specific thoughts you wanted to share?"

I rubbed my temple. "I don't know. It's so much to take in. But I was having a hard time even *thinking* with him sitting there staring at us."

"Are we really considering tying ourselves to this guy?" Kaige asked, grimacing.

"If what he said is true, then we've been tied to him all along," Wylder pointed out. "He's apparently been skimming money from the Noble businesses for years. Dad's never mentioned anything—maybe this Devil's Dozen organization really does have methods to take their tithe that can go unnoticed. I guess it wouldn't be impossible with all the stages of money laundering and the rest. There's a lot of cash changing hands all the time."

Kaige shook his head, the chain with his father's dog tags sliding against his neck with the movement. "It's wild, though. A shadowy organization created by creepy old men with an obsession with the full moon, and they run all the criminal business in the world? It feels like I've tripped into some crazy movie."

"It might sound strange, but I've always had the impression there might be a higher force above us," Gideon said. "Certain things happen too smoothly or conveniently."

Kaige snorted. "I think you're confusing Jesus with code-named gangsters."

Gideon rolled his eyes at the bigger guy before turning to us. "I definitely don't see any reason to doubt the Long Night's version of what's happened in the Bend. Think about it: the Storm's and the Red Shark's people showed up seemingly out of nowhere, and we'd never heard about them before. That's because they aren't just regular street gangs fighting for territories. They're the true kings of the underworld."

"And if we hope to win against one of them, we probably need the inside knowledge this guy can give us," I said. "The Storm has too much power over us right now, at least if we want to end things quickly."

"Can we trust the Long Night to keep his word?" Rowan said.

"I sure as hell don't," Kaige muttered, swiping his hand over his dark buzzcut. "He calls himself the Long Night, for fuck's sake. He's fucking looney tunes."

Gideon nodded. "I don't know about his sanity, but he could be playing at something he's not telling us about, manipulating us." He paused. "Although this is a very elaborate ruse, if so."

"Any deal with him is a deal with the devil," Wylder said with a growl in his voice. "He admitted it himself—he's one of them, which means he's equally or even more dangerous than either the Storm or the Red Shark. Look at what he's already threatened to do."

I sucked in my breath, my thoughts finally settling into some kind of order. "I totally agree that he's dangerous and that we can't really trust him. But how can we say no? The alternative is to let him come in and steamroll over not just the Storm's people but all the rest of us. From the way he's talking, he doesn't care if he has to paint the whole county in blood just to clean the slate—people from all the gangs, innocents caught in the crossfire. It'll be awful."

Wylder frowned, but I could see the wheels turning in his head.

"He gave us one week," Kaige said. "We can't do shit in that."

"It's still better than the no time at all we'd have if we refuse to even try," I said. "The Long Night is going to give us information and resources—that help might be enough for us to get the upper hand quickly."

Rowan tipped his head toward me. "I agree with Mercy. This way at least we get a chance to do things our way and survive. Lord knows what will happen if he sends his own men in."

"Chaos," I said, thinking back to my vision. "Utter, bloody chaos." The Long Night's words echoed in my head, *There won't be anything left for you to call home.*

Wylder let out a rough breath. "I see what you're saying, and I know you're right. No way in hell am I giving up and rolling over. Winning this war is going to be hard for more reasons than just the Storm, though."

I looked at him with a tug of my heart. "What do you mean?"

"This guy came to me instead of my dad. Dad won't be happy about that, which is just going to add to the friction that's already there between us." He closed his eyes for a second, his expression tightening, and I knew he'd made a decision. My heart thumped faster.

I couldn't fight for the Bend on my own, and the other guys would follow Wylder's lead. I needed him by my side.

Wylder opened his eyes to gaze at the closed door for a long moment. Then he said, "There's nothing we can do about Dad's hurt feelings now. We have to make the best of what we have. And that means fighting as hard as we fucking can. It's still our territory too, and we're not going to let any asshole crash in and take it from us, no matter what special secret group he's part of."

My body began to thrum with anticipation. Now that we were agreed, I didn't want to wait to get started. I could feel the seconds passing us by.

"They'll never own Paradise Bend, not really," Wylder finished.

I sat up straighter in my chair and looked at the other guys. "Everyone's on board?"

Rowan and Gideon nodded despite their solemn expressions.

Kaige sighed. "I still think this is insane, but I don't think it's going to stop being insane no matter what I do. I'll always have your backs."

"I guess we'd better let him know, then," I said.

Gideon scanned the room again. "Is there a button somewhere we can press, or...?"

We examined our surroundings for a few minutes, and finally Rowan went over to the door and knocked on it loudly. One of the men in the collared shirts opened it and peered inside. Behind him, I could see the long stretch of a corridor with big bay windows at the end, the green of foliage showing through the glass.

The building must be huge. I couldn't think of any

place like this in Paradise Bend. Where exactly were we?

"We're ready," Rowan said. "We'd like to give the Long Night our answer."

The man's lips thinned. "I hope for your sake that it's the right one."

Rowan returned to the table, and we sat there in silence. A few moments later, the door swung open, and the Long Night walked in. This time he was alone.

The dull thud of his loafers on the plush carpet was the only sound in the room. Instead of sitting down, he stopped behind one of the chairs, his hand clasped over the top. "So, what have you decided?"

"We'll take your deal," Wylder said. "We get one week. You don't make a move on any of us until then. And you fill us in on anything useful you know about the Storm."

A triumphant smile came over the Long Night's face, and his silver-blue eyes almost glistened. "I'm glad to know you've decided to take my help after all. I must admit, I was starting to have my doubts. Stubbornness could become one of your fatal flaws, Mr. Noble."

"I like to see it as a virtue," Wylder retorted.

My throat had constricted now that we were setting this deal in motion. "What exactly are your conditions?" I said abruptly. "We don't have to take down the Storm himself, do we?"

The Long Night let out a low, humorless laugh. "Of course not, girl. You'd never get close enough to him. I doubt he'll even set foot in your little county himself. I'm not going to ask for the impossible. I only want his men out of Paradise Bend—permanently. You need to beat them and beat them well enough that they'll have no interest in returning." He gave us all a narrow look. "Do you accept those terms?"

For a second, I couldn't breathe. Beat them that definitively—in a week. It was hard to imagine. But like I'd said earlier, what choice did we have but to try?

"I'm in," I said.

"We all are," Wylder put in, speaking for his inner circle as well. The other guys tipped their heads.

"Excellent." The Long Night rubbed his hands together. "I'll have you driven home and see that you receive the resources I promised immediately. I'll even give you a small reprieve—your week will start tonight rather than right at this moment. Seven nights from today, I want all trace of the Storm gone from Paradise Bend. Good luck."

Wylder

I TUGGED AT THE BLACK TIE AROUND MY NECK. IT felt like a noose, slowly choking off the air to my lungs. I loosened the knot, but that didn't do much.

The tie wasn't the problem—I was. I'd been on edge since the moment the lid on that crate had popped open to reveal my brother's mutilated body, sent by Xavier.

I gazed at the freshly dug grave and the casket that'd just been lowered into it. It was made of polished mahogany with embellishments along the edges. Nothing but the finest for my brother.

We'd only just made it back to the city in time to change our clothes into something more fitting and get to the ceremony before it started. Dad had been eyeing me from the moment I'd gotten here, with an expression like he wanted to lay into me but wouldn't in this kind of company.

Or maybe it was Mercy, standing next to me, that he was shooting his periodic death glare at. He probably didn't want her here after he'd done so much to drive her out of our lives, but she was back, and she was staying. Dad would have a fight on his hands if he tried to challenge me on that subject again.

I couldn't stop my mind from tripping back a few hours ago to the immense mansion where the man who called himself the Long Night had held his impromptu meeting with us and made his demands. Did Dad have any idea that he'd been working under someone else all his life, while he made such a show of being the head honcho? How the hell was I going to tell him what I'd learned? I could only imagine how pissed off he'd be... if he even believed me.

Now, at the priest's direction, he dropped a handful of dirt onto the coffin. Anthea stepped forward too, her expression tight. I wondered how she felt about all this. She'd never talked much about my brother, but I knew she'd grown up alongside him, much closer to his age than mine, more like siblings than aunt and nephew. But then she'd been sent into that horrible marriage and Roland had taken off... The opening of the crate was the first time she'd seen him since his disappearance, just like it was for me.

Like usual, she kept her emotions close to her chest. But as she stepped back, she quickly swiped at her eyes.

Then it was my turn. The sun-warmed soil was gritty against my fingers, and it fell onto the polished surface with a faint patter.

As I stepped back, a fresh wave of guilt surged over

me. A part of me had always thought Roland would come back. There'd been times early on when I'd wished he would so Dad would lay off on me. But after everything that'd happened with Laurel, I'd lived in horror of the idea all the same. I hadn't wanted my brother to swoop in and take what was mine after I'd sacrificed so much for it.

And now he was gone. There was no way he'd ever return to us for any reason. No way I could have my brother back and see if we could fix our broken relationship.

The priest said his prayer. The Nobles who'd gathered for the ceremony listened in silence, a few of them poised farther back from our circle to stand guard. When the prayers were over, Dad took his spot to speak.

He cleared his throat, revealing more emotion in that sound than he usually showed in an entire month. "He was my son, my blood. I wanted so much more than this for him. He was born to be exceptional, and we'll never see how much of that promise he might have fulfilled if he'd come back to us another way." His voice caught. He lowered his head for a moment to gather himself. "You will never be replaced or forgotten."

I didn't want to take his words personally, but they felt like a jab directed at me, a reminder of the fact that he didn't consider my performance as his heir to be particularly promising.

As Dad stepped back, he made a motion for the grave to be filled in. My pulse stuttered.

"Wait," I said. "I want to say something for my brother."

All eyes turned to me. Dad's face hardened a fraction, and his lips thinned. Ignoring him, I took his place at the head of the grave.

The words started slowly and then tumbled out. "I can't talk about Roland the way I'd want to because we weren't really all that close. He was five years older than me, and always committed to helping Dad manage the family business." Until he hadn't been, I didn't mention. "But the times he did spare to hang out with me always stuck in my mind. I wanted to be just like him. And then, when he left, I realized he'd been doing even more than I'd ever noticed, never letting the stresses or challenges of the work affect how he treated me."

I took a deep breath as memories rushed up inside me. The relief that'd been mixed in with my horror at seeing Roland's body had been nothing to do with him. It'd been Dad's fault, like so much else. He was the one who'd pitted me against my brother by bringing out the threat of his possible return whenever he felt I'd screwed up, comparing me to him at every turn.

I peered down at the coffin, wishing I totally believed that my brother's spirit might be around to hear this. "Roland, there are a lot of things I wish I could go back and change—one of them being trying harder to bring you home and fix our relationship. I let us both down. But I won't now." I raised my hand, clenched into a fist. "I will avenge you."

Soft murmurs spread through the small crowd at my

declaration. Dad was looking at me with an unreadable expression. Only the pit of the grave separated us.

The priest murmured another prayer before a few men took up spades to fill in the grave. I went back to Mercy, who slipped her hand around mine and gave me a gentle squeeze of reassurance. Dad's cool gaze lingered on us. The rest of my inner circle must have noticed, because the three guys drew a little closer around us as if they thought we needed protection.

Which, given how Dad had acted over the past several weeks, might not be wrong.

But it turned out it wasn't him we needed to defend against. Just as we were about to walk back to the cars, several sharp *bangs* crackled through the air.

Gunshots.

The guards shouted in alarm, as if we needed a warning to realize we were under attack. I ducked instinctively, pulling Mercy toward the ground with me and reaching for the gun at my waist.

The priest who'd performed the ceremony toppled over onto the freshly churned soil, blood gushing from multiple bullet wounds. A few of the underlings at the edges of the gathering were crumpling among those rushing for cover.

A bunch of men with rifles hurtled toward us over the rise of a nearby hill, taking more shots seemingly indiscriminately. I aimed to shoot back at them, but there were too many of our own people milling around. None of us had been prepared for an assault on this scale, not here during a fucking funeral. There was nothing but gravestones to take shelter behind, and our attackers had the high ground.

"Get to the cars and get out of here," Dad hollered with a wave of his arm, and for once I agreed with his order. Several underlings closed tight around him to shield him. They took off for his car.

Staying low with Mercy and my men around me, I hustled backward toward the other vehicles parked along the graveyard's driveway as quickly as I could. But that didn't mean I was going to stop fighting. I managed to take a few shots when I got an opening. One caught a charging guy in the jaw, but the attackers were moving too quickly for any of us to get a good aim.

"The Storm rules here and everywhere!" one of the other pricks yelled, and Mercy tensed even more than she'd already been beside me.

"Xavier," she muttered, as if there'd been much doubt about who would orchestrate an attack like this.

"Let's just get the fuck out of here," I said through gritted teeth.

I'd come in my car, and Rowan had brought his as well so we weren't packed in like sardines. We dove behind the statue of an angel for extra cover and then bolted for the vehicles. Mercy ended up at mine with me, the three guys at Rowan's.

Kaige moved to rejoin me, but I motioned him to stay where he was. More Nobles were racing around us, Dad scrambling into the back seat of his own car with bodyguards around him, shots echoing over the grassy hills. I just wanted us gone, fast and uninjured.

I tossed the keys to Mercy. While she unlocked the car, I got in a couple more shots, including one to the shoulder of an asshole who'd thought he could blast away my woman. The second she yanked the door open, I shoved her inside toward the passenger seat and dove in after her.

The wheels screeched as I careened along the driveway and onto the street beyond the gates. My heartbeat thumped in my ears so hard my bones seemed to rattle with it.

"Fuck, fuck, *fuck*," I spat out. "The fuckers didn't let us have one day of peace. My brother didn't get a proper good-bye even in his death."

Mercy looked over at me, her own expression taut with anger. "They're all jackasses, and I wish we could have taken them all down. But—" Her shoulders stiffened as I jammed on the accelerator. "We'll deal with them. We've got the Long Night backing us up against the Storm and Xavier now."

I couldn't shake the anger coursing through me. The buildings beyond the windshield were unfamiliar. I had no idea where in the city we were now, and I didn't care. I slammed my fist against the steering wheel.

"He killed my brother, mutilated him almost beyond recognition, and now this." I shook my head, all the horrible thoughts from the last few days washing over me. "But Xavier isn't the only monster here."

Mercy frowned. "What do you mean?"

"You know what I felt first when I realized it was Roland in that crate? Not horror or pain or grief that my brother was gone. I was *relieved*. Because I knew he wasn't coming back to take my life away from me and that automatically cemented me as the Noble heir, regardless of Dad's intentions."

"Wylder—"

I glanced at her, my grip on the wheel tightening. "I'm fucked up."

She shook her head. "No, you're not."

"I am. My first reaction was to see my brother's death as a personal gain."

"It isn't like that at all," Mercy said. "Your father drilled it into your head that you had to be perfect if you wanted to be his heir. He used your brother to get to you, to mold you into what he wanted you to be."

I laughed shakily. "And he's got that now."

Mercy spoke with total certainty. "Wylder, you're nothing like your father."

There was no pity in her light blue eyes, only concern for me. The heat of my anger started to simmer down. My foot eased up on the gas, and she tipped her head toward a vacant lot we were just coming up on, the cracked cement dotted with sprouting weeds. "I don't think anyone's following us at this point. Maybe you should stop and take a few breaths."

She was right. Like she was so often. I exhaled raggedly and twisted the wheel to bring us into the lot, parking close to the shabby building next door so we wouldn't be easily visible from the road. Then I cut the engine and pressed the heels of my hands against my forehead.

"How can you be like this?" I asked.

Mercy blinked. "Like what?"

"You're so fierce, and you take no prisoners, but

somehow you can be so understanding when it comes to me and my fuckups."

"I'm not any more perfect than you are," she said. "But I think that's okay. You and I are both human, and at the end of the day, we're simply trying our best. Neither of us had parents who made it easy for us."

I brought my hand to her cheek and caressed it. My rage was simmering deep inside me, but I was no longer directing it at myself. I was still wound up from the encounter with the Storm earlier, and all I could think about now was finding some way to release that energy.

There was one way we'd both enjoy.

I tugged Mercy toward me, and she met me halfway. Our mouths caught together like a snare. We kissed deep and fast, our tongues tangling with each other.

My fingers sank into her hair, loose from its usual ponytail for this formal occasion, and a growl reverberated from my throat. The fire inside me was raging hotter now, but it wasn't all anger anymore. In an instant, I'd gone achingly hard.

This wasn't enough. I unbuckled my seat belt before reaching for Mercy. I caught her by the waist and lifted her on top of me, loving the little gasp of surprise that spilled out of her. She sank onto my lap, already diving in for another kiss.

As our mouths melded together, I shoved the seat as far back and down as it would go. My fingers leapt to the back of her dress. I yanked the zipper all the way to her ass and dragged the straps over her arms. Mercy fumbled with my suit jacket and then the buttons of my dress shirt at the same time. She tossed my tie to the side.

The second her naked breasts brushed my chest, I groaned. When I nipped Mercy's bottom lip with my teeth and flicked my tongue over the spot, she moaned in turn. We were burning up together, our skin scorching everywhere we touched.

She ran her hands over the plane of my chest, and my muscles flexed under her eager fingers. I ground my hips up into her. The feel of her against my rigid cock made me want to explode right there.

She made a rough sound against my lips, and I bent down to take one of her nipples into my mouth. As I sucked and nipped, the impatient noise changed into a whimper that got me even harder. I switched from one breast to the other, and Mercy swayed back toward the steering wheel, her eyes at half-mast and her lip bit beneath her teeth ever so temptingly.

When I released her nipple with a loud, wet *pop*, she leaned toward me again. She put her hands against the headrest and pressed her hips toward me, rubbing against my erection. When she lifted up to free me from my slacks, her ass bumped the middle of the steering wheel.

We both flinched at the sudden honk. Mercy's hands froze on my belt buckle. "Do you think someone heard us?" she asked.

I raised my eyebrows at her, practically panting in need. "Do you care?"

A naughty look came over her face. "No."

She jerked at my pants, and my dick sprang from its

confines. Mercy wrapped her fingers around its length, sending pulses of pleasure through my veins. She stroked me from base to tip, swiveling her thumb over my piercing with a more potent jolt of pleasure. I leaned back against the seat, unable to hold back a grunt.

When I was aching and wanting, she stopped, but only to grab a condom out of her purse. I helped her roll it over my cock. She set her palm on the roof to balance herself as she slowly sank down on my dick until I was completely sheathed inside of her. I could feel her pussy tremble around my cock. The sensation drove me nuts.

I put my hands around her waist and pulled her up, only to slam her down on my dick. Her greedy cunt easily swallowed my cock to the hilt. She circled her arms around my neck, the heat of her body coiling against mine. As she rode me hard and fast, her perky breasts bounced up and down, the nipples brushing against my chest.

The sounds of our pants and moans filled the car as we moved urgently against each other. Gripping her hips, I swiveled them just as I buried my dick inside her again. Her eyes rolled back with a piercing keening. Her brown hair fanned wildly across her shoulders, sweat streaking down her neck.

I swept the strands back from her face, wanting to see her clearly. A storm of emotions coursed through my body, almost overwhelming me. I was a walking inferno, and I would probably have burned myself down by now if it weren't for her. She burned just as brightly, but the fire in her made my own burn hotter and clearer in all the right ways, showing a path through the chaos.

The realization crashed into me hard and fast: I never wanted to lose her. And she deserved to know what she meant to me after all the crap I'd put her through.

I rolled my hips beneath her again and felt her pussy start to clench around me. She was so close. I grasped her face so her eyes met mine and said with all the truth I had in me, "I love you, Mercy. So fucking much. I love you."

At the same moment, I bucked even deeper into her. Mercy's legs shook, and a cry tumbled out of her as her pussy walls convulsed around my cock.

The sensation set off my own release. I came with a shout, the force of the orgasm making me clench my teeth.

We slowed together, our breaths coming ragged, her body going slack over me as we eased down from the peak together. Mercy's heart thundered where her chest came to rest against mine, echoing my own frenetic pulse. My dick was still buried inside of her.

Before more than the slightest twinge of worry could hit me that she hadn't said anything back yet, she raised her head and planted another kiss on me, long and lingering and more tender than anything we'd shared in the past several minutes. Then she drew back just a few inches. An emotion I'd never seen before shimmered in her bright eyes.

"I love you too," she said, her voice rough. "I just

hope—you *are* okay if I feel the same way about certain other people too?"

A bubble of exhilarating happiness exploded inside of me. I laughed. I couldn't help myself.

"Mercy," I said, cupping her face in my hands. "You might not believe it, but I've decided I actually prefer it this way. You're not just my girl; you belong to all of us. Together. I'm lucky that I get to be a part of this amazing thing we've found."

A smile curled her lips, and I knew I would do anything to preserve it. "Do *you* really believe that?" she checked.

I nodded. "You're our woman, and we're yours." Images from our collective romp in the van came to my mind. It'd been the most erotic experience of my life, and seeing how much pleasure Mercy had gotten out of it...

Nothing would make me walk away from this. I trusted the three men of my inner circle more than family, and she belonged with us. That was all there was to it.

And that wasn't all we were going to do together. I hugged her tighter and then gave her my fiercest grin. "You got my head on straight. Now it's time to crush the Storm and Xavier, just like they deserve."

4

Mercy

It felt strange, being back in the Katz house with the remainder of the Claws forces sitting at the long dining table and standing by the walls around me. Like I'd stepped right into my father's shoes with them barely cooled from his death. But there wasn't any time to ease into my role as Queen of the Claws. We had a hell of a lot of work ahead of us.

Despite the invaders who'd come through my childhood home, it still smelled the same, wisps of old cigar smoke and gin hanging in the air. Someone had rigged up a chandelier over the table that wasn't quite as nice as our old crystal one but did the trick, its warm glow spilling over the assembled crowd.

I'd summoned them as soon as I'd gotten back from Wylder's brother's funeral, and they'd arrived in the falling dusk. It was full night now, the yard dark beyond the window. Our one week had begun.

"All right," I said, resting my hands on the table from where I was standing at its head. "You're all here because you're willing to go up against the Storm and do whatever we can to stop him—or any other outsiders—from taking over our home. We've got a limited amount of time to make that happen before someone who might be even worse crashes the party. So I want to figure out what we have to work with. I want to hear what you're particularly good at, any strengths or expertise you've got that might help us win this war."

The men around the table shifted in their seats. I was only starting to learn their names, other than Kervos at my right hand, who'd already pitched in plenty, and Sam next to him, the red dye not yet totally washed out of his hair from when he'd played the role of a substitute Wylder in an earlier gambit. A pang formed in my chest at the thought of Roy, who'd come to warn us about Colt's ambush weeks ago and maybe saved my life... and then lost his own life at Xavier's hands.

Jenner, the most senior member of the Claws who'd stuck around, hadn't shown up yet. I hoped that wasn't a bad sign.

After a moment, Kervos spoke up. "I've handled a lot of stolen car operations." He motioned to a younger guy with spiky black hair across the table from him. "Quinn and I can hotwire any vehicles we need for getting around or transporting supplies. And I'm not bad with a gun, if I do say so myself."

Quinn nodded, and several others around the room chuckled. "I'm a good shot!" someone piped up, and another voice added, "Yeah, me too," and in a few seconds it sounded like I had a whole house full of desperados.

"Okay," I said with a small smile, holding up my hands for the chatter to die down again. "That's good to hear, because I wouldn't be surprised if we need to do a lot of shooting."

"That means we're going to need lots of guns," Sam pointed out. "Me and a couple of the other guys have some connections there, and I know where your dad had a stash that I don't think Colt or Xavier ever touched."

"Perfect." I pointed at him. "I'm assigning you and whoever you want to take with you to get those weapons and bring them back here to distribute. None of us should be going out on the streets unarmed, and I'm going to need a few of you stationed around this house, our base of operations, on a rotating guard. The Storm's people have proven that they're ruthless—we can't give them any vulnerable moments to take advantage of. Is there anyone who's particularly good at other kinds of fighting, or at things like climbing and breaking into places if we need to?"

One by one, different men raised their voices. I made mental notes, studying their faces and picturing them carrying out the skills they mentioned. It felt natural, much easier than I'd expected, as if I'd been preparing for this all along without realizing it. But then, maybe I had. I'd committed a lot of details to memory over the years watching Dad from the sidelines, wanting to be ready for whatever trouble might be coming for him—or for me, from his hands.

I glanced at my notes on my phone. During the ride back to Paradise Bend in the Long Night's posh car, the resources he'd promised had started arriving, including reports on several business ventures the Storm was involved in. We might need to mess with those to get the upper hand.

"Does anyone have experience with or at least knowledge about sports gambling?" I asked. "Organizing bets on games and that sort of thing?"

A couple of guys lifted their hands. I got their names and committed those to memory too. "Good, I might need you for a special mission at some point. And how about property management? I know my dad owned a bunch of buildings in the Bend."

There was a momentary silence. "Meso handled a lot of that," Sam put in. "He— The Steel Knights took him out. He refused to go over to Colt's side when everything first went down."

Kervos nodded with a grim expression. "I haven't seen anyone who worked with him on that side of things around lately either."

I let out a breath. Well, I couldn't expect to have everything handed right to me. And Rowan had done some negotiations involving property for Ezra, so that might be all we needed.

"How about—" I started, and paused at the creak of footsteps.

"How about you all wait a few minutes before getting started without your elders," Jenner grumbled in a good-humored way, coming in to join us. He limped a little with an injury he'd taken during Xavier's attempt to wipe the last of the Claws out of existence, and shadows darkened the skin under his eyes, but he stood steadily enough. And he wasn't alone.

A girl who looked about ten years old, with her blond hair in two braids and wearing a sparkly unicorn T-shirt, kept close to Jenner's side. He rested his hand on her shoulder.

My eyebrows rose. "Who's this?"

The kid's mouth stayed shut tight, her eyes widening as she took in the crowded room.

Quinn frowned at Jenner. "Why'd you bring Sarah over here?"

"I couldn't exactly get a babysitter with how everything's been lately," Jenner said. He turned to me. "This is my daughter. She won't get in the way."

I couldn't blame him for not wanting to leave her alone with the rampages the Storm's people had been going on. I hadn't even known he *had* a kid... There was so much catching up I had to do with the Claws men.

My Claws.

I nodded. "It's fine. Sarah, is it? I like your name. Mine's Mercy."

"Won't you say hello to her?" Jenner asked patiently.

Sarah pulled a little away from her father, gripping his arm. "Hi, Mercy. It looks like you're really busy."

Beside me, Kervos chuckled. "This is why I like kids. They tell it how it is."

"We were actually just finishing up the most important part," I said. "Why don't I show you where you can hang out for a bit, and catch your dad up." I glanced around at the others. "The rest of you can take a break. There's beer in the fridge—just don't go crazy. We've still got a lot of planning to do."

Sam let out a little whoop, and half of the group tramped over to the kitchen. I led Jenner and Sarah over to the living room and turned on the iPod one of the guys had mounted on a portable speaker. "Do you like listening to music?" I asked her.

She smiled shyly. "I love Billie Eilish."

"Let's see... You're in luck." I started the album playing and patted the sofa. "You can hang out here, even sing along if you'd like."

She hopped up and started swaying with the tune. I stepped off to the side with Jenner and cocked my head at him. "I'm assuming there's a good reason she's here? This is the first time I've seen her."

Jenner sighed. "I need a drink first."

We walked over to the kitchen, and he squeezed past the other guys to the fridge to grab a beer. With it in hand, he came back to the entrance to the living room and looked across it toward his daughter. He tipped the bottle to his lips and chugged half of it without stopping.

"So...?" I prodded as he lowered the beer.

Jenner made a face. "She mostly lives with her mom. Mostly *lived* with her mom. That woman took off two days ago. She got scared with all the violence going on around here, which I can't blame her for, but she skipped town alone, leaving Sarah behind. I guess she didn't want to have a kid with her, slowing her down. I got a text message from her and by the time I showed up at the house, she was already gone and Sarah was waiting without even a suitcase."

My heart tugged at the picture he'd painted. My hand brushed over my pocket where I had my bracelet from my own mother on me like usual. Had my mom left for the same reasons Sarah's had—thinking it was easier to make a run for it without me by her side?

A lump filled my throat. "I'm sorry."

Jenner took another swig of the beer. "I didn't make the best choices in partners when I was younger, obviously. And maybe it's my fault too that I haven't been around to pitch in as much as would be ideal. I don't know. But I don't want anything to happen to Sarah. I've always tried to be there for her as much as I can even with the kind of life I live." He paused. "I haven't got a clue how to keep her safe, Mercy. It's hell out there right now."

It was. And for some of us girls growing up in the gang life, it'd been hell all the way through, since way before the Storm had ever shown up on our doorstep.

I watched Sarah bob with the melody, and resolve coiled tight around my chest. I wasn't my father, not one bit, and I was going to see that no other girls in the Bend grew up the way I had if I had anything to say about it. Things could be better for them than they'd been for me.

"You two can stay here," I said abruptly.

Jenner blinked at me. "What?"

"Until the mess with the Storm is cleaned up, Sarah can stay here and so can you, so she'll have you with her.

There are too many rooms in here, and the silence practically echoes. God knows I need company. Since I'm running the Claws out of here again, people will be coming and going all the time anyway, and it'll be the best protected building we've got. I don't want her out on the streets in harm's way."

Jenner's voice roughened. "Mercy, I—"

I held up a hand. "You don't have to say anything. It's the only answer that makes sense." I lifted my chin toward where Sam and Kervos had gone over to join the girl, Kervos offering her a chocolate bar he must have grabbed from the stash on the kitchen counter. "Besides, she already seems to enjoy the company of our men."

Jenner cracked a small smile. "She does, crazy as it sounds. They're good to her."

"Now that we've gotten that settled..." I elbowed him lightly. "Let me fill you in on what we already discussed, and then we'll get everyone back to business."

I filled him in on the basics of the Long Night's deal and what we'd learned from him. Jenner's expression turned more serious by the second.

"If you need anyone else on the betting side of things, I was involved in a little of that when I was starting out too," he said. "And I know most of the guys here fairly well if you want advice on who to give what job to, who *shouldn't* be working together, that kind of thing."

"Thanks," I said. "That'll be a huge help."

He tipped his head to me. "I can already tell you're

going to be a very different kind of leader than your father was, Mercy—and I'm thinking that's a good thing."

His vote of confidence warmed me for the five seconds it took before I noticed that Sarah had wandered away from the sofa. She crept over to the doorway that led to the basement stairs, and my pulse hiccupped.

I hurried over, forcing myself to slow as I reached her so I didn't freak her out too much. Flashes of the horrors I'd experienced in that dark space flitted behind my eyes, sending another chill through me.

I tugged Sarah gently back, shut the door, and fished out my keys so I could lock it.

"There's nothing down there you'd want to see," I said, keeping my voice carefully even. "Nothing good at all. Promise me you won't go down there even if someone leaves it open, all right?"

"I promise," she said in a soft voice.

"Perfect." I gave her arm a quick pat. "Now do you want to keep chilling out with the music, or do you want to hear what we're discussing? I think you're big enough that you've got a right to know what's going on if you're interested."

Jenner's mouth tightened, but after a moment's contemplation, Sarah just said, "I'll go back to the music." But her "Thank you" as she headed back to the sofa sent a sharper twang of foreboding through me.

If we couldn't get the Storm's people out of the Bend in the next seven days and the Long Night made good on his promise to clean the slate, it wouldn't be just the men in the next room who'd suffer. Every kid with any ties to the local powers would pay for our failure too, including Sarah.

The clock on the mantel seemed to tick louder, each second inching us toward our possible doom.

5

Gideon

WYLDER PACED BY THE CHESS TABLE AS I DELVED deeper into the files the Long Night had sent us this afternoon. A lot of the information I hadn't been able to examine thoroughly via my phone on the trip back, and we'd hurried to Roland's funeral right after. This was my first real deep dive, but Wylder wasn't exactly patient. Especially after the attack we'd just faced.

"We have to strike back," he muttered. "Hit them where it hurts, give them no time to recover. Just keep hitting them again and again, until they're forced to leave."

Kaige looked up from where he'd been watching the fish cruise by in my aquarium. "Well, obviously. But we don't know how, do we?"

"I'm working on it," I said shortly. "There's a lot to sort through here. Information on the Storm's business activities, his strongholds, the drug trade... And I have to cross-reference it with what's actually happening around the county right now. Finding out about some arrangement they've got in Timbuktu isn't going to help us."

I grabbed a company name and fed it into my usual search app. The results turned up nothing remotely inspiring. I sighed and went back to the files.

"Has the Long Night said anything about manpower?" Rowan asked. "I got the impression we're on our own as far as putting people on the streets."

I nodded. "It sounded like the whole reason he brought us on is to avoid putting his own men in the line of fire. We have Mercy and the Claws who've stuck around, and at least some of the Nobles..."

I glanced at Wylder sideways, but he just kept pacing without saying a word. He hadn't talked to his dad about the Long Night's proposal and the deal we'd made with him yet. I didn't see how we had a hope in hell of pulling off a victory without the full power of the Noble forces behind us, and we weren't getting that without Ezra's go-ahead, but I wasn't going to question my best friend right now. Not when he'd just watched our enemies tear apart his brother's funeral.

Not when I was at least partly to blame for that funeral being necessary in the first place.

I ran another search, and my spirits lifted slightly. My fingers sped over the keys as I homed in on the bit of data that'd shown a little promise. After a few minutes, a smile stretched across my face.

"What?" Wylder asked, coming over to lean against the desk. He'd picked up on my good mood.

"I think I've got something. The Long Night has this company listed as the Storm's main weapons supplier in the States. I'm seeing evidence that they've got a major shipment headed toward Paradise Bend—it should arrive around late evening tomorrow."

"More weapons," Kaige grumbled. "Perfect."

I searched through the records I'd dug up, and my heart started to sink again. "Maybe not just that. The truck they're using is outfitted with seating as well. From the looks of it, the Storm is bringing in a contingent of new men too."

Wylder spat out a curse. "Over my dead body."

I very much hoped it didn't come to that.

"We won't let them get far," I said, checking my maps for possible routes. "I think we can hit them on their way into the county. They won't expect us to have figured out the shipment is coming, considering we only realized thanks to the Long Night's inside information. We'll take them by surprise, mow down all their new soldiers, and confiscate the weapons for ourselves."

Rowan hummed. "The first step to pushing them out of the Bend is not letting them get any more of a foothold than they already have."

"I like it," Kaige said with a jerk of a nod. He cracked his knuckles. "I just wish we didn't have to wait until tomorrow."

"We work with what we've got," Wylder said. "It's a good plan. You can figure out where we'd need to ambush them, Gideon?"

"I think so. It should be easy to track the truck through street cams and other footage now that I know what to look for. We'll stay ready to course-correct if they deviate from the most obvious route. And I'll..."

I hesitated, trailing off. I'd been going to say that I'd be right there with the others, directing them on the ground. But the image had flashed through my head of Xavier looming over me, a knife flashing in his hand and a cruel grin stretched across his scarred face. Even though I wasn't facing the slightest bit of exertion, my lungs started to constrict.

"You can give us instructions from here just fine," Wylder said. "That's what you've always done before. Or you can come along—it was your idea. Whatever you think would work best."

The fact that he was letting me decide what I was most comfortable with only made me feel more guilty.

I couldn't say I'd been wrong to get more involved in the hands-on fight against the Storm and his men, but my last major plan had backfired on us. I'd gotten a good ally killed, I'd nearly been killed by Xavier, and my friends and my woman had needed to risk their lives to rescue me. The one victory I'd scored during my capture, the tracker I'd managed to stick to one of Xavier's boots, hadn't turned up any useful intel yet.

Some good had come out of the initial plan, at least. I'd been able to pass on all kinds of data from the computer I'd hacked in the Storm's local headquarters, some of which had helped me put together the pieces for our current plan alongside the Long Night's data. But ultimately, I'd been a liability. I wanted to destroy Xavier and the Storm any way I could, with bullets and fists as well as my computers if need be, but what if I only screwed things up again?

I set the question of whether I'd join the ambush in person aside and focused on another matter we could no longer ignore. "We'll need a lot of people. The Storm could be bringing in as many as twenty, maybe even thirty men on this truck. They'll be well-armed. We want to outnumber them enough that we can deal with them easily without many—if any—casualties on our side."

Rowan frowned. "Between the Claws and us, we'd only have a small advantage in numbers."

"We shouldn't have to rely only on ourselves and Mercy's people," I said, and looked at Wylder. "We have the Nobles too. At least, we should have them when your father understands what we're really up against here."

Wylder let out a huff of breath. "Or he'll kick me to the curb for making up stories that sound crazy to him."

I could tell that even though he was balking, he knew I was right. His mouth twisted as he grappled with the idea.

A sudden resolve gripped me, a flicker of anticipation coursing through me alongside it. I might not be a whole lot of use in the middle of a battle, but I had plenty of other strengths. The largest was that I knew my data. Wylder's current problem was one I could actually tackle.

"We should go talk to him now," I said. "Give him time to wrap his head around it before we need to get into the thick of preparing. I'll come with you—I'll bring my tablet, show him all the evidence, and lay out a case for why his cooperation is necessary to *his* survival as well as everyone else's."

"He's not going to like hearing that either," Wylder said, but then he sighed and offered me a smaller smile. "But I'm not leading us into a slaughter just because I hate talking to him. Let's go take him on together." He glanced at Rowan and Kaige. "You two, get some sleep. I want you totally fresh tomorrow."

He marched toward the door, and I hurried after him. As he strode down the hall, his gaze snagged on one closed door, and his steps slowed for just a second.

My gut knotted. That room had been Roland's back before the guy had run off.

A surge of emotions, more than I was used to dealing with, swept through me. I bit my tongue, and a metallic trickle of blood seeped through my mouth.

I couldn't keep quiet about this. Wylder deserved to know.

I stopped completely, and Wylder immediately turned to me with a quizzical look.

"I need to tell you something," I said. "But first you should know how incredibly sorry I am that I fucked things up so badly."

Wylder's forehead furrowed. "What the hell are you talking about?"

My throat tightened, but I forced myself to keep talking. "It's my fault. That Xavier targeted Roland. I— when he was questioning me, and I was doing whatever I could to distract him so that maybe I could get the tracker on him, I babbled a bunch of random things, and one of them was that you had an older brother. Most of it was bullshit. I claimed that Roland was off training to eventually come back and take over, that you were some kind of decoy..."

I winced inwardly at the memory, knowing how close that idea came to the fears that had driven Wylder to pull out all the stops to live up to his older brother's legacy in Ezra's eyes.

"I was just shooting my mouth off, saying the first things that popped into my head that I thought would catch his attention," I went on. "I had no idea—I mean, none of us knew where Roland even was. It never occurred to me that Xavier would manage to track him down and do something like that. But I shouldn't have brought him up at all—I should have realized what a mistake that was—"

Wylder was staring at me. The vice-like sensation crept around my lungs again, until I could barely breathe.

"I'm sorry," I added again, hating how weak my voice sounded. "I should have told you sooner."

My best friend dragged in a breath, ragged with emotion. Then he let it out in a rush and stepped forward to clasp my shoulder. "I know you were only trying to help every way you could. And you really *couldn't* have known that Xavier had the kind of resources to track Roland down when not even my dad has been able to. And—hell, I can't imagine what it was like, being captured by that guy. I'm impressed by how well you did keep your head together."

What, that I hadn't completely fallen apart? "Any of the other guys—" I started.

Wylder shook his head. "It would have been hard for any of us. But yeah, it was probably harder for you because you're not usually out there fighting people face to face. I recognize that. I'm not going to blame you for what that sicko did." He squeezed my shoulder. "Roland might have been my brother by blood, but you're my brother in every other way that matters. I know you would never purposefully betray me or the Nobles."

Relief I still wasn't totally sure I'd earned trickled through me. I ducked my head. "Thank you." Maybe there was more I should have said, but I couldn't find the words. And besides, we had another possible villain to tackle that needed to take priority over my self-doubt. The seconds were ticking away before the Long Night swept into Paradise Bend.

We walked around the landing to the opposite wing and down the hall to Ezra's office. Wylder knocked on the door. There was no response. We waited a minute, Wylder trying again. Then he checked the handle and found it unlocked. We glanced at each other.

Ezra never left his office unlocked unless he was in it.

Wylder turned the knob and pushed the door open so we could enter.

Ezra was sitting at his desk, a glass in his hand. He took a long swig of whiskey before he turned to us with a glare. "I'm not entertaining anybody."

Wylder's jaw locked. "It's important."

"Go away," Ezra muttered before he poured some of the fire-colored liquid into his glass.

"Dad," Wylder said, his tone stiff. "It's important. The lives of every man working under us are on the line. So please put the fucking whiskey away and let us talk to you."

Instead of answering, Ezra hurled the glass at us. Wylder ducked, and it shattered on the wall behind us. Wylder turned to Ezra with a glare that his dad returned with a tight smirk. He was more out of it than I'd realized.

"Ran off with your whore today while I had to fight for my life at the cemetery," he sneered.

"You got out of there before we did," Wylder answered calmly. "I saw you driving away before I'd even gotten into my car. I'm not sure what you expected me to do after that. And you don't call Mercy a whore."

Ezra's lip curled with a sneer. "I'll call whoever I want whatever I want."

"No. Not with her." Wylder took a few steps until he was standing right in front of Ezra's desk. Something had changed in him. I could feel that, and maybe Ezra felt that too. He fell silent, staring up at his son.

Wylder seemed to take his silence as an opening. He sat down in one of the chairs opposite his dad, and I took the one next to him.

"I had an interesting meeting earlier today," Wylder said. "Have you ever heard of the Long Night?"

I studied Ezra's expression carefully. He knit his brow, looking only puzzled. It didn't appear to be a show. Maybe he really hadn't had any idea that there were powers calling the shots over his head.

"The long night?" he repeated. "What's that?"

"It's a who," Wylder said. "That's the name he goes by."

"And who is this 'he'?"

"A very powerful man who brought me, my men, and Mercy in to talk to us about the war in Paradise Bend."

Ezra considered his son for a long moment. "Go on."

Wylder quickly recounted the story of the darts and how we'd woken up in the immense mansion, the explanation the Long Night had given us about the organization he and the Storm were part of, and the proposal he'd given us.

"But he's only given us a week, starting tonight," he finished. "He wants this dealt with quickly, or he's threatened that he'll put all his own men to the job and wipe the whole county clean so there's no one left who answers to anyone but himself."

Ezra's jaw worked as if he were chewing on the idea. "I'm supposed to believe that some lunatic who named himself after a full moon has been manipulating our business pursuits without me having the slightest idea—"

"You don't need to believe it," I broke in, with a hitch of my pulse that I ignored. Arguing with Ezra Noble rarely went well for those who dared to. "You know I deal only in facts, Mr. Noble. The fact is that what we saw out there was clearly the domain of a man with far more resources than even you possess. He's given us some of those resources as they relate to the Storm, information we had no hope of getting on our own." I held up my tablet. "I can show—"

Ezra cut me off just like I'd done to him, his gaze snapping back to Wylder. "And *you're* the one he offered this deal to?" His tone had gone icy cold.

Wylder's expression hardened. Apparently he'd given up on trying to be tactful after his dad's earlier reception. "Maybe that isn't so surprising considering that Mercy and I have been the ones out there in the Bend trying to fix this problem while you've spent most of the past couple of months denying there even is one."

Ezra stiffened in his seat. "I still rule the Nobles, as you'd better remember."

"Of course you do," Wylder retorted. "But who the hell cares who's sitting on the throne if in a week there'll be no Nobles at all. Can you set that crap aside for long enough to save our hides, for fuck's sake?"

Ezra's eyes flared. Before he could speak, I jumped in, keeping my tone carefully even. "We have plenty of intel, and we're already making plans. But we need all of the Nobles on our side, fighting with us, if we're going to have any hope of reclaiming Paradise Bend in the timeline we've been given. With enough manpower and the information the Storm can't imagine that we have, we can strike quickly and decisively and maybe have a real chance."

"Or else we'll all end up like Roland in a week's time," Wylder added.

Ezra scoffed lightly. "Maybe you should have

thought twice before agreeing to a devil's deal. The Nobles won't be taken down that easily." But I saw the way his knuckles had whitened where he'd clasped his hands together. Between the two of us, we were managing to convince him of the gravity of the situation.

"He didn't give us much of a choice," Wylder said. "It was either this or have him start the slaughter immediately if we said no. And I'd rather not take my chances against twice as many enemies. We need the Storm's people gone from Paradise Bend anyway. You know what a menace they've been."

"You have the Claws on your side courtesy of your plaything, don't you?"

Wylder took a few deep breaths to calm himself, but I could feel the anger radiating off him. "Think about it, Dad. If the Long Night makes good on his promise, it's game over for all of us. Is it really worth risking that on the assumption that there couldn't be anyone more powerful than you? Let's clean up the Bend once and for all—you, me, and the rest of the Nobles, together."

Ezra was silent for a few beats. Then, with a long suffering sigh, he said, "Fine. The deal's been made without my input, and there's nothing I can do about that now. And we do need the Storm's forces cleared out. But anything that happens, it's on you. You can call on any of the Nobles when you need to, but I want to be kept informed if and when that happens."

"Shall I send you a file or would you like notes over dinner?" Wylder said dryly. There it was again, that edge in his voice. My relief was quickly swallowed by the tension stretching taut between them.

"That's alright," I said hastily. "I can fill Ezra in."

Both father and son turned to look at me. I swallowed hard. "I mean I can act as the go-between, keep you both appraised of what's going on and any new developments. It's better this way since my job is staying behind the scenes anyway." Anything to reduce the chances of a blow up between the two reigning Nobles. My efforts might not be enough, but at least I was contributing something.

And it terrified me less than the thought of confronting Xavier face to face another time. I'd take Ezra Noble over that monster any day.

"I find that satisfactory," Ezra said. "Now get out of my office. You got what you came for."

Wylder stood stiffly, and I followed him out the door. Taking in his rigid posture, I couldn't help thinking that Ezra had been totally wrong. Wylder hadn't gotten what he really wanted out of his father at all.

But I wasn't sure he'd ever get the respect I knew he craved, not while Ezra could still dangle it over his head like a carrot on a stick.

6

Mercy

I SHIELDED MY EYES AGAINST THE SUN ON THE horizon. Evening was falling quickly, casting an ominous shade of orange across the scattered clouds as if foretelling horrible things to come.

Our first day out of the seven we had to drive the Storm's people out of the Bend was almost over. I just had to hope it'd finish with a strong step in the right direction.

I took a deep breath as I looked below the steel railing that ran the length of the old Bailey Bridge. The river churned beneath our feet, and the wind made the girders groan. Next to me, Wylder checked the bullets in his gun and rubbed his fingers over the smooth metal surface of the muzzle. Rowan and Kaige stood nearby, and a huge force of Claws and Noble men was assembled around us.

We were staked out on either side of the bridge that

led into the Bend, not the most popular route into the county but a shortcut to the interstate lines—one Gideon had discovered that the Storm's transport company had frequently used before. He'd confirmed just a few minutes ago that the new truck was headed straight toward us.

As I watched the occasional car or truck zoom past us, I shifted from foot to foot restlessly. Anytime I spotted a vehicle approaching that looked remotely larger than a standard car, my pulse sped up. But unless the transport truck broke several rules of physics, it wouldn't be here for about ten more minutes.

Rowan had turned to talk to the nearest Noble men. I watched him direct them to different strategic positions along the sides of the bridge where they could duck down out of sight behind the beams, ready to leap out the second we had the truck cornered. We had a truck of our own, albeit a smaller one, waiting for our signal at the other side of the bridge. The plan was all coming together.

"The anticipation is killing me," Kaige muttered.

"I know it's not your strong suit, but be patient," Wylder said. "It'll be better for us the darker it is once they get here."

He was right. We'd have more shadows to hide us, more of a false sense of security for the Storm's people. But I shared Kaige's sentiment. I wanted to get this done.

Wylder clicked the pistol's chamber into place and took aim at the distance. The dark water of the river looked almost ominous as it flowed past us below. A faintly fishy scent drifted up on the breeze. I wrinkled my nose.

"At least your dad came through," I said, glancing back at the forces gathered behind us and offering my own people a nod. "We'll overwhelm these assholes for sure."

"He didn't have much choice once we explained the situation to him well enough," Wylder said, his voice going terse. "After everything that's already gone down, it took hearing that we'd all be dead in seven days for him to finally get off his ass. I can't believe that for all this time I thought he ruled things around here."

"In a lot of ways, he did," Rowan said as he rejoined us. "It's not as if he knew the Long Night was siphoning off profits from his successful ventures."

Wylder let out a disgruntled sound. "Either way, my dad is directly responsible for the mess we've got here now."

"So is mine," I said. I didn't like acknowledging the role my father had played in the conflict, but I couldn't deny it.

Wylder's eyes flashed. "Maybe so. But tonight we begin our first step toward getting us back on the path we should be on."

The headset he was wearing crackled. I faintly made out Gideon's voice speaking into Wylder's ear.

"Got it," Wylder said, and swiveled to face the men, both those we could easily see and those disguised in the shadows. "The truck will be here in just a few minutes. Everyone's in position, so just do the job you were given, and we'll come out of this on top. The

Storm fuckers don't stand a chance. We want to destroy every man in that truck if we possibly can. They all die here."

A low cheer passed through the assembled force. A shiver traveled down my back at the same time. I knew why that was the plan—any man left alive was one who might kill us in the future. But at the same time, my stomach clenched.

The people I'd killed before had already been attacking the Bend. The men arriving tonight had never set foot here before. We knew why they were coming—it wasn't any mystery—and anyone working under the Storm was obviously a threat. But still, the thought of a full-out massacre reminded me a little too much of Colt and his men mowing down my family at our rehearsal dinner.

Wylder must have caught something in my expression. "You okay?" he asked me.

"Yeah," I said nonchalantly. The shadows were rapidly gaining on us. The moon peeked out of the clouds overhead, its glowing face staring down at us. "We have to do what we have to do."

"We wouldn't need to go to these extremes if they hadn't torn through the Bend first."

"I know." I let out my breath. "I'd better get into *my* position."

Because I wasn't as practiced with a gun as most of the men, my job was to hang back by the end of the bridge and pick off anyone who broke away from the pack and headed this way. I walked over to one of our cars that was parked a short distance away, which I was going to use for cover, and took out my gun. Leaning my elbows against the hood, I waited.

It barely seemed like a minute before the headlights of a huge truck appeared in the distance. Anticipation coiled in the pit of my stomach.

The last of the regular cars drove off the bridge. Two pickup trucks driven by Nobles roared onto the road, cutting off both lanes and blocking the transport truck's route into the county.

The truck started to slow, and snipers, one of them from the Claws, popped up on either side of the girders. With silenced shots that were still loud enough to echo through the night, they blew out the tires on each side.

The truck screeched, careening to the side and then jerking to a halt as the driver must have slammed on the brakes. As the other truck of Nobles roared toward it from the far end of the bridge, men sprang out of the cab and the back of the cargo hold. Guns gleamed in their hands.

We were ready for them.

Wylder and the rest of the Nobles and Claws leapt out of hiding all around the truck. More bangs thundered through the air.

The Storm's driver tumbled to the ground by his open door, blood blooming on his forehead. Several figures who'd been charging out of the back crumpled in a tangle of bodies. More bullets pinged off the metal sides of the truck.

The Noble and Claws forces swarmed the doorway before many more of the Storm's men had a chance to burst out. Shouts and groans carried through the darkness as our people mowed down those too packed inside to have much chance of defending themselves. A fresh trickle of queasiness wrapped around my gut.

But I had to stay focused. A few of the Storm's people had managed to scramble away from our onslaught. A couple of them hefted themselves up onto the steel beams to try to use them for shelter and a higher vantage point to pick off our men.

And a couple dashed for the larger shelter of the city buildings, straight toward me.

One of them was already bleeding pretty badly, staggering with his steps. Steeling myself, I aimed and got a clear shot at his head when he paused to catch his balance against a lamppost.

Really, he looked half-dead already. I was just putting him out of his misery.

Bam.

The pistol jerked in my hands, and the man fell, blood and brain splattered across the side of his face. I didn't have time to feel anything about it, because another man was running past me, this one much faster than the first.

I took a hasty shot at him, but he was moving too quickly. The bullet thudded into the brick side of a building instead. He was past me now, dashing toward the streetlights farther down the road.

Swearing under my breath, I shoved away from the car and sprinted after him. I took another shot, but he ducked, and it probably would've have gone wide anyway. I had hardly any experience with shooting while running.

This was my one job—I couldn't let my men down. If I could get close enough to use my knife...

My feet pounded against the asphalt, my lungs already starting to burn from the extreme exertion. I was starting to gain on the runaway. Just another ten seconds, and I might—

I was just raising my hand to fire at much closer range when a sedan roared up the road, its headlights blinding me. As I whipped up my hand to shade my eyes, the car veered right in front of me with a screech of its tires.

Even as I backpedaled, the door swung open, and a massive figure stepped out into the hazy light. Xavier sneered at me. "Hello, Mercy."

The headlights behind him made his profile even harsher, the X-shaped scars on his cheeks turned absolutely grotesque. A few of his men spilled out of the car behind him. He took out his gun.

My heart lurched. I lunged for the closest shelter: a mailbox at the edge of the sidewalk.

Bullets spewed in my wake, several thumping into the side of the mailbox. I sent a quick mental apology to the people whose letters had just gotten blasted in my defense and sprang for an alley several feet away. Heavy footsteps thumped after me.

"You thought you could pull a stunt like this and I wouldn't find out immediately?" Xavier hollered after me. "Where are your boyfriends now, Mercy? Not around to keep their kitten safe anymore, it looks like."

I didn't waste my breath replying. I didn't need anyone but myself to keep me safe.

As I hurtled into the alley, I leaned into my momentum and threw myself at the wall on one side. The second my feet and reaching hand smacked into the concrete surface, I shoved myself toward the opposite wall as hard as I could.

Back and forth, I ricocheted up the walls, gaining a few feet in height with every leap. As Xavier and his men charged through the mouth of the alley, I heaved myself onto the roof of one of the buildings.

I crouched there by the eavestrough, panting to catch my breath. Xavier motioned to his men to fan out around the building. "I'm going to catch you one of these days, little kitty," he called, peering up at me. I couldn't tell whether he could actually see me in the darkness or was just guessing at my position.

My gaze darted around. I'd inadvertently run myself into a dead end. This building was the last one of the block before the corner, where I didn't have a hope in hell of leaping the entire street. The only way off it was to jump to the building on the other side of the alley— right over Xavier's head.

If he sent his men up here, I might be screwed.

Sweat beaded on the back of my neck. I inched along the rooftop slowly, aiming to get a little distance from Xavier, but he prowled further into the alley at the same time. "Mercy," he said in a sing-song voice. "Come out, come out."

Then he whipped up his hand. I'd only just yanked myself back from the edge when a bullet clipped the corner of the roof just inches from where I'd been watching him. I chomped on my tongue and winced.

"Hiding away like a scaredy cat," Xavier taunted. Something far darker than a sneer came into his voice. "Josey gave up her life for you just so you could become a total chickenshit? What a fucking waste."

I froze in place. How the fuck could he know that name?

Xavier kept going. "I'm looking forward to flaying the skin right off you. Riddling your bones with bullets. Grinding you into a pulp."

He shot at the roof again, but a few feet farther along. He assumed I was still moving. I dragged in a breath, forcing myself to focus through my shock.

It didn't matter what he'd said. I couldn't worry about that now. If I wanted to stay alive, I had to get moving.

I eased a couple of steps back so that I could straighten up and eyeballed the opposite roof. The flattest spot was right across from me. As long as Xavier didn't double back right away, I should be fine.

Should being the operative word. I was staking my life on that hope.

I swallowed hard and backed up a little more to give myself a running start. Xavier had stopped talking, so I had no idea where he was, but as soon as I peeked over the edge, he'd know where *I* was. I had to go in blind.

I braced myself and then hurtled forward with all the strength I could push into my legs.

My feet practically flew across the hardened tar. If Xavier heard me coming, I didn't stop to worry about that. All my attention narrowed down to the need to propel my body across the six-foot gap between the buildings.

I hit the edge of the roof and sprang. The air whipped over my clothes and through my hair. A shot rang out, and I half expected to feel pain searing through one of my limbs—but I hit the shingles of the opposite roof with a quick roll, planting my hands to steady myself.

A tug in my gut called for me to stay, to see what else Xavier might say. Whether he'd mention something that would explain the taunt he'd made. But I couldn't trust a single word that came out of his mouth. I had to get somewhere safe and make sure the rest of my men had stayed safe too. I had to warn them that Xavier and others had arrived.

I took off across the roof, running over that building and onto the next where there wasn't any gap between them. As I fled, I yanked my phone out of my pocket and tapped out a hasty text to Wylder. When I felt safe enough to stop, I'd give him my location and ask someone to pick me up.

My heart was still hammering away in my chest. I made another, smaller leap and spotted a telephone wire arcing across the street that I could use like a zipline to get across.

As I reached it, I couldn't help glancing up toward the stars twinkling into view overhead. Those words Xavier had said replayed in my mind again. *Josey gave up her life.*

How the hell did he know my mother's name—and how was he so sure she was dead?

Mercy

Ezra did not look pleased with our victory. He kept stalking around the sitting room where the guys, Anthea, and I had gathered to discuss the results of yesterday's ambush and our next steps, his mouth set in a rigid line. About a dozen Noble men were staked out in the yard around the mansion. I wondered if he was getting paranoid. Maybe the news that he wasn't really the top dog around here had gotten to him.

"So, Xavier showed up?" Anthea was saying. "How did he find out?"

Gideon looked up from his tablet. "I'd imagine he was tracking the shipment. He must have been able to tell the truck had stopped for longer than made sense and immediately rushed over."

"Thankfully all our people got out of there in time— with the truck and all the weapons," Wylder said with a tight smile. "The prick got distracted by his obsession with Mercy."

"Seems to be a common problem," Ezra muttered without stopping his pacing. Wylder shot him a brief glare, and then everyone pretended he hadn't spoken.

I rubbed my hands over my knees, which were scraped under the fabric of my jeans from my leap across the rooftops. The faint sting barely penetrated my thoughts. My fingers drifted up to trace the line of my *Little Angel* bracelet in my pocket.

The way Xavier had said Mom's name: *Josey*. The familiarity in his tone. His certainty that she was gone. I hadn't mentioned it to the guys because I knew we had much more important things to focus on—like, oh, the fact that the Long Night was counting the hours until he'd send his people in to slaughter us all—but my nerves were still rattled.

I'd never known what'd happened to my mother. She'd just vanished one day—all her things gone from the house when I'd gotten home from school. Dad had refused to say more than that she'd "left." I hadn't known whether to believe him, knowing how he was... but how could Xavier know anything about her fate?

It didn't make any sense at all, and I didn't like that.

I pushed those thoughts aside. "All's well that ends well. We struck a good blow, and now we have more weapons and the Storm has fewer people here. How do we hit them next?"

"Yeah!" Kaige smacked his hands together. "I'll punch as many of those assholes as we need to."

As I gave him an affectionate kick from my seat

next to him on the couch, Ezra scowled. But my gaze was drawn to Gideon, whose face had darkened as he peered at his tablet's screen.

"We definitely hit them hard," he said, "but the Storm is stepping up his game too."

"One of our properties was attacked this morning," Ezra snapped. "Let's not beat around the bush."

"We had to expect some kind of retaliation," Rowan said. "It didn't go that badly. The men at the factory were able to defend it, so the Storm didn't take anything from us. There was one casualty, but that's it, right?"

Ezra's scowl didn't shift. "One too many."

I bit my tongue against pointing out that if he'd pitched in more from the start of the conflict, it might never have gotten this far.

Gideon cleared his throat and raised his head. "There's actually another thing, one I've only just confirmed. The truck last night was the biggest consolidated influx of Storm troops to come into the city in the past day, but it wasn't the only one. At least three other smaller trucks arrived. From what I can tell from the footage I've been able to dig up, they've still added a couple dozen men to their ranks."

Wylder muttered a curse. "And there are probably more coming. Can we catch them before they get here like we did with the transport truck?"

Gideon grimaced. "I haven't been able to find a pattern yet that would allow me to predict which trucks are associated with the Storm and when they'll be arriving. These were much more low key than the big one. I'm working on it, though."

Ezra let out a snort but said nothing.

"Fucking hell," Kaige said, running his fingers through his short, dark hair. "So yesterday was for nothing?"

"Not exactly," Anthea pointed out. "You took their weapons and at least half of the manpower they hoped to add to their forces. If the strike hadn't hurt, the Storm wouldn't have pushed back at us right away. Xavier's pissed off."

"Anthea's right," I said, grateful for her logical thinking. "We can't give up. We still made *some* progress, and we're only just getting started with the new intel we got from the Long Night."

"Right." Kaige perked back up again. "So, when are we going to go shoot them all down? That'd be a quick way to deal with the pricks."

Wylder shook his head with a crooked grin. "While I appreciate the sentiment, going head to head against the Storm's people without surprise on our side is only going to mean a bloodbath for all of us—and I don't know that we'll come out on top even then. We have to play this strong but smart."

"But we have to do something."

"And we will," Wylder promised. "Thankfully they can't know that we've secured the alliance of the Long Night. That's our wild card."

"I'm with Wylder on this one," Gideon said. "And with the new information we've gotten, I have been able to identify a few locations where the Storm may be storing vital equipment. It's not clear what exactly is in each place, but we're talking weapons, vehicles, possibly stashes of Glory."

Kaige growled at the mention of the drug. Gideon brought up a map on his tablet and pointed out four buildings he'd marked with a red X. Two of them were deep in the Bend and two others near the border of Paradise City.

"I'm not sure yet which one is most active, since I've only just narrowed my search down to those," Gideon went on. "But I'm keeping a close eye on them, and hopefully by tonight we'll have a solid idea of which would make the best target. That seems like a reasonable direction for our next attack."

"So, I'll get to punch or shoot *someone* then?" Kaige asked. "Just to be clear?"

Wylder gave him a baleful look. "You didn't spill enough blood last night? Yes, I'm sure there'll be guards, and someone will need to dispatch them."

Ezra had remained silent for this part of the conversation. He turned abruptly toward the doorway. "My advice to you? Don't get killed." He strode out of the room, muttering under his breath something about needing a drink.

Anthea sighed. "Should I go talk to my brother?"

"Don't bother," Wylder said. I could tell from his tone that his patience with his father was at an all-time low. "The longer he wallows, the less he can interfere in what we do."

Anthea nodded reluctantly. Things had gone so wrong between Wylder and his Dad that I couldn't help but feel a little responsible, knowing it was in part because Ezra disapproved of his son's relationship with me. But I had to admire the change in the Noble heir at the same time. He finally had enough leeway to take charge for himself, and he was making good use of the opportunity.

He clapped his hands. "All right. I'll send out a few small teams on foot to investigate those buildings and the activities around them—from a distance, without alerting the Storm's people. Gideon, you keep crunching the data, including the reports those teams send in, to figure out our best target. Kaige, maybe you and I could—"

Gideon cut him off with a sudden exclamation and a loud ping of his tablet. We all jerked toward him. "Is something wrong?" Rowan asked.

"No." Gideon's gray eyes had lit up with an eager gleam. "We've finally got something—from the tracker stuck on Xavier's boot. He's left the county, going somewhere new. He's got to be doing something to prepare for *his* next attack against us. Maybe he'll lead us to an even better target."

We all gathered close around to peer at the tablet's screen. Gideon had switched to a different app with a map view. A little blinking dot moved across the road at a quick pace.

"He's in a car, obviously," Gideon said. "Driving fast. Taking a lot of sudden turns like he wants to be sure he isn't being followed." He chuckled to himself almost gleefully. "Little does he know."

Rowan leaned on the back of the sofa to watch. His hand drifted over my shoulder, and I raised mine to squeeze his fingers in return.

"That's a good sign," he said. "He wouldn't care about being followed unless he was going somewhere important."

"Exactly." Gideon watched the screen avidly. "No sign of slowing down yet. I think we should see where this leads before we make any decisions. But it could take a little while. I doubt he'd go *too* far from the county while we're on the offensive, but it could still be hours."

Anthea stood up with a brisk swipe of her hands. "Well, it's just about lunchtime. I'll whip something up so we'll all be well-fueled in every possible way."

My mouth immediately started watering at the thought of one of Anthea's meals. "Count me in."

We ended up gathering around the island in the kitchen, Gideon leaving his tablet propped up in the middle so we could all follow Xavier's movements. Wylder sat close enough to me that our knees touched, and a quiver of warmth ran up my leg remembering our passionate interlude in the car after the funeral. And more than that, the words he'd said to me.

Love wasn't something that came up all that often in our kind of life. My dad sure as hell hadn't been in love with my mom or any of the other women he'd brought around. I wasn't sure I'd have said it to Wylder if he hadn't said it first so I knew it was something he'd have wanted to hear. But damn, was I glad it was.

These were good men, all of them—the four I'd found myself tangled up with. I leaned against Kaige's shoulder for a moment, and he pressed a quick kiss to my temple. Anthea clucked her tongue at us, murmured something about "young love," and got to work over the stove.

Xavier's dot didn't stop until we'd all polished off the juiciest hamburgers I'd ever eaten along with a heap of Anthea's famous fries—or at least, they should have been famous. I was just licking ketchup from the corner of my mouth when Gideon leaned forward.

"He's stopped." He cocked his head to the side, giving the screen a puzzled frown. "There's nothing on the map there. It's way out from any town—no buildings even showing up."

"I guess it makes sense that the Storm would have some kind of secret bases set up," I said, studying the image. "These people are obviously very good at staying under the radar."

"And he's got to realize how easily someone with the right skills can use traffic cams and so on to spy on his movements, like Gideon already has," Anthea pointed out. "Somewhere way off the beaten track would be hard for anyone to trace."

"Right," Rowan said, shooting a smile at Gideon. "We'd never have known about this if you hadn't managed to get the tracker on Xavier."

Gideon's laugh sounded a little raw. "I'm glad something good came out of that SNAFU after all."

"The Storm has got to have some pretty important stuff stashed there if he keeps it so carefully hidden," Wylder said. "Especially if Xavier's going there now while he's gearing up to get his revenge for the bridge ambush. I say that's our target. We hit it tonight."

All of us around the island nodded. I hopped off my

stool. "I want in, but I should check with my men back in the Bend and see how many Claws are up for another mission. Let me know when you've worked out our best approach."

I'd only just turned toward the door when a couple of Noble men hustled inside. They were ushering a boy who looked to be in his mid-teens ahead of them. I paused, frowning. The kid couldn't have been out of high school, with sandy blond hair a few shades darker than Rowan's and a sharply regal nose that didn't quite fit the boyishness of the rest of his face. I'd never seen him before.

It appeared that Wylder hadn't either. He got to his feet, casting a critical glance over the boy. "What's going on?"

"This kid turned up outside saying he wanted to talk to the leader of the Nobles," one of the guards said. "I wasn't sure if we should bother Ezra with it."

Wylder hesitated, and I knew he was debating whether he could claim that leadership himself. How would Ezra react to this new arrival in his increasingly hostile state? On the other hand, how would he react to Wylder going over his head again?

Before he made his decision, I stepped forward and pointed toward the Noble heir. "Wylder speaks for the Nobles. Anything you need, you can talk to him about it."

Wylder's gaze snapped to me, but he didn't argue. The guard shrugged, and the boy eased away from them. His eyes flicked nervously from side to side, but then he drew his chin up with obvious determination. "Thank you for hearing me out."

Rowan's voice took on the gentle note it always did when he was putting someone at ease. "Why don't you start by telling us who you are?"

The boy took a deep breath. "My name is Beckett. You don't know me, but I know about you. I'm the son of the man you call the Storm."

8

Rowan

I narrowed my eyes at the kid. Something about his appearance had heightened my instincts. I kept my attention on him, my gaze skimming over him carefully.

There was no way of telling if his story was true. We'd never met the Storm, so I couldn't check for family resemblances. Why would the son of the man we'd been fighting against want to talk to *us*?

Beckett opened his mouth to go on, but Wylder raised a hand to stop him. The Noble heir looked around as if he expected his dad to appear around the corner any second. If Ezra did find out who'd supposedly walked into our midst, I could only imagine the scene he'd make. The kid would be lucky to live a minute longer.

"Not here," Wylder said gruffly.

Beckett frowned. "What's wrong?" The kid looked spooked, as if he was expecting somebody to charge him from the door. I was still having a hard time wrapping my head around the idea that the Storm had children—or any family really.

But I guessed he was a person like the rest of us—like the Long Night, who might have had kids and even grandkids for all we knew—no matter how much power he held.

"Let's take this to the back sitting room," Anthea said briskly, and I was immediately grateful. Both Wylder's office and Gideon's would hold too much information relating to our plans. The back sitting room had a door that locked, but it was small enough that no one used it for anything official often.

Wylder nodded and motioned for Beckett to head out of the kitchen ahead of him. The Noble men started to follow us, but Wylder shook his head at them. "I'll handle him."

I half expected them to argue, but apparently the Noble heir was making strides in winning over his father's men. They stepped back with respectful dips of their heads. It probably helped that Axel wasn't around anymore, spewing his venom.

In the hall, Wylder took the lead, Kaige and I falling into step on either side of the kid and Mercy, Gideon, and Anthea bringing up the rear. He wouldn't be able to get away with much. We tramped into the cozy space with its antique sofa and chairs set and heavy velvet curtains, which Wylder jerked shut over the window. I locked the door behind us.

Wylder gestured to me. "Rowan, pat him down."

Beckett's eyes twitched even more nervously as I

stepped toward him, but I kept my expression mild. "Stand with your legs a foot apart and your arms raised," I instructed, and he moved right away.

I briskly checked him over, paying particular attention to obvious pockets and typical places to conceal a holster. When I turned up nothing, I backed up and crossed my arms over my chest, considering him. "It was a big risk coming in here totally unarmed."

The kid shrugged, but the flick of his tongue over his lips showed he wasn't really all that nonchalant. "Would you have trusted me otherwise?"

"We still don't," I had to point out.

"Well, I was hoping to talk, not get into a fight. I'm counting on you wanting information about my father more than you want to shoot up some teenager who's put himself at your mercy."

Wylder pointed Beckett to a chair. He sat down, taking a quick swipe at his forehead, where sweat was starting to shine. Anthea pulled out a water bottle from a mini fridge and handed it to him.

Beckett eyed it suspiciously before snatching it from her hand. I raised an eyebrow at her as she walked toward me. Anthea shook her head to indicate that she hadn't put anything in it, as adept as she was with chemical effects. I guessed a kind overture couldn't hurt anything.

Wylder dropped into a chair across from the kid. "So, you're really the Storm's son?"

"That's what I said, didn't I?" Beckett replied.

"Are you having second thoughts about coming here?" Wylder asked.

Beckett froze, his jaw tightening before he seemed to come to a decision. "No, but I'll admit I'm still not sure this wasn't a stupid idea. I just... I didn't know what else to do."

"You said you have some information about the Storm," I put in. "How can we know whether you're actually who you say you are and whether you're telling the truth rather than trying to throw us off?"

The kid gave me a look that seemed to imply I was being an idiot. For all his nerves, he had a lot of bravado too. That did line up with him being a child of privilege. I could tell his clothes were custom tailored and good materials too.

"I don't know how I could prove it to you," he said, a little haughtily, "since you don't know enough about who my father is to recognize whether I'm telling you something only his son would be aware of. But the fact that I came here at all should show that I'm putting *my* trust in you. And if you use the information I can give you, then you'll see pretty quickly that I'm being honest."

"Your father has been making things very difficult for us," Mercy said. "His people have hurt this county way more than anyone else in the entire time I've been alive. That doesn't exactly make us want to welcome anyone associated with him."

Beckett's mouth twisted. "I can believe it. And if I had any say in it, he and his shadow would be far away from here. Things were bad enough before—" He cut himself off with a sharp breath. "I want the war here to be over too. That's why I came, and why I'll help you."

"Where did you say you're from again?" Gideon prompted, obviously trying to prod him for more details about the Storm that he might not have meant to give away.

"That's not important," Beckett said, dodging the question easily. "If Dad and the rest of his men leave Paradise Bend, they won't bother you anymore, no matter where they go from here. That's all you really care about, isn't it?"

Abruptly, Kaige loomed over the kid's chair. "I still don't see why we should listen to you at all. Maybe this is one of your asshole dad's twisted plans, huh? Why would you come here wanting to *hurt* him?"

Beckett's voice tightened. "I don't want to hurt him. I want to save him from the mess he's created."

"Oh, and we're supposed to feel sorry for *him* now?"

"Can you please back off?" Beckett said, looking straight at Kaige. I had to give it to him: the kid had balls. "I'll explain if you give me the chance."

"Kaige, stand down," Wylder said, quiet but firm. Kaige grumbled under his breath and sat down on one of the chairs, which creaked in protest under his brawn.

"How old are you?" I asked Beckett.

"Sixteen," Beckett said. "But I've been on the sidelines of my father's business since I was twelve, and I knew about it for much longer than that."

Just like Ezra had drawn in Roland from the start, from what I understood, and then started shaping Wylder into his vision of an heir as soon as he'd lost his older son. Despite myself, I felt a trickle of sympathy I quickly tamped down on. Maybe that reaction was exactly what he—and the Storm —wanted.

Beckett was non-threatening. Even though he was almost as tall as us, he still had his boyish features, barely on the cusp of adulthood. But looks could be deceiving.

"Growing up like that must have been tough," Mercy said evenly, but I thought I caught some pity in her tone. She knew what it was like being dragged into this kind of world as a child better than any of us in this room.

"I guess, but it was the education I needed," Beckett said. "It's a brutal world out there, especially for a family like mine, constantly surrounded by people who'd like to take a grab at our empire, but we still have to play nice with them. You should know that without my help, you're unlikely to win this war in the long run. The Storm is far more powerful than you think. He has the resources to keep going and going until everyone who stands against him in this city is wiped out."

"And why would you want to stop him from doing that?" Gideon asked, with a cock of his head as if he were genuinely curious rather than looking for proof. Knowing him, he probably was.

Beckett took a deep breath. "Over the last few years, Dad has become increasingly hungry for power. He's been taking over any territories he can by whatever means necessary. He saw a power vacuum in the Bend, and decided to make a move, but the resistance you've been giving him has only made the change I saw before more extreme. He's pushing our men harder than ever, giving more control than ever to that loose cannon Xavier, and neglecting our usual businesses."

"Xavier isn't the only one to be blamed," Mercy said. "Your father sent him here."

Beckett sighed. "I know. Dad would never have given him this much authority in the past. He's... He's insane. The things I've seen him do just around us..." He swallowed hard. "But he gets the job done, and these days that's all Dad seems to care about. Unfortunately, that means that Xavier has gained considerable power, more power than I'm comfortable him having."

"And now you're feeling sorry for us here in Paradise Bend?" Anthea said.

Beckett shook his head. "I won't pretend or lie to you. What happens to this place isn't my concern. It's my father I'm worried about. This new aggressive approach is earning us all kinds of enemies and setting a standard for the people who work for us that I hate. I'm afraid we'll be dealing with the fallout for decades, long after his empire becomes mine. I want to inherit something more stable and even peaceful, not an organization built out of violence."

Wylder raised his eyebrows. "Well, I hope you didn't come to us thinking *we* care what happens to the bastard or your family's 'empire'."

Beckett glanced around the room, his posture stiff. "I know, and I don't expect that. You just have to understand that I love my dad despite the path he's been going down, and despite our differences I don't want to see him hurt. I want to see this crusade of his over with, and I also want it to happen without him ending up dead or with much more bloodshed on either side. I can give you information on his operations that will help you tackle him quickly, more effectively—and without the slaughter getting even worse."

"Too bad," Kaige growled. "Because I'd like nothing better than to get my hands on that cunt and rip him apart for bringing war to our doorstep."

Beckett swallowed visibly. "You've got to understand. I know he's done terrible things to you. But he's still my dad, and he hasn't been a bad father most of the time... He's all the family I really have."

A pang radiated through my chest. Every sign I could pick up on said he really was worried about his father, and I hadn't noticed any holes in his story. I could usually spot a lie once someone really got talking. And something about his explanation and the anguish on his face resonated with my own past, bringing out a surge of emotion from deep inside me.

I'd always wanted to save *my* family, to protect them from the crap I'd inadvertently brought into their lives and then my dad's poor decisions. I'd failed. How could I tell this kid he deserved to fail too?

Whatever he could tell us might be useful. We'd gotten extra intel from the Long Night, but he wouldn't know his opponent's secrets as well as that opponent's own family.

"Kaige, enough," Wylder said. He turned back to Beckett. "Why are you here *now*? The Storm has been tearing through the Bend for weeks now."

"I heard about the ambush and the massacre of

Storm men last night," Beckett said, his voice rough. "My father was upset to the point of stomping around ranting about it. He gave Xavier more freedom to do whatever he feels he needs to do, which I know is only going to make things worse... I felt like I had to do *something*, and if I waited any longer, it might be too late for everyone."

Could Xavier really get worse than he already was? Had his previous actions actually been *restrained*? I shuddered inwardly at the thought.

"You've put a lot of faith in us," I said, watching him carefully. "Aren't you worried that we'll hurt *you* or use you against your father somehow?"

Beckett gave me a pained smile. "That's a risk I'm willing to take. Anyway, taking me hostage will only make the situation worse for you, not better. Dad'll go totally berserk. You don't want that any more than I do."

I believed he was telling the truth about that too. I paused and glanced at Wylder. "I think we should give him a chance. See what information he can give us and how we can use it."

Wylder gave me an assessing look. "Are you sure?"

He might not trust the kid, but he trusted my judgment. I studied Beckett again, wanting to be sure I didn't misuse that trust. But every instinct in my body told me I was looking at a kid who was terrified of the situation he'd been watching unfold and desperate to turn it around.

I nodded, my gaze darting to Mercy. "I can recognize what he's going through to some extent. I gave up a lot to try to protect my family. If he's willing to offer anything that'll benefit all of us, we should let him. Lord knows we need it right now."

Wylder appeared to contemplate my words for a few moments. Then he focused on Beckett with a lift of his chin. "Can you tell us anything about a facility belonging to your father that's about an hour north of the city, several miles off any major road? Someplace Xavier might have had a reason to go."

Beckett's face twitched with surprise. "How did you —?" He shook his head as if he'd decided the question didn't matter. "That could actually be a good place to start. My dad has a base out there that he's been using to funnel resources and men into the Bend and other operations in this state. If you could destroy that, it'd strike a real blow against his efforts here and show he's up against even more opposition than he was ready for. Maybe that'd be enough for him to rethink continuing his campaign."

"If this place is that important, I assume it'll be heavily guarded," Mercy prompted. "How do you see us managing to take it down?"

Beckett gave her a small smile, and I caught the hint of ruthlessness in his eyes—no doubt cultivated by his father without the Storm ever realizing that one day his son might turn it against him.

"What if I told you there's a way to destroy it without anyone ever knowing you were even there?" he said.

Wylder leaned toward him, his interest piqued. "Tell me more."

9

Mercy

WE TRAMPED THROUGH THE FOREST, OUR flashlights set on the lowest brightness so they only lit up the underbrush a few feet in front of us. We had to be sure we wouldn't be seen from a distance. Around us, thick branches of trees tangled together with a thick canopy of leaves that all but blotted out the moonlight. It'd rained briefly in the afternoon, and the smell of damp soil filled my nose.

Something snapped a few feet away. Wylder and Rowan whirled around. There was a flash of bright eyes and a reddish-brown body as a small fox scurried away.

"There used to be some of them in the city around the parks," Rowan murmured as we walked on. "I haven't seen one in ages."

"Well, at least there aren't any snakes," Kaige said, and then looked to the others for confirmation. "Right?"

Wylder gave him a reassuring swat and motioned for him to get a move on.

We were about half a mile away from the Storm's secret facility and drawing closer with every step that we took. Beckett had informed us that the buildings were surrounded by a high chain-link fence that was electrified, and armed guards patrolled the property. But he'd given us a way in that would avoid all of the security measures.

A metallic glint caught my flashlight. It was the jaws of a hunting trap with a rabbit caught inside it. It looked like the trapper hadn't come around in a while, because the fur was eaten away by maggots. Its empty eye sockets stared at me as I walked past it.

"Still think this is a good idea?" Kaige asked.

I took a deep breath. "Rowan's a good judge of character. If he thinks the kid was being genuine, I'm okay trusting him with this. It's not like we won't be careful."

"It'd be an awfully convoluted plan for screwing us over," Rowan pointed out. "And I think we all know a thing or two about growing up quickly and wishing we could change the course our parents set us on." His dark blue eyes scanned our little group.

He was right about that. There was one thing we all had in common—our parents had thoroughly fucked us up.

Wylder nodded. "We had to do something. We're already through the second day of our week. I don't totally trust the kid, but that's why we're here—to find out whether we *should* trust him. At least we're taking the risk ourselves. My dad would probably have sent his least favorite underlings out to take on the danger." He grimaced.

"I think anyone who sends us stumbling around in a forest in the middle of the night has bad intentions," Kaige grumbled, before turning to me. "Mercy?"

I peered off into the darkness, and my stomach twisted. "So many people have already died. If Beckett can give us a way to win this war without tons more death and collateral damage, I think we should take it. Maybe this and a couple more definitive strikes will be what it takes to end this once and for all." I paused, ducking my head. "I'll fight as long as it takes, but I've got to admit I'm getting tired of it."

Kaige grunted. "I never get tired of fighting. But I *am* tired of seeing assholes trying to gun you down, so if this means that part's over, I guess I'm okay with it."

"Glad to have your support," Wylder said dryly, and then held up his hand, bringing us all to a halt.

Unless we'd deviated from the directions Beckett had given us without realizing it, the faint pinpricks of light that showed between the trees from up ahead were the distant security lights of the Storm's facility. There was another short stretch of forest and then an expansive field between us and the compound, but the "doorway" we were looking for should be right around here.

Wylder cast his flashlight around, veering to the right as he scanned the ground. After several seconds, he let out a triumphant sound and pointed his beam at a tree with a subtle marking on the bark. We hurried over and helped him pull over a layer of moss that covered a circular metal hatch in the ground.

The four of us eyed it cautiously. Wylder rubbed his jaw. "Let's take the lay of the land up here first, make sure everything looks the way the kid led us to expect." He reached into the pack he was carrying and pulled out a pair of binoculars. "Want to do the honors, Kitty Cat? You're the best climber between us."

I smiled and accepted the binoculars. Glancing around, I picked out the nearest tall tree with branches spaced decently well. With a running start, I leapt up to grab a lower branch and hoisted myself onto it. It took less than a minute for me to clamber above the thicker canopy to a spot where I could see more easily between the thinning treetops.

I raised the binoculars to my eyes, my other arm pressed against the rough bark of the tree trunk, and peered toward the security lights. With a couple of flicks of the dials, the building came into focus.

The place looked like some kind of storage facility. Beyond the metal fence, I spotted a few men going about their usual patrol. A narrow dirt road snaked away from the facility and probably led back to the main road. Two huge trucks were parked just inside the gate. Beckett had told us that his father moved shipments of supplies through this place, sometimes stashing things there for later use, and that some of his underlings went through additional training inside the building.

I climbed down and reported everything to Wylder. The Noble heir cocked his head. "That all matches up with what the kid told us." He turned to the hatch.

"Now for the real question: is this a brilliant plan or a devious trap?"

We all knelt down around the hatch. I swept a few stray bits of soil away from a small electronic keypad off to the side. Rowan tapped in the code Beckett had passed on.

Immediately, a faint sound of air whooshing reached our ears. Wylder snagged his fingers around a small latch and pulled it up with little effort. He shone his flashlight into the opening, where the steel rungs of a ladder fell away into the thicker darkness of a tunnel that supposedly led under the ground to the Storm's facility—a secret escape route for the inhabitants. Now it'd become a secret entrance for us—although we weren't even going all the way into the building.

Some of us weren't even going into the tunnel itself. I wished I could have joined the guys, but I'd anticipated the effect the sight would have on me. Taking in the tight space and the darkness pooled inside it, my skin crawled with an eerie chill. My heart started to thump faster.

I closed my eyes against the prickles of panic, focusing on the hoot of a nearby owl and the brush of the breeze over my bare arms.

"It's okay," Rowan said gently. "None of us can do everything. Wylder and I will manage just fine."

"Anyway," Kaige said, "*someone* needs to stand guard."

"And from the looks of things, you'd block up the whole tunnel if we tried to squeeze *you* down there," Wylder teased. He hefted his bag. "Let's go."

Rowan attached his flashlight to the pocket on his

shirt and scrambled down the ladder. There was a faint thud as his feet hit the ground. We all gazed down at him. Seeing him in the dark, narrow space made my chest clench up all over again. I forced myself to keep looking.

He was taking on this danger when I couldn't because I was too weak to get over my stupid claustrophobia. The least I could do was see him off. My brain had to figure out that I wasn't going to be suffocated or buried alive when I wasn't even *in* the damn tunnel.

Rowan ducked deeper into the narrow space to make room for Wylder's descent. When the Noble heir reached the bottom, Kaige leaned farther over, frowning. "This place doesn't look too stable to me. Just don't get trapped in here."

"We won't," Wylder said. "Send us an alert if you see any movement nearby, and don't get seen yourselves. If this all goes according to plan, we'll be back in less than half an hour."

They vanished into the darkness, and I finally let myself look away. Kaige wrapped his muscular arms around me and nipped my earlobe, offering a welcome distraction with the heat of his body. "Guess it's just us now. I can think of a few interesting activities to keep us busy."

As much as I enjoyed having him this close, I pushed him away with a playful shove and an arch of my eyebrows. "We're *supposed* to be standing guard. There might be Storm men around. We should keep a close watch."

Now that I was no longer looking into the dark passage, my panic was easing, leaving only a leaden feeling in my arms and stomach. Even just standing next to him, Kaige's massive, solid presence bought me comfort.

"What do you think they'll find down there?" Kaige asked as he stepped back from the hatch, his gaze scanning the woods around us.

"The underground entrance to the compound," I said. "So far everything else has gone the way Beckett said."

He shook his head doubtfully. "I just hope it's not a trap. It would be too easy to get us in there together and then bury us."

I shivered at the thought. Kaige's brows came together. "I'm sorry. I shouldn't be talking like that. Don't think about it—there are a hell of a lot of easier ways to trap us if they really wanted to, right?"

"Probably." I rubbed my arms, willing away the renewed chill. "I just wish my fear didn't hold me back in situations like this."

"How often does it even come up? Like Rowan said, none of us can do everything." Kaige stepped closer to me again, putting an arm around my shoulder. I couldn't help leaning into him. He looked down at the hatch, and his expression turned momentarily serious. "I couldn't have come up with a plan like this. My brain just doesn't work in all these fiddly sneaky ways. I know that tackling our enemies like this is better for us in the long run, especially when we're up against people as powerful as the Storm, but the only way that ever occurs to me is to crack some heads."

I lifted myself on the balls of my feet to give his cheek a quick peck. "You've got more than muscle to offer."

He shrugged without meeting my eyes. "Gideon and Rowan, they're smart and quick on their feet. Wylder and you—you're natural leaders, and I've seen the way you coordinate with each other and the people under you during fights. What am I except a couple of fists? Very powerful fists, sure, but I'm nothing without my body."

The doubt in his tone squeezed at my heart. "You don't really believe that, do you? Because I don't."

"I know what people see when they look at me—I know what I am." Kaige seemed to shake off his momentary pensiveness. "But hey, there are some benefits to being a guy who's all about the body. Think of all the amazing ways I've been able to handle this one." He traced his fingers down my side to my hip.

I elbowed him lightly. "Focus on keeping watch. You can show me more of those bodily talents later."

Kaige gave me a flirty grin, though I thought I saw a hint of his earlier uneasiness lingering in his deep brown eyes. "Is that a promise?"

I wagged a finger at him. "If you promise to keep your eyes on the woods instead of me until we're done here."

"Aww, you're no fun." He pinched my hip.

I rolled my eyes as I returned my own gaze to the

darkened forest around us. "I think I've proven that's not true at all."

Kaige snickered, but he fell into a companionable silence, watching for any movement between the trees. My pulse kept pounding, not from claustrophobia now but the basic uncertainty of what Wylder and Rowan would have found at the end of that tunnel. Beckett had seemed sincere, sure, but how could we trust *anyone* in this kind of life?

On the other hand, look at how many great things had happened because my men and I had found a way to trust each other.

At a rustling near our feet, my gaze jerked down. Rowan was just climbing up the ladder. Dirt speckled his hair and clothes, and he had a smudge on his temple, but otherwise he looked no worse for wear. He panted a little as if he'd run the whole way, though.

"Are you okay?" I asked as Wylder clambered out of the tunnel after him.

"Perfect," the Noble heir said with a grin. "The explosives were exactly where Beckett said they'd be, just waiting to cut off the escape route and destroy all the evidence inside if the Storm's people were making a run for it. Of course, with our way, they'll be the ones getting destroyed."

Rowan matched his smile. "We laid the fuse all the way out here. There's nothing left to do but light it."

Wylder held up the end of the thick rope we were using as a fuse. We'd soaked it in kerosene before bringing it out here, and the chemical tang wafting off it itched in my nose. He snapped his fingers. "Lighter?"

I held out the one I'd been carrying for this purpose. All four of us stood around the mouth of the tunnel as Wylder flicked on the flame. He held it to the end of the fuse and dropped the rope the second it lit up.

It fell to the floor of the tunnel, the flames already streaking along its length out of view like a serpent made of fire. Kaige grabbed the hatch and slammed it down. "Let's get the hell out of here before the place blows!"

We turned and jogged through the forest as fast as we could in the darkness, not daring to even turn on our flashlights now. I didn't think it'd been more than a minute before an earth-shaking *boom* split the air and rattled the branches around us.

I spun around. Orange light danced and flashed in the distance in the tiny gaps between the trees. The initial explosion was followed by a thundering crash of thick walls collapsing. In my mind's eye, I pictured the hail of concrete and mortar—and the bodies engulfed in the blaze.

I leaned against a trunk to catch my balance. The breeze licked over me, carrying a trace of acrid smoke. My throat constricted around it.

We'd mostly wanted to obliterate this resource of the Storm's, to show him we could tackle him on his own turf. But at least some of the men in and around that facility would have died in the explosion—some of them men who might have had nothing to do with Paradise Bend.

But that was what this war had come to. How many

innocent people had fallen in the Bend because of the Storm's reign of terror?

My people were safer now because we'd managed to strike a major blow against our enemies.

Kaige raised his hand to request a high five from Wylder. Wylder smacked his hand, but his expression was somber. He wasn't unaffected by the lengths we'd gone to for this victory either.

"It looks like Beckett set us on the right path," Rowan said. "He didn't know we'd found out about this place until he showed up at the mansion, and he hasn't had a chance to leave or do anything unmonitored since he arrived. I don't see any way this could have been a ploy to convince us."

Wylder nodded. "The kid's legit. Now let's get home and find out what other ways he's willing to help us rain havoc down on his dear ol' dad."

I gave the flickers of the flames one last look and hustled with the others through the forest toward our car.

Mercy

THE GUYS DROPPED ME BACK AT MY HOUSE WITH A promise to pick me up early next morning to regroup and strategize. I waved goodbye to them and watched them drive down the darkened street. It was past midnight, and all but a couple of the lights in the house were off. I hoped Sarah was sleeping okay in her new room. I'd managed to find an old bedspread from my childhood with pink and purple clouds printed on it that she'd squealed over on sight.

A few of the Claws men had come to a stop on the lawn near me, braced to leap to my protection, but the street around us was dead. I nodded to them with a smile of thanks and headed up the front walk to the house.

Sam was hanging out in the living room with a couple of the other guys, passing a joint around as they discussed some new job they were putting together to increase our income. "Everything good?" I called to them.

Sam grinned at me. "Yep."

I'd noticed a change in their morale ever since we'd successfully carried out the ambush on the weapons truck. While it hadn't been as all-encompassing a blow as I'd hoped, it seemed to have had a positive effect on the Claws men in general.

I picked up a target practice board that'd been knocked to the ground. It was splintered with knife gouges. When I passed through to the dining room, I found the table laid out with an assortment of weapons from the ambush—guns of all sizes, from pistols that would easily fit into one of my hands to semi-automatic rifles.

We were definitely well-armed now. Jenner figured we could sell a bunch of the extras to help fund our continuing operations.

I sighed deeply. My body still buzzed with the adrenaline of our forest mission, and I knew sleep wouldn't come easily.

Instead of making my way upstairs, I walked through the house and opened the door to the backyard. Maybe the cool air would help soothe the growing restlessness in me. It almost felt like I was holding in a breath and waiting for something, but I didn't know what.

The sky was clear, stars twinkling through the thin haze of city smog. It was so silent out here that I could hear the crunch of a few fallen leaves under my feet. The grass was overgrown, in desperate need of trimming, not that landscaping was a big priority at the moment. Wild tufts of weeds knotted along the edges of the white picket fence that towered a good seven feet off the ground. Dad had always liked to keep the neighbors out of our business.

I'd have to clean this place up better... when I had time. It was hard to wrap my head around the idea of doing anything that wasn't directly toward our fight against the Storm. Who cared if my backyard looked a bit ratty when we might all be dead in less than a week?

I sucked in the cool night air and tipped back my head, letting the breeze lick over my skin. Of its own accord, my hand dropped to my pocket, where I was carrying my childhood bracelet like usual. The one that'd been my mother's last gift to me.

A sudden urge came over me. I tucked my fingers into my pocket and pulled out the thin silver chain. It gleamed in the faint light. I ran my thumb over the words engraved in the narrow panel: *Little Angel.*

We'd played out here all the time. Flashes of memory passed through my head: Mom swinging me around over the grass. Us tumbling onto the lawn together and rolling all the way to the flower bed, giggling. Her boosting me up so I could perch on the lowest branch of the tree. I'd always demanded to get up there, and she'd gone along with it, even though she'd hovered nervously beneath me in case I'd fall.

I never had. What would she think of my climbing abilities now?

I glanced back toward the house. The memory of the last morning I'd had with her was fragmented too.

I'd only been six, and I hadn't known it was going to be my final glimpse of her. I could picture her willowy figure swaying through the kitchen, humming a tune under her breath as she prepared pancakes for me with sweet maple syrup on top.

She'd always been there. It'd never occurred to me that she might leave. She'd given me the bracelet on my sixth birthday, kissed my nose, and told me I'd always be her angel, no matter how old I got.

And then less than a month later, she'd disappeared.

She and Dad hadn't been married—I knew that much. And they'd argued sometimes. I had shaky memories of those moments too: of cringing in a corner when he'd lay into her for some small oversight. She'd been the only woman who'd ever given him a kid, and he'd blamed her for not managing to produce a son for him. I wished I'd had the guts to point out to him that if he couldn't knock up *any* women, the problem was obviously below his belt, not theirs.

Mom wouldn't have left me with him all alone on purpose, would she? Or would I rather that she had than think that Dad had *forced* her to leave in some permanent way? How well had I really known her anyway? Sarah probably hadn't believed her mom would ever run off on her.

A thump at the fence brought my attention jerking to the far end of the yard. At the sight of the massive form crouched on top of the white pickets, my stomach flipped over.

It was Xavier, poised like a tiger about to spring, with a menacing grin stretched across his face.

I dropped the bracelet, my dominant hand leaping to the gun wedged in the back of my jeans. Before I'd managed to raise it, Xavier pointed his own pistol right at my face.

"Hello, Mercy," he said like he had yesterday night, balancing on the narrow top of the fence without the slightest waver. I hadn't even heard him coming. For all his bulk, he was obviously agile and stealthy as well as strong.

Of course he was. How else could he have snuck onto the Noble property to leave me all his horrible "gifts" like the creepy drawing and the severed cat tail— not to mention the rest of the cat's corpse and the rotted body parts he'd dug up?

I could never forget that I was dealing with a total psychopath in him, someone who didn't operate according to typical human standards.

I kept my fingers curled around my gun, afraid to raise it in case Xavier shot me before I could shoot him, afraid to turn my back on him to run toward the house. I took one step backward, and he clicked off the safety.

"You're staying right there," he announced, so coolly and confidently I had no doubt that he'd put a bullet in my brain the second I made another move. Then he started to whistle an eerie tune under his breath, as if he were taking a casual stroll down the street.

There were supposed to be a couple of guards keeping an eye on the back of the house, but he must have managed to keep out of their view. I held myself still and considered my options, fear tickling up my spine.

"Don't even think of raising the alarm either," Xavier warned. "Or it's going to be a bloody massacre for not just you but all your pathetic followers. But I think you know a thing or two about that. Do you have any idea how many men you blew to bits tonight? Most of those idiots weren't even headed for Paradise Bend. But what do you care about the havoc you wreak?"

"The only person wreaking havoc around here is you," I said, pitching my voice just a little higher than usual so it wouldn't be obvious I was trying to catch the guards' attention, but loud enough that I could hope that they would hear me anyway. "And we're going to keep destroying the Storm's resources until he realizes it costs too much to stay in the Bend."

"Why do you feel the need to explain that to me?" Xavier asked in a taunting voice. "Oh, that's right." He waved the gun toward me. "Under all the pretense of a badass leader, you're a just a little girl with a gun. You're a weakling with no spine, and you have no idea what you're up against. So far, you've gotten real lucky, but that's only because I was toying with you. Now it's time to put you down for all the misery you've caused me."

"The misery *I've* caused you?" I retorted in a disbelieving tone, letting my voice get just a little louder. "I'd never have had anything to do with you or the Storm if you hadn't barged into my home. Maybe you're the weakling, scared of this little girl." If I got him angry, affected his focus, I might have the chance to take a shot after all.

But Xavier just snorted in response. "Scared of you?

Oh, no. I loathe you. I loathe your very existence. You took away the only thing I've ever cared about."

Genuine anguish reverberated through his fierce voice. I frowned, racking my brain to figure out what he might mean. Had one of the Storm men we'd taken down been important to him? It'd never seemed like he cared about their lives.

"What the hell are you talking about?" I demanded.

Fury clouded Xavier's face. Unfortunately, his gun hand didn't dip. "You took Josey from me," he snapped.

My heart stopped. The words tumbled from my mouth before I could think better of them. "Don't you dare try to use my mother's name to mess with me."

Xavier shifted his weight. His voice came out thick with rage. "Before she was your mother, she meant much more to me than she could ever have mattered to you. She was my entire world."

"Stop fucking with me," I said, but my voice faltered. I gathered myself and put more force into my next question. "What the fuck do you mean?"

Had any of the men nearby caught on that I was in trouble yet? They might be sneaking closer to make sure they were in a good position before they jumped right into the fray.

And maybe I didn't want them to jump in yet. I wanted to know what connection this sick bastard had to my mother.

Xavier's pupils were dilated and the veins on his forehead pulsed as he began to speak. "Your mother and I grew up together, and somewhere along the line, we fell in love. Or at least I thought she loved me back until she ran off someplace too far for me to find her until years later. She said I was hurting her. As if I'd ever do anything that wasn't for her own good." His tone had taken on an odd rambling quality.

He laughed suddenly, the sound echoing around the backyard. He wasn't even trying to hide himself now. He dropped down on the lawn in front of me, and I instinctively drew a step back. Anger emanated from his every pore. His eyes were bloodshot, his face tightened into a mask of pure fury—all directed at me.

"She looked just like you," he went on. "Innocent and pure, and you wouldn't even suspect that she schemed behind my back to leave me. Took off one night while I was on a job—I came back to the apartment and found her and her things gone."

My stomach twisted. Maybe I didn't really want to hear this story after all. But I needed to understand—and to give any help that was coming time to get into the right position to take this monster down.

"How's that my fault?" I asked. "I wasn't even born yet."

"No." He gave me a dark look. "I spent a long time looking for her, looking for my answers. But it was only after she was completely gone from this world that I discovered where she'd ended up. She came here and decided to play house with that prick Tyrell Katz, got herself pregnant by him... I treated her like a princess only for her to become another man's whore. And then when I finally had my chance to get her back, she was already out of reach. All that was left was him and you, the two people she left me for."

He wasn't making any real sense. How could Mom have left Xavier for me when I hadn't existed yet? But in Xavier's mind, it was obviously my fault somehow.

He hadn't loved her. He'd been obsessed with her. He'd thought he owned her, just like Dad had thought he owned me. Josey had escaped one monster only to get wrapped up in another one's life. Maybe my father hadn't been quite as awful as the man in front of me, but they were cut from the same cloth, weren't they?

How could I doubt that she'd ever been with Xavier when she'd given Dad at least seven years of her life? She'd had a type, one that really wasn't good for her.

"You're lying," I challenged him, even though I didn't really believe that.

Xavier stared at me as if he wasn't really seeing me. Maybe he was imagining my mother superimposed on my features. "She would have come back to me. She would've come back where she belonged if it wasn't for *you*. She stayed so she could pretend to have her happy little family, and by the time I found her, it was too late." His voice cracked. "My Josey was dead."

He sounded so sure. "No," I said, shaking my head. "Maybe she got away from you *and* my dad like she deserved."

Xavier focused in on me again. His expression hardened. "*You* never deserved her. And you'll pay for stealing her from me. You'll pay and pay and pay some more. The Storm would have never cared about a pathetic little place like this if I hadn't pointed it out to him. I convinced him that taking over Paradise Bend would be a good investment. I wanted to get to Tyrell, but he was already dead before I got here. Now I've got the next best thing. I've got you, Mercy, and it's time for you to die."

He leaned forward, his aim steadying. Just as my muscles tensed to throw me toward shelter, a shot rang out from a different direction.

A bullet clipped Xavier in the shoulder. He flinched and ducked, his aim faltering. In that split-second, I jerked my own pistol up. But even as I pulled the trigger, the enormous man was vaulting over the fence and thumping down on the other side.

A couple more *bangs* of gunfire split the night. I dashed to the fence, hoping I could get in another shot, but when I scrambled up to see over the pickets, I couldn't make out his hulking form at all. He'd raced off through the yards.

Had anyone hit him more than that wound on his shoulder? He obviously hadn't been hurt enough to really slow him down.

Damn it. My teeth set on edge, but at the same time, I suspected I was lucky to simply be alive.

Claws men spilled into the backyard around me—half a dozen of them, Kervos among them. "I'm sorry, Mercy," he said. "We'd have taken a shot sooner, but we were afraid he'd kill you if we missed."

"It's okay," I said, pulling my spine straight even though my gut felt like jelly. "You got here in time. That's what matters."

"If we could have taken him down..."

I let out a shaky breath. "There would still have been the Storm to deal with. He's the real problem. But we definitely need more guards—all around the property."

"Of course." He strode over to the other men and started giving hasty orders in a severe tone. A couple of the guys hung their heads as he must have chided them.

I peered at the ground, searching the grass until I caught the glint of silver I was looking for. Bending down, I picked up the bracelet I'd dropped. As I brushed bits of dirt off the chain, my insides tangled up all through my abdomen.

Xavier was insane. But his story explained a few things: why he'd targeted me at the start, why he'd wanted to torment me instead of just killing me. Why he was attacking my home so viciously in the first place. This was all some kind of psycho revenge for events I'd had no control over. I'd been *six* when Mom had vanished from my life, for fuck's sake.

Kervos rejoined me, studying my face. "Are you okay?"

"Yeah," I lied. I was pretty shaken up, but I didn't want to show him that. I needed to process everything Xavier had told me—decide how much was true and how much insane ramblings.

Did Xavier really know what had happened to Mom, that she was definitely dead, or was he simply guessing?

Kaige

I TOOK A LONG SWIG FROM MY ENERGY DRINK AND grimaced at the bright kitchen lights. It'd been another long night with barely any sleep. My typical insomnia was only harder to overcome with the adrenaline that kept buzzing through my veins.

We'd pulled off so much in the past couple of days... but it didn't feel like anywhere near enough. And I had no idea what more we could be doing.

The other guys were pulling together a hasty breakfast, the smell of butter and burnt crumbs filling the air. Gideon chugged his precious coffee with one hand while he tapped on his tablet with the other. Wylder smacked a plate of toast on the island.

"Five more days," he said. "And Xavier's going as far as coming right up to Mercy's home. We can't let him get away with a move that bold."

My hand tightened around the energy drink can to

the point that the metal started to crackle. I wanted to plant my fist in that motherfucker's face, and that was all there was to it... if I hadn't known he'd put a bullet in my brain before I got close enough. Asshole.

Rowan put on a calm front, but I could tell he was shaken by the danger our woman had been in too. "Whatever our next move is, we need to do significant damage. Maybe we should focus directly on Xavier. From what Beckett said, the Storm has pretty much given him free reign here. He's making the decisions."

"The rest of the troops will have trouble staying focused if he's out of the picture," Gideon said with a nod.

"Right," Wylder said. "We've wanted to bury that prick from the moment we found out he existed. So far, we haven't had any opportunities that panned out. It didn't sound like the kid has any inside line to info on Xavier's psychotic plans, so he won't be much help there. If we could just—"

Before he could finish that thought, two Noble lackeys rushed into the kitchen. "Mr. Noble," one of them said in an urgent tone. "There's—there's a problem."

I could see Wylder suppress a groan. "This early in the morning? Fine, what the hell is it?"

The men exchanged a worried glance. "We're not totally sure what's going on—or why, anyway. But a bunch of people are going around on the streets along the border between the city and the Bend smashing up stores and other buildings."

I frowned, and Rowan drew himself up straighter. "Is it the Storm's men?"

The other lackey shook his head. "It doesn't look like it. They seem to just be regular people—not trained at all, no weapons. Our guy down there reported that a few of them have been muttering something about Glory, so maybe they're druggies on a bender?"

Every nerve in my body jangled onto the alert. I hurled the near-empty can into the sink with a clatter. "Is that fucking crap making even more of a mess?"

The lackey who'd spoken flinched. "I'm not sure what they're talking about. But they also cracked the windshield of the Noble guy who spotted them while he was driving by. We just thought you'd want to know."

Wylder nodded with a jerk of his head, pushing aside his plate. "And it's good that you did, because we need to deal with this—whatever it is—fast." And we couldn't count on Ezra to handle it well, he didn't have to say.

I wondered if the lackeys had come to Wylder rather than his father on purpose. The lower Nobles had to be picking up on what an asshat Ezra was being these days, right?

But none of that mattered if Xavier and his toxic drug were destroying the county even more than they already had. I flexed the muscles in my shoulders. "We have to go." Find out how bad the damage was. Beat whoever was responsible into a pulp. The Storm's people couldn't keep using Glory to manipulate the regular people of Paradise Bend—we couldn't let them all turn into junkies like my parents.

Wylder motioned to the men. "Gather a couple of cars of back-up, and we'll head down there to deal with it. And be quick about it!"

The two guys scurried off. Wylder adjusted the gun tucked in the back of his jeans and motioned us to follow him. As he strode down the hall and into the foyer, he called out to a few of the men we passed, ordering them to join us out front. He was already enough of a leader to know who he wanted supporting us out there.

The landing overhead creaked, and I glanced up to see Anthea and Ezra standing by the top of the stairs. Anthea's eyebrows had drawn together. "What's going on, Wylder?"

"We're going out to check on a disturbance," Wylder said. "Seems like a bunch of people are riled up— probably the Storm's involved somehow."

Ezra remained silent. He was watching Wylder with his mouth pursed. A fresh flare of anger rose up inside me. For as long as I'd been here, I'd seen Ezra push Wylder harder and harder to become the leader he wanted. He'd never seemed satisfied. I'd used to think he always wanted more because he was trying to hone Wylder's capabilities as much as possible.

But now that Wylder had finally stepped up to his role as heir and the men were responding well, something had shifted in Ezra. He didn't seem so happy about the turn of events. What the hell did the guy want?

All I knew for sure was that I didn't trust that

asshole much more than I trusted Xavier, which was not at all.

We marched out to the garage, and I made a beeline for my favorite of the trucks in common use. It'd go faster than Gideon's surveillance van. As I jumped into the driver's seat, the other guys got in around me. Doors slammed as the other Noble men Wylder had called on got ready to follow.

I tore out of the garage and onto the street with a roar of the engine. "Whoa, there," Rowan said as we raced down the hill so fast my stomach lurched. "We'll get there faster if we don't crash on the way."

"I know how to handle a car," I growled, gripping the steering wheel harder, but I did slow down just a little so it was less likely some idiot cop would chase after me.

We flew through the city streets, already getting busy as the morning rush got going. Gideon made a faint noise when I blew past a red light, but I didn't care what he thought. His job was letting me know if there was anyone nearby who'd care about the traffic laws I broke.

Wylder was checking texts and looking at a map on his phone. "Right around here..." he said.

At the same moment, the sound of shattering glass reached my ears. I turned a corner and spotted the vandals easily enough.

They were spread out across a few blocks up ahead, at least a couple dozen of them. Some carried hockey sticks or baseball bats, others random debris like a broken tree branch or a length of pipe that they must have scrounged up somewhere.

They didn't seem to be working together, just focused on whatever destruction they could carry out on their own. A guy over there was smashing at a restaurant awning with a dusty board. A woman across the street from him was heaving what looked like a bowling ball through a barber shop window.

They seemed intent in their destruction, but the lackey had been right—they didn't look like the Storm's people to me. A few were teenagers, and others older men and women with graying hair. It was like a bunch of random strangers had suddenly decided it was time to riot. What the hell?

I parked the truck by the curb, and the other Noble cars stopped behind us. None of the vandals appeared to have noticed us yet.

"Jesus Christ," Gideon muttered under his breath.

As we got out, a middle-aged guy down the street yanked down a big inflatable sign outside a gas station and tore it open. Closer by, a teenage girl was scrambling out of a store through a smashed window, carrying what looked like a broken piece of the checkout counter. It was total fucking chaos.

Watching them, an uneasy shiver crawled up my back. There was an air of desperation to them, and a lot of them hardly seemed to notice *anything* going on around them except what they were doing with their two hands. I spotted glazed eyes and sweaty faces.

When I inhaled, I no longer smelled the asphalt

road or felt the heat on my skin. Memories of drugs and pain washed over me.

I shook myself out of the momentary daze and concentrated on the present. I couldn't let my past eclipse what I needed to do.

I turned to Wylder. "They're out of their minds. They all look like druggies to me."

"All of them?" Gideon asked.

I squinted at the ragtag bunch again and nodded. "I'd say so."

Rowan frowned. "Why would a bunch of junkies be smashing up buildings like this? That's not going to get them more drugs. They don't seem like they're hallucinating—and Glory hasn't made people aggressive in the past."

I shifted my weight, restless and on edge. All I wanted to do was to barge in and set every single one of them straight, no matter how far I had to go to do that. But I'd messed up big time the last time I'd rushed in without listening to Wylder, and I'd gotten Mercy into trouble.

I trusted Wylder. I knew he'd run things right. Letting him call the shots and telling me when it was time for me to crack some heads wasn't really giving up that much control but showing I could control myself enough to be part of this team.

Thinking of it that way helped keep me focused.

Wylder walked up to the closest vandal and yanked the bat he was holding out of his hands. He waved it at the guy. "There's nothing you want here. Go home."

The man wobbled on his feet. "Why you got to go

and do that, man?" he mumbled. "I just want some peace."

"Is this your idea of peace?" Wylder asked, gesturing to the mayhem around us.

The man coughed. "I just want Glory. I don't want no trouble."

"Then get going and quit smashing up other people's property," Wylder ordered him.

The man cringed, but he wandered off. Wylder shook his head. He motioned for us to follow him.

Up ahead, a man and a woman were punching and kicking at each other as they fought over what looked like a chunk broken out of a store sign. The woman hit the man in the ribs, and his grip on the hunk of plastic loosened, but before she could drag it completely out of his grasp, he snatched it back and slammed his foot into her shin. She hissed through her teeth.

Wylder glanced at me and tipped his head toward them. That was all the signal I needed.

I marched over and caught the man around the waist in one swift motion. He was so skinny he felt almost weightless as I hauled him over my shoulder. Rowan snatched up the sign piece that clattered to the ground.

The woman swayed from side to side, looking like she was still considering making a grab for the piece of trash. I wrinkled my nose at the BO wafting off the guy I'd grabbed and chucked him onto the opposite sidewalk.

"She's taking it away," he protested. "Don't let her take it away!"

I furrowed my brow. What the hell was he talking about?

Wylder advanced on the woman, looming over her with a menacing glower. He pointed at the chunk of sign. "Why do you want this? What the heck do you think you're going to do with it?"

The woman just sputtered furiously at him and ran off in the opposite direction.

"I'm not sure intimidation is going to work all that well on people this strung out," Rowan put in. "Let me give it a shot?"

Wylder motioned to the vandals still merrily wreaking havoc farther down the street. "Have at it, smooth-talker."

Rowan walked over to a young woman who was yanking at a plaque fixed to the side of a bank. He held up the piece of sign, and her head whipped toward him, her eyes widening as if he was showing her a lump of pure gold.

"You want this, don't you?" he said, keeping his tone patient and gentle in a way I could never have managed. "What's so special about it?"

The guy I'd grabbed scrambled up, looking like he was going to charge at Rowan, but I stepped between them with a glower. He backed down fast enough then and staggered off across the street.

The woman Rowan was talking to extended her hand toward the chunk of plastic. Her fingers opened and closed as if she thought she could snatch it up without even being close enough to touch it. "I don't—I don't know if I'm supposed to talk about it," she said weakly.

Rowan's voice softened even more. "We're not here to hurt you. We're not the cops, so you don't have to hide anything from us. We just want to know what's going on around here. If you can explain, I'd be happy to give you this. You can do whatever you want with it."

Her face brightened so suddenly it was almost funny. I swallowed down a laugh. And then any humor in me died as she rasped out her answer.

"The people who sell the Glory... they told us anyone who brings back a piece we can show we grabbed off some store or whatever in Paradise City, they'll give us a whole pound of Glory for it."

Wylder frowned, stepping up beside Rowan. "They asked you to bring a piece of a sign?"

The woman shrugged. "Anything, really. As long as they can tell we pulled it off a building here in the city. They said... They said the city people are too uppity and they want to see us bring them down a peg."

She was from the Bend, obviously. Even as my hands clenched, I could see how easily the Storm's men could have persuaded a bunch of their customers to take them up on their offer. A lot of them resented everyone who got to live on cleaner streets. I should know—I'd been one of them once.

"And you went along with it," I couldn't help grumbling anyway. "Very smart."

She winced, and Wylder held up his hand to quiet me. I reined in my anger.

That fucking Xavier. Using the people's emotions and their weaknesses against them to tear apart our home even more. My gaze swung around wildly, and I had to tense all my muscles to stop myself from pummeling the nearest utility pole to let out my frustration on something.

Rowan's expression had turned thoughtful. The wheels must have been turning in his head, because he tipped his head toward the woman. "What if I told you that you get to have a pound of Glory for doing absolutely nothing."

My jaw dropped. What was *he* on? We weren't going to go around handing out drugs... were we?

"What do you mean?" the woman asked, her interest obviously piqued.

"I mean you get to walk away from this and in return we give you what you want," Rowan said. He turned to Wylder. "We still have that stolen truck that we got from Colt, right?"

"Yes," Wylder said slowly. "I think I see where you're going with this."

"I don't," I snapped. "Are you insane? It's bad enough Xavier giving them—"

"Kaige," Wylder said sharply, and I managed to shut my mouth, my face burning almost as hot as the rage inside me.

My weaknesses were getting the better of me now. I forced myself to breathe deeply, hating every second of it.

"It's just lying around anyway," Rowan said. "Better that they get it from us in return for *not* destroying the city or listening to the Storm's people rather than letting the Storm keep the upper hand."

Wylder nodded and turned to me. "It'll only be temporary. We've got less than a week before either none of this matters or we've run the Storm out of town anyway."

I growled under my breath, but I couldn't come up with a coherent argument. Every bone in my body resisted the idea.

The problem was, I didn't have any better ones.

Wylder raised his voice to carry down the street. "Attention, everyone! I've got news about how you can get your Glory."

Several heads turned our way. Most of the vandals stopped what they were doing at the name of their drug of choice.

Wylder clapped his hands to catch even more of them and pitched his voice even louder. "We'll give you a pound of Glory right now if you back off and leave the buildings around here alone. And we've got *another* pound for you if you lay low for a week and we don't catch you messing with any other property or going to your usual dealers. That's all it costs. Chilling out and minding your own business. Sound like a good deal?"

Junkies weren't exactly the ambitious type. An offer that involved less work was obviously going to sound better to them. All along the street, the vandals set down their makeshift weapons and drifted toward us.

Wylder motioned to one of the Noble lackeys. "Go to the truck and bring over enough Glory to 'pay' all these good people so we can get them home."

As I watched the guy dash off, my stomach sank. Wylder caught my eye. He gave me a tight smile, sympathetic but unyielding.

He was the boss. The plan even made sense. I could deal with it—but only because I knew Wylder would only have run with this plan if we hadn't been pretty fucking desperate right now ourselves.

How much farther would we have to stoop before this war was over?

Mercy

THERE WAS SOMETHING A LITTLE WEIRD ABOUT having Gideon in my bedroom—and weird that it felt weird, considering how intimate we'd gotten on multiple occasions. But this was the room I'd slept in since I was a child until very recently, and I'd never had a guy over here. I'd never wanted to expose any of the men I got together with to my father's unpredictable temper and the operations of his business through the house.

But Dad was gone now, and I decided what the rules were. And frankly, I liked being able to perch on the edge of my queen-sized bed next to the tech genius who'd proven to be so passionate under his analytical demeanor. He'd come in with his tablet already out, ready to get to work, but he paused for a moment to take in the warm violet walls and the maple dresser and vanity that matched the bedframe.

"The room smells like you," he said.

"It *is* my bedroom," I pointed out. "I guess that's to be expected."

A corner of Gideon's mouth quirked upward. "Mercy Katz's natural habitat. I have to admit I expected something more fiery..."

I rolled my eyes. "Just because I don't put up with any crap doesn't mean I don't enjoy getting to relax when, y'know, I'm actually trying to *sleep*."

His gaze homed in on a photograph on the dresser of me when I was eight, standing on the lawn with my legs apart and my hands on my hips in clothes a little too big for my skinny body. His smile widened. "You were a badass even back then. I need to show this to the others." Before I could protest, he clicked a photo of it.

I scowled at him. "I thought you had something important to go over with me. The druggies who were bashing up the stores haven't started up again, have they?" Rowan had called me to fill me in on the latest development in our war against the Storm a couple of hours ago.

"No," Gideon said, his expression turning sober. "But I took a bunch of photos of them while we were handing out the drugs to bribe them into laying low. Most if not all of them seemed to have come from the Bend. I wanted to run their faces past you in case you recognize any of them and know they're more than just some random junkie."

That made sense. I leaned back on my hands, my

fingers sinking into the worn but cozy duvet. "Sure, I'll take a look."

He handed the tablet to me, and I crossed my legs to prop it on my lap. He'd already opened the Photos app. The first picture showed a haggard-looking man in grungy cargo pants. I flicked him away to study the next figure and the next, my stomach twisting with each image I dismissed.

They all had an air of desperation around them that I knew Xavier had taken advantage of. A lot of them looked as if they hadn't had a square meal in a month or longer. The youngest ones, teenagers with scruffy hair or wild eyes, tangled me up the most. They'd barely gotten started in life, and they were already way too far down a bad path.

Maybe we could change that once the Storm was gone for good. We just had to get on with kicking him and his men out of here.

Without thinking about it, I pulled my childhood bracelet out of my pocket and twisted it between my fingers. The memory of Xavier looming over me on the backyard fence flickered through my mind, along with an echo of the momentary helplessness I'd felt. It was hard to fully concentrate on anything with his words running through my mind. Especially the way he'd talked about Mom and her supposed death.

I shook away those thoughts and focused on the rest of the photos as well as I could. When I'd reached the last one, I handed the tablet back to Gideon.

"A few of them look vaguely familiar, probably from

seeing them around town. I've never had a bad run-in with any of them—nothing significant I can think of." I paused. "Is Kaige okay? With the whole drug bribery thing, I mean?" I knew how much he hated seeing Glory distributed on the streets. Watching his own people hand it out must have been even harder.

"He understood why we're doing it," Gideon said. "He definitely wasn't happy about it, but he managed to keep himself together. It's only until this war is over with." He sighed. "I wish we could have gotten more use out of the tracker I placed on Xavier. He must have realized we used it to trace him to the Storm's secret facility, considering we blew it up the night after he went out there. It's still active, but it hasn't moved since last night. I think he's just stuck it somewhere to throw us off his trail."

"Figures."

He glanced at me. "I particularly wish I'd been able to see that he was heading to your house so I could have warned you."

I reached over and squeezed his hand. Gideon sometimes got it into his head that he wasn't doing enough to protect me just because his ways were with data and devices rather than kicking ass, but that was ridiculous. "It's not your fault. Anyway, maybe it's a good thing that Xavier had a chance to vent at me so I could find out why he's so obsessed with me and taking over Paradise Bend."

"Yeah." Gideon exhaled in a huff. "Him and your mom, way back when. Who would have thought?"

"Maybe we *should* have thought there was some kind of connection like that considering the way he was going after me." My thumb slid over the engraved panel on my bracelet, and a sudden inspiration sparked in my head. "Gideon, how difficult is it to dig up information on people who have been missing for a while?"

Gideon raised an eyebrow. "Do you have somebody in mind?"

I hesitated. I'd never talked about my mom much with the guys, and it wasn't as if knowing the truth about what'd happened to her fifteen years ago was all that urgent. "I don't want to burden you if there's more work you need to do to get ready for our next assault on the Storm."

"It's no problem," Gideon said. "I've already scoured the files the Long Night sent over at least a dozen times. Right now, we're waiting on Beckett to get back to us with more information before we commit to our next moves."

I clasped my hands together on my lap. "I'm hoping you can find my mom."

Gideon blinked, and then understanding lit his eyes. "You want to find out if Xavier's right about her."

"Yeah. All *I* know is that she took off... or something... when I was six—fifteen years ago. She just vanished one day, and my dad claimed she'd skipped town. I've never been sure whether that was true, but with the things Xavier claimed—I need to know whether she's out there, or if she's actually dead. Just to get the questions out of my head."

"Of course. I'll see what I can find." Gideon tapped through to a different app so eagerly that a rush of affection filled my chest. If anyone could get me answers, it was him.

"What do you know about her?" he asked. "The more details you can give me, the easier it'll be for me to narrow down the search."

I worried at my lower lip with my teeth. "Not much, unfortunately. I'm sorry. Her first name was Josey, although for all I know she'd have switched to a different name if she was trying to hide from both my father and Xavier after she left here. I never knew her last name. If she was with Xavier for a while before she came to the Bend and met my father, I guess she was living here maybe seven or eight years. She'd have been in her early twenties when she had me—my dad only went for younger women—so she'd be in her early to mid forties now if she's still alive."

Gideon's fingers flew over the touchscreen. "Anything else? Did she mention any places she liked? Did she have any favorite activities...?"

I thought back to those long-ago days as hard as I could. "She loved the outdoors. She always wanted to get out of the county to the state park nearby or places like that, but Dad didn't like her taking me too far away from him. He was probably worried she'd take off on him and he'd lose both of us. She had a thing for Indian food—that was how I first got to try it. I don't know how helpful that is. I was so little that I didn't really pay much attention."

"That's understandable," Gideon said, more gently

than I was used to from him. "I'll see what I can dig up. It might take some time, but there aren't many people who can escape me if I put my mind to it." He shot me a grin.

The thought of just sitting next to him while he worked made me restless. I squirmed on the bed for a moment and then got up to see if anyone else needed anything in the rest of the house. "I'll be out there if you need me," I said.

When I pulled open the door, I found Jenner on the other side, a plate with a sandwich in his hand. When I startled, he smiled sheepishly. "I didn't mean to surprise you. I thought you could use some lunch. I haven't seen you in the kitchen since this morning."

"Thanks," I said, unexpectedly touched. There'd been a time when Jenner had been willing to kill me for the new allegiances he'd made. We'd come a long way since then.

I took the plate from him and headed to the stairs so I could eat in the dining room. Jenner followed. He stopped me at the bottom of the staircase.

"Look," he said, "I didn't mean to eavesdrop, but I heard a little of what you were saying to your friend there... You're having him search for your mom—for Josey?"

Any appetite I'd had abruptly fled. "Yeah. Did you know her?" I wasn't sure exactly how long he'd been working for my dad.

Jenner nodded, his mouth slanting at a pained angle that put my nerves even more on edge. "Why are you wondering about her now? It's been so long..."

I shrugged with forced nonchalance. "Xavier said some things about her—and, I mean, I've never really known what happened to her. Dad wasn't exactly super open with me."

Jenner glanced at the floor and then back at me. It was obvious he didn't want to say whatever was on his mind. He dragged in a rough breath. "I'm so sorry, Mercy. I thought you knew. You're not going to find her. She's gone."

All the air squeezed out of my lungs. "You mean dead."

He inclined his head, and even though I'd been prepared for that fact, it hit me so hard the plate slipped from my hands. It smashed on the floor, the halves of the sandwich falling apart. I ducked down, my legs a little wobbly, and grabbed at the pieces to clean up the mess.

"How do you know?" I asked, keeping my head low in case my eyes decided to spill over. I still needed to keep a strong front around the men working for me.

"One of the Claws men I was working with at the time helped Tyrell dispose of the body," Jenner said. "He mentioned it to me—and maybe a few other people, one of whom told Tyrell he was talking, because then we never saw that guy again either. You know how your father was when people went against him."

I inhaled shakily. "Is that why he had my mom killed? She 'went against' him somehow?"

"I don't know the details. I'd heard him complaining about her, that she was paranoid and thought someone might be after her, that she hadn't managed to get pregnant again, that she fussed over you too much." Jenner paused. "I didn't agree with any of that. She was a good mom to you, from what I saw. But Tyrell... Tyrell didn't really have that paternal instinct, did he?"

A choked laugh sputtered out of me. "No, he sure as hell did not." I straightened up with the pieces of plate and sandwich clutched in my hands and carried them over to the kitchen garbage can. All these years, somewhere in the back of my mind I'd held on to a little hope, but it'd all been for nothing. She'd been out of reach the whole time.

Jenner came with me. "I'm so sorry, Mercy. I wish there was an easier way to tell you. I assumed you'd already found out one way or another."

"Don't apologize," I told him, forcing myself to meet his eyes and willing back the tears that were burning in the back of mine. "I'm glad you told me. I needed to know. Thank you for being honest with me."

Of course Dad had killed her. Of course he'd never owned up about it to me. It'd been the most obvious answer the whole time, but suddenly I was more furious with him than I'd ever been before. I'd have given anything to bring him back to life just so I could kill him all over again.

She'd loved me, tried to look out for me, and he'd taken her from me like he'd taken so much else over the years.

I couldn't imagine eating anything right now. Shock was still surging through me, numbing the turmoil of my emotions. I headed back upstairs. There was no point in wasting Gideon's time with a search that would lead nowhere.

Gideon raised his head as I came into the room. At the sight of my face, his smile vanished. "What's wrong?"

"You can stop looking," I said, my voice coming out rough. "I got my answer. She isn't out there to be found. She's in an unmarked grave somewhere—wherever my dad had her dumped."

His eyes widened. He set his tablet aside and motioned me over. I sank down on the bed next to him, and he slid his arm around me.

"I'm sorry," he said. "That's awful. I—is there anything I can do? What do you need?" He peered into my eyes, so awkward but earnest in his desire to comfort me that it brought an ache into my chest.

Dealing with people's emotions wasn't something Gideon had much experience with. Usually he avoided them completely. But for me, he was trying his best. That meant more than any suave condolences would have.

I leaned into his embrace. "I'm just glad you're here. Having you with me makes it easier to deal with the news."

His expression turned doubtful, as if he couldn't compute how that could be the case. "Are you sure? If you want me to bring you back to the mansion so you can be with all of us..."

I reached up and touched his cheek. The jagged tufts of his blue hair caught the sunlight, turning it as vivid as the summer sky. He really didn't understand how much he meant to me. Maybe I hadn't even known how much he did until right now, in this moment, when all I wanted to do was fall into him away from the awfulness of my past.

He wouldn't pry for answers or demand I act in any specific way, just take me as I was. And if he could do anything to make it better, I knew he'd leap at the chance in an instant.

The feeling that had been building inside me since the first moment we'd kissed, only getting stronger when he'd opened up about his own past scars and shown me how far he'd go for me, filled my throat. I let it spill across my tongue. "You're enough. You've always been enough. I love you."

Something lifted in my chest when I said those words out loud. Gideon stared at me, emotion flashing through his normally cool gray eyes. His throat worked, and he brought his hand up to run his fingers into my hair. "I love you too. I didn't know I could feel this much about anyone, but I—I don't know what else to call it."

Joy bloomed inside me. I smiled at him. "I think those words work just fine." Then I leaned in for a kiss.

Gideon tugged me closer, his mouth capturing mine with all the intensity I'd come to expect from him and more. His tongue slipped between my lips, teasing over my own, and his free hand trailed down my side. Heat flared low in my belly. All at once, I wanted everything he could give.

I nipped his lip ring and tugged at the buttons on his collared shirt. A sly, knowing grin stretched across his ethereal face. As he started undoing the buttons, he leaned me back on the bed with him over me. With every caress he offered, more pleasure and longing washed away the grief that had filled me minutes ago.

When Gideon's chest was bared, I swept my hands over his smooth skin and the darkly divine figure inked on it. "My dark god," I murmured, and more lust flared in the tech genius's gaze.

He kissed me harder, splaying my legs around his hips so he could rock against my core at the same time. The press of his growing erection against my pussy had me desperate for more in an instant. He pulled back just long enough to yank off my shirt, and I pawed at his slacks, determined to have those off too.

Gideon proved just how many ways he could use those nimble fingers by stripping my jeans off me even as he sucked the tip of my breast into his mouth. Without raising his head, he flung the jeans aside, swiveled his tongue around my nipple forcefully enough to make me gasp, and kicked off his own pants. Then, moving his mouth to my other breast, he delved his hand under my panties.

The first stroke of his fingers had me gushing against them, pleasure surging from my cunt. I growled and yanked his mouth back to mine.

"I want all of you inside me now," I muttered against his lips, our hot breaths mingling together.

Mischief sparked in Gideon's eyes. "The queen of the Claws should get whatever she requires," he said, tugging my panties down. He spread my legs wide again and lined himself up. As the head of his cock rubbed over my clit and down to my opening, I noticed the faint raggedness creeping into his breath.

"We can flip over," I said, desire flooding my body as I remembered the time I'd ridden him. I didn't want him to strain his injured lungs.

But Gideon shook his head with a look of determination I'd become familiar with, though it was normally aimed at his computer screens. "You're mine," he said intently, "and I'm going to take you every way I want to."

I practically came just at those words and the intensity of his tone. He slammed his mouth into mine at the same time as he plunged into me all the way to the hilt, and my moan was muffled by that blissfully violent kiss. If this was what he wanted, I sure as hell wasn't going to argue with him.

Gideon snatched one of the pillows and shoved it under my hips to raise me to an angle that let him drive even deeper into me. With each thrust, a hint of a rasp sharpened in his breaths, but he showed no other sign of needing to slow down. He devoured my mouth and nibbled his way down the side of my neck, all the while pounding into me with enough force to send me soaring in a matter of minutes.

"Fuck," I gasped out, and then I was clenching around him, a shudder running through my body. Gideon groaned, thrusting even harder, with a stutter in his chest as he followed me.

He stayed braced over me as we came down from the high of our orgasms, kissing me more sweetly now. I wrapped my arms around his shoulders and pulled him down next to me so I could tuck myself against his slim but solid frame.

Right here, in the present, I was loved so thoroughly I didn't know how it was even possible. No matter what Dad had done, no matter what I'd lost, I knew I'd come out of this lucky in the end.

Mercy

I PLANTED A BOWL OF NACHOS IN THE MIDDLE OF THE coffee table in my dad's old office, and Kaige immediately dove in. From the way he gulped down the chips, he'd recovered from any lingering trauma of dealing with Glory earlier today.

I tsked at him. "Save some for everyone else."

"Want one?" Kaige mumbled around his mouthful, nudging the bowl toward Rowan, who laughed and shook his head. Wylder snatched up a handful and leaned back on the narrow sofa. Gideon finished arranging his tablet at the other side of the table to his satisfaction and straightened up to take a chair. When his eyes met mine, the gleam in them made me think of the words we'd exchanged earlier—and how thoroughly we'd proven them to each other after. I smiled back at him.

"When exactly are we expecting Beckett to call?" I asked.

"He left a message indicating that he'd try tonight," Gideon said. "Obviously he has to work around everything else going on in his life. We don't want him to get caught any more than he does. But it sounds like he was able to find some information on one of the Storm's business associates from the list of names we passed on that we got from the Long Night: Anderson."

"Anderson Cooper!" Kaige said with a triumphant air.

Wylder rolled his eyes. "It was Evan Anderson, you dork. He's a real estate guru, not a TV personality."

"The way the Storm's been tearing down the Bend, it's funny to think he's had that much interest in real estate *development*," I muttered.

"Hey," Rowan said lightly, "even Ezra's dipped his toes into that area. It's an easy way to pursue legitimate business activities once you've got some money to throw around. I'd guess a guy like the Storm, who's keeping his less legit activities super-secret, needs a legal front—or several—even more than any regular criminal organization."

"True." I waved a chip at Gideon. "You haven't found any evidence that this Anderson guy is involved in the underground stuff too, have you?"

Gideon shook his head. "He seems totally on the up and up. Lots of deals with prominent businessmen and public figures. I think there's a good chance he doesn't know anything about the Storm's other types of business."

Wylder smirked. "Which could be good for us. Exposing the Storm would be an easy way to attack him from a totally different angle. He needs to know that we're not letting up on him and that he can't predict how we'll strike next."

"But without the kid's guidance, we're going in mostly blind," Gideon reminded us. "We didn't get much more than the name and a few properties Anderson has managed for the Storm from the Long Night. No more than that for any of the other business associates he mentioned either. That's not really enough to make a solid plan."

"Beckett will come through," Rowan said confidently. "He wants this war over nearly as much as we do."

I nodded. "His information before was good. Let's just wait instead of getting all impatient." A shiver ran down my spine at the thought of what the kid might face if his dad caught on to how his own son was double-crossing him. Somehow I didn't think the Storm would see it as a loving gesture meant to protect his dad from getting into bigger trouble later, the way Beckett clearly intended it.

Wylder checked the time on his phone and sighed before grabbing more nachos. Kaige was still munching happily away. I sat down behind my dad's old desk and picked up the crystal paperweight so I could turn it over in my hands.

It felt strange sitting there. The leather of the chair bit into my ass, but Dad had always preferred not to get too comfortable. According to him, staying a bit on edge helped ensure you didn't miss anything when it came to important decisions.

Below the window, one of the Claws men moved through the darkened yard on his patrol. We had enough guards staked out around the house to be confident Xavier couldn't set one foot on this property again, at least not without taking several bullets in the process. Still, the evening shadows outside brought an uneasy sense of gloom over me.

A ringing sound pierced the air. Gideon jerked forward and tapped the screen of his tablet, which he'd connected to a burner phone to take the call.

"Hey, Beckett," Wylder said in his typical cocky voice. "I hope you've got something good for us."

Beckett's voice filled the room, slightly scratchy as if it wasn't the best connection. "I'm here."

Wylder frowned. "Perfect. Gideon said you indicated you've got something to share about this Evan Anderson guy."

Instead of answering right away, Beckett paused. After a moment of silence, Rowan cleared his throat. "Beckett, are you still there?"

"Yeah." The kid's voice had dropped to a whisper. "Yeah, sorry, I just—my dad has a lot of people in the house, and he's been restless, so I've got to be careful. Today was—today was bad."

Concern jolted through my nerves. "Why? What happened?"

Beckett let out a ragged breath. "Xavier came to the house where we're living right now. He was pissed off and going on about how my dad isn't supporting him enough. Ranting about how many people they've lost, insisting that he needs even more to work with if he's going to crush everyone in Paradise Bend. He sounded totally unhinged—I have no idea what he's going to do next. Or who he's going to do it to."

My stomach knotted. I wanted to be glad about how much our assault on the secret facility had thrown Xavier for a loop, but we had other things to consider too. Xavier definitely wouldn't go easy on Beckett if *he* found out that the kid had been in contact with us.

Which Beckett had obviously already realized, because the next thing he said was, "I kept freaking out that he'd realized what I'd done—how I helped you make that strike on the storage and training facility. He sounded ready to tear someone in half, anyone he was angry with. And I..." His voice got even quieter. "I don't know if my dad would be able to stop him. I don't know if he'd *want* to if he knew."

"You haven't seen any sign that he or your dad suspects you've reached out to us, have you?" Rowan asked.

"N-no. I think I've been careful." Beckett swallowed audibly. He sounded so raw and frightened it brought a lump to my own throat. "But who knows how it'll go in the future. I'm walking a perilous line here. I know it. I thought it'd be okay, that it'd all work out for the best..."

"That's what's important," I said, unable to stop myself from jumping in. Maybe we were asking too much from him. He was only sixteen. And I knew all too well what it was like to be afraid of your own parent, to not be able to trust that they'd have your best interests at heart.

We did have to end this war—for Beckett's sake too.

"You don't have to tell us anything else if you think your safety is at risk," I went on, ignoring the sharp look Wylder shot me. "You've already done a lot for us to help us shift the tide in our favor. Any time it's getting to be too much, you can back off. I promise your secrets will always be safe with us, and we're obviously very thankful that you offered your help at all."

Gideon's forehead had furrowed. "But, Mercy, he's the one who—" he started to protest.

I held up my hand and shook my head. The information Beckett could offer could make a huge difference to us, but it wasn't worth getting it at the expense of a teenager's life. I *wasn't* as brutal as my father, and I intended to keep what conscience I still had intact. There were lines I wasn't going to cross.

We could hear Beckett breathe. When he spoke again, he sounded annoyed with himself. "I'm being stupid. Freaking out like a kid."

I didn't think he'd appreciate me pointing out that he *was* technically a kid. "It's understandable that you're shaken up," I said. "Xavier's fucking terrifying, excuse my French. Being cautious around him is *smart*, not stupid."

"But nothing gets done if people are too scared to do it," Beckett said, sounding as if he was talking to himself more than me. He inhaled again with a rush of air. His tone got gruffer. "Sorry for melting down a bit. I want to do this. I *have* to do it, for me and Dad, for a better future. I'm not going to chicken out."

I wished I could reassure him more that none of us saw him as a coward, but I couldn't think of words he'd believe. I settled on, "I think you're going to make a great leader someday, Beckett."

The guys around me stayed silent, waiting as our conversation played out. I shot Wylder a grateful smile for his patience.

Beckett didn't respond to my compliment. There was a rustle as if he'd straightened his posture. More of the confidence we'd seen in him when he'd first come to speak to us came back into his tone. "Okay, I managed to overhear a conversation that Dad was having with one of the guys he does business with. Someone on your list—at least, his last name was Anderson, like I already told you."

Wylder leaned forward. "What were they talking about?"

"I was wary of getting too close in case he noticed me eavesdropping, but from what I could tell, Dad was pretty irritated. He was talking fast and telling Anderson how he wasn't happy about where he was taking the deal. It sounded like the guy wanted a better arrangement than he's been getting from Dad, and Dad was insisting he wasn't going to get better elsewhere and didn't like that Anderson was trying to squeeze him for more money—a higher percentage or something."

Kaige's eyebrows rose. He might not have been much of a strategist, but even he would be able to figure out that friction between the Storm and his associates could work in our favor.

Rowan spoke up. "And as far as you know, the kind of business they were talking about was all above board, nothing illegal, right?"

"Yeah," Beckett said firmly. "The only things my dad is directly involved in are totally legitimate. He's very careful about that, believe me. You're not going to be able to pin anything on him that way."

"That isn't quite what I had in mind," Rowan said.

"Okay. I didn't mean— I guess I'm still kind of keyed up."

"That's understandable," I said. "Is there anything else you found out that might help us?"

"I don't think so. I'm going to keep listening in as much as I can. I'll contact you again if there's anything. I should probably go now, though. I don't know how close an eye he's keeping on me."

"Thanks," Rowan got in before the line went dead.

"So," Wylder said, looking around at the rest of us, "the Storm is having trouble keeping his associates under his thumb. They're starting to want more than he's offering."

I wet my lips, an idea hitting me so abruptly that I felt almost giddy. "Your dad *was* getting into some real estate deals. Is there any reason we couldn't too? Maybe we could steal the Storm's business with this guy right out from under him."

Kaige frowned. "Are we really in the big leagues enough to approach some international real estate whatever-exactly-he-is?"

A smile was creeping across Rowan's face. "He doesn't have to know our background. We can control how we present ourselves and put forward a compelling offer. Then we just need to reel him in. Money talks more than anything else. We do have plenty of that to work with." He glanced at Wylder. "If you don't mind dipping into the Noble accounts."

Wylder waved a hand. "Absolutely, if you can pull this off. Let's steal everything that used to belong to the Storm that we can get our hands on. And this Anderson guy could be a great asset to have on our side in the future too."

Gideon cocked his head in thought. "Rowan negotiated the waterfront deal for Ezra. Ezra was very happy with how that went down—and he's hardly ever actually happy. Obviously we should have Rowan do the talking for us."

A hint of a flush colored Rowan's cheeks. He'd always been a little too modest to know how to take a compliment without getting embarrassed. "Of course, whatever you need me to do," he said to Wylder. "I do have the lingo down at this point."

"You shouldn't have to go alone," I said. "You can do most of the talking and fill me in on what I'll need to know, but this'll be a joint venture, Nobles and Claws. That way we can put more clout behind it. My dad left behind some capital I can access."

Kaige thumped his hands on the table. "In that case, why don't we all go? I'm in!"

Wylder raised his head, but I spoke up before he could encourage the idea. "I don't think we want to

intimidate this guy. All of us together could be kind of...
overwhelming. He's a regular businessman, not a gang
lord we need to make a huge show of power with. I
think this probably needs a little more delicacy."

"I can be delicate," Kaige said, but then he cracked a
smile, because he couldn't even say it with a straight
face. Gideon snorted.

"I think just Mercy and I would be perfect," Rowan
said. "It's better this way and less messy. But all of that
aside, I'm guessing it won't be easy getting to Anderson.
Someone that well-connected and in-demand probably
has meetings and events scheduled out months in
advance."

Gideon had started furiously tapping away at his
tablet. After a minute, he raised his head and grinned.
"Well, we're just in luck. There's a charity fundraising
auction happening tomorrow afternoon, and Anderson
is one of the sponsors. You can meet him there."

"What if the Storm's there too?" Kaige asked.

"I don't get the impression he's paying enough
attention to Paradise Bend to have bothered to find out
what we even look like," I said. "He's letting Xavier
handle everything while he pretends he's a regular
business mogul."

Rowan nodded. "But events like a charity gala tend
to sell out their tickets well in advance."

"Which is why it's always good to be friends with an
expert hacker." Gideon jabbed at his screen some more
and then rubbed his hands together triumphantly. "Your
names are now on the guest list."

Kaige guffawed. "You're fucking magic, man."

"You are," I agreed. "Now we just need to figure out what these deals are that the Storm is getting pissy about so we can steal them out from under him."

"That's right." Wylder leaned back in his seat, crossing his arms over his chest. "We're going to show the Storm what it means to mess with us. He needs to know that if he keeps on attacking us, we're more than capable of taking away not just his men and his supplies, but his livelihood as well."

Mercy

"Don't you like it?" Anthea said.

I realized I'd been frowning as I stared at myself in the mirror, examining the flowing turquoise dress she'd lent me. It clung to my curves, but not so tightly or exposing so much skin that it'd look out of place at an elegant gala, and it complemented my dark hair just like Anthea had said it would.

But I hadn't gotten dressed up like this since the guys had fully accepted me—since I'd come into my own as queen of the Claws—and I'd forgotten one thing I now took for granted.

"It's gorgeous," I said. "I just feel kind of naked without a gun. And there's nowhere to tuck one away wearing something like this, is there?" I motioned to my back where I'd normally have shoved my pistol into the waist of my jeans or sweats.

Anthea snapped her fingers. "I have just the solution

for that." She went to the closet and popped open one of the built-in drawers. When she turned back to me, she was holding a gun no longer than her palm, bubblegum pink in color. She raised her eyebrows. "This is what 'proper' ladies carry in their purses."

I took it from her and turned it over in my hands, unable to hold back a snort. It was a third of the size of my usual pistol. "It's very cute."

"I know it doesn't look like much, but it'll get the job done," Anthea said. "A bullet between the eyes will still do the trick just fine, no matter how big a gun was shooting it. Hopefully you won't run into that kind of trouble at this fancy fundraiser, though."

I swallowed thickly. "Yeah."

Just the thought of being around all those posh businesspeople made my chest clench up. It wasn't likely they'd start firing shots, but they had their own ways of going on the attack that I had no experience with at all. It was so far from my scene, I might as well be traveling to Fiji.

I tucked the gun into the purse Anthea had also lent me and stepped into the stilettos that completed the look. Anthea stepped back to take in the full picture and nodded with satisfaction. "You look beautiful. You'll fit right in. Now go get those rich bastards."

I had to laugh, her enthusiasm loosening a little of the tension inside me. "Thank you. I'll do that."

Rowan was waiting outside by the car we were taking. He'd exchanged his usual silver Toyota for a sleek black convertible, and he'd upgraded his own look too. He always dressed pretty snappy these days, but this was a completely new level. His dark tailored suit and crisp white shirt fit him perfectly, and he'd slicked back the spikes of his blond hair with gel. I stopped in my tracks, drinking the image in.

I liked his usual boy-next-door vibe, but there was no denying that he looked particularly delicious right now. And definitely not as a boy but a man.

"Wow," he said, giving me a similar onceover and then a soft smile. "You look fantastic. I'll be beating guys off with a stick."

Another laugh spilled out of me. "Then you'll have to lend me the stick after so I can beat off the women who'll be drooling over you. Come on, let's get going." It was early in the morning still, but we had a long drive ahead of us. The gala was happening two states away.

Rowan took my hand as if I really were some kind of lady and led me around to the front passenger seat. As my fingers twined with his, I couldn't help admiring his profile too. He'd grown up so much, and for the better, I thought, even if he wasn't always so sure of that. He'd become even more confident and passionate, ready to fight for the people he cared about.

A swell of affection filled my chest. I had the urge to kiss him hard—I would have if it wouldn't have ruined the lipstick Anthea had painstakingly applied.

Had I ever really stopped loving Rowan? I wasn't sure. Underneath the anger and the sense of betrayal, I'd still held a candle for the first guy who'd ever won my heart. Now, the rush of feelings swept all the words out of me.

I'd told Wylder and Gideon I loved them. I should

say it to Rowan too. But this didn't feel like the time, not when we were practically playing dress-up. I didn't want him to think I was only caught up in the moment or that I preferred him this way.

I'd tell him later, when we were back to our regular selves, because it'd be just as true then.

Rowan waited until he was sure I'd gotten my skirt out of the way before shutting the door for me, all gentleman-like. He got in on the driver's side but didn't start the engine right away.

"I wanted to show you something," he said. "I figured why not now, since we'll have a lot of time to kill."

My curiosity was instantly piqued. "What?"

He reached to the back seat and handed me a sketchbook. "I've been getting back into old habits over the past week or so. I thought you might like seeing the results."

He'd been drawing again? "Yes, of course," I said, my heart lifting. As far as I knew, Rowan hadn't done much drawing at all since he'd gotten involved with the Nobles. He'd told me that he didn't feel he deserved to have art in his life. I hadn't agreed with him then, and I was relieved to hear he'd changed his mind too.

As he drove down the driveway and onto the street, I flipped open the sketchbook. I lingered on each page, taking in every detail of the lines of pencil before turning to the next.

He'd started with random objects around the house, it looked like. There was a fruit bowl from the kitchen, a sitting room with armchairs and side tables drawn with every carved flourish in the wood, even a sketch of Wylder's Mustang in the garage. They all looked so real I could almost believe they'd spring right off the page. I ran my fingers over them, careful not to smudge the pencil lines. "Wow. You're really getting back into it, huh?"

Rowan looked abashed. "Just a little. It's felt good, exercising those old muscles again. And there's been lots of inspiration for me to use."

"Well, I'm glad you're getting your groove back so quickly," I said with a smile.

A few pages farther in, the pictures began to change, getting more ambitious. They were full scenes that filled the paper all the way to the edges, some of them with figures. I found Wylder and Gideon poised around the chess table, and Kaige lounging in his hammock. Rowan had captured their personalities perfectly with a few strokes of his pencil.

But most of those more expansive drawings featured me.

The first one showed a familiar building—an abandoned auto shop—and a woman who was suspended mid-leap. Then I was facing a few men, jabbing my finger at them, my hair pulled back in a ponytail and my face fierce with determination. Another showed a forest draped in dark shadows, with the flashlight in my hand bringing only the shapes within its glow into sharper focus. Toward the end, I found one that was just my face, a wide smile curving my lips as I gazed into the distance.

A lump rose in my throat. There was no mistaking

the fondness in every line Rowan had drawn to depict me. He'd made me beautiful in a way not even Anthea could have managed—he'd made me *art*. And not just when I was wearing a pretty dress but when I was out there getting things done the way I needed to.

For a few minutes, I couldn't speak. Finally, I found my words. "Rowan, these are incredible. Really."

His gaze darted to me as if checking to make sure my reaction was genuine. His expression relaxed with a grin. "Thanks. I'm glad you like them."

I beamed back at him. "It's great to see you reconnecting with this side of yourself again. The gang doesn't have to be your entire life, you know?"

"I didn't really know that until you came back, Mercy," he said, his gaze fixed on the road again. "It's like you're my muse. There's nothing I enjoy drawing more than you. I hope you don't mind."

"Are you kidding me?" I said. "This is the most flattering thing anybody has done for me."

"Even more flattering than taking a three-hour train and getting you snow cones and cheesecake from Beach View?" he said, a teasing hint in his voice.

I punched him playfully on his arm. "Half of it had already melted by the time you came back."

"Sure, but that was also the moment when I realized how special you were to me," Rowan said, his face turning serious. I felt that familiar squeeze in my heart again and the words that I hadn't said to him in years, ready to burst out of me.

Wasn't it amazing that we'd been able to go back to our former selves, able to enjoy each other's company without the shadows of our troubled past hanging over us? I'd missed this vibe so much. I'd missed *him*.

I cleared my throat, pulling my mind back to the business at hand. "Should we go over our strategy? I want to make sure I'm totally clear on everything, since this isn't really my wheelhouse."

"Sure," Rowan said. "But I know you'll do fine. And I'll be taking the lead."

As we left Paradise Bend far behind, we went back and forth on our story, making sure we were in sync and polishing up our proposal. We weren't going to lay out all our cards upfront, but we needed to show enough for it to sound like a lucrative and appealing offer.

By the time we reached the city where the gala was being held, I was still anxious, but my nerves were under control after all that prep. I gazed up at the skyscrapers catching the mid-afternoon sunlight, twice the height of any building around the Bend. This was where the big players did their work, people like the Devil's Dozen and their associates.

In my earlier research to prepare for this event, guided by Gideon, I'd discovered that the building where the gala was being held was a hotel built in the late sixties that Evan Anderson had helped broker a deal around last year. The subsequent renovations had left it newly cleaned up and extravagant. The marble panels on the exterior were so polished they practically glowed.

Rowan gave the car to a valet, and we joined the current of attendees streaming into the building. Anthea had chosen well—we fit right in with our fancy clothes. I definitely wasn't overdressed. I saw a woman wearing a feather boa and another with a hat with so many whorls of fabric protruding from it I had no idea how she kept it balanced on her head. All the men sported fancy suits or even tuxedos. The place was all glitz and glamor.

Uncertainty clenched my stomach as we approached the door, but the security didn't give us a second glance as they checked us off the guest list and motioned us into the premises. The vast foyer inside was pristine white with gilded walls and marble floors.

We climbed a winding staircase to the ballroom already buzzing with the people inside. The air held a decadent mix of expensive alcohol and cloying perfume. Smooth jazz trickled from hidden speakers. The lights from the fancy chandeliers hanging throughout the massive room dazzled me.

"Quite the place," Rowan said, letting out a quiet whistle as he glanced around.

My heart thumped as I scanned the room for Anderson. It took a minute before I spotted him deeper inside the room, surrounded by a crowd who appeared to be hanging off his every word.

He wasn't afraid to make a style statement, that was for sure. The pattern on his suit resembled zebra stripes, but somehow it worked on him perfectly rather than looking out of place. His silver hair fell in sculpted waves to the tops of his ears, and a diamond stud glinted in one of his earlobes. He had to have tons of money, but he wasn't flaunting that part of his persona as much as a lot of the other patrons.

We needed to get him alone, and when he was in a mood to be open to offers. I studied him surreptitiously from across the room. "Maybe we should wait until after a few of the auctions have happened? If they go well, he'll be in good spirits."

"That sounds like a plan," Rowan said. "The program said the auctions would be scattered throughout the afternoon—in between refreshments and time to socialize, I guess." He nodded to a painting mounted on the stage set up along the far wall. "I believe that one's up first."

As if on cue, Anderson walked to the center of the ballroom, clapping his hands to catch everybody's attention. As soon as he had it, somebody handed a mic to him.

"Attention, everybody! We shall now begin the auction of our first item." He walked to the painting and flourished his hands at it. "First up is a 2012 masterpiece by one of the most celebrated artists of the United States, Augustine Cavallaro."

We wove through the crowd to get closer to him, and my thoughts whirled in my head. We weren't here to buy any paintings, but Anderson would also be more open to talking to us if we showed a willingness to open our wallets right away, wouldn't he?

"The bidding starts as ten thousand dollars," he said. "Do I have ten thousand?"

"Ten," I said, raising my hand. Anderson's eyes sought me in the crowd. He tipped his head at me in approval.

Somebody else called out, "Twelve thousand."

"Fifteen," I said.

"What the hell are you doing?" Rowan whispered next to me, his smile twitching with a mix of amusement and confusion.

"Just showing we can play with the top dogs," I said.

I tossed in another couple bids as the number quickly soared, but stepped back when there were still a few other bidders in the mix so there was no chance of the painting going to me. It was won by a short, balding man who looked very happy with the now one hundred thousand dollar purchase.

"A great showing for our first auction," Anderson said. "Remember that all our proceeds from today's event will go to charitable foundations that work with displaced children and veterans."

We circulated through the crowd, keeping an eye on Anderson and waiting out the next two auctions. I didn't bid again, but Rowan did in the third, picking up my strategy. After that was over, I noticed Anderson going over to the corner to consult with another man, maybe a colleague. The other guy hustled off, and for that moment, our target was alone.

"Come on," I said, tugging on Rowan's suit jacket.

We hurried over as quickly as we could while still pretending to be as posh and poised as everyone around us. Rowan grabbed a glass of champagne from a passing waiter and held it up in a cheers gesture to Anderson as we reached him. "The event seems to be going well."

The real estate guru looked us over. "It has," he said. "I'm sorry neither of you has scored anything you were interested in yet, but I appreciate you throwing your hats into the ring all the same."

Rowan flashed his smile, the one that always seemed to put people at ease. I simply stood there and looked pretty, which was my main job while he did the talking. I was totally okay with that for the time being.

"That's all right," Rowan said. "Obviously there are people here more fanatical for art than we are. But we had our sights on a bigger score."

Anderson raised his eyebrows, clearly intrigued. "What would that be? What line of work are you in, by the way? I don't think our paths have crossed before."

"Not surprising," Rowan said breezily. "We're venture capitalists, and we've spent the last two years hustling to expand our business to the point where we can compete on a national scale. We already have holdings in a few different states."

"Anything I'd have heard of?"

"For now, we mostly operate in smaller cities. Our most prominent business is based out of Paradise Bend."

Anderson showed no sign that he'd ever heard of the county, which wasn't surprising, considering that it sounded like the Storm kept his illicit activities very separate from his legitimate business ventures.

"But I take it you're looking to expand," he said.

"Yes." Rowan let his smile turn a bit sly. "We've cultivated a lot of... connections to keep us abreast of any interesting developments where we might have an opportunity. I understand one of your regular financiers is balking at agreeing to fairer terms—which seem truly deserved considering how much you've done for his company."

Anderson's gaze flickered, but otherwise he kept his expression impassive. "Who would have suggested a thing like that?"

Rowan shrugged. "I don't want to get anyone in trouble. I just wanted to let you know that if you're looking for someone who'll meet your conditions and give you the percentage you're worth, possibly even offer a little extra bonus as a show of trust in a new partnership, we'd love to talk further."

Anderson glanced at me, and I figured it was time I showed that I had a brain as well as a body. "We think it could benefit both us and you," I said. "We're impressed by what you arranged for this hotel, and we've seen several of your other projects. You clearly have a good eye."

"I'm not sure," Anderson said. "I don't like to make any kind of deal on the fly like this." But he was clearly intrigued.

"We're expecting a boom in the real estate business in our county and the surrounding area very soon," Rowan said. "With the right partnership, we could have a gold mine on our hands. We definitely don't expect you to commit to anything upfront, but I'd love to submit some documents to your office for you to look over. We'd just need to hear within a couple of days. We're looking to set up multiple investments, but we can't wait too long to get started."

An eager gleam had come into the businessman's eyes. He rubbed his hands together. "Yes," he said, pulling a business card out of his pocket. "This is the card I only give people I *actually* want to hear from. Send your proposal to this address, and I'll take a look right away."

As Rowan slipped the card into his suit, a couple of women dragged Anderson away, but not before he gave us another encouraging nod.

As soon as he was out of view, I turned toward Rowan. "We did it! I think he'll bite. You already have all the paperwork done up, don't you?"

"Yeah." Rowan chuckled, looking a bit dazed. "I spent all yesterday getting it perfect. We can contact Gideon as soon as we've left and he can send it before we're even back at the mansion. If Anderson bites—it'll be amazing for the Nobles and the Claws even without the fact that it's undermining the Storm's business at the same time."

"Then let's celebrate with a little partying, since we are here at this fancy party, after all." I grinned at him.

We drank a little more champagne and gulped down dainty hors d'oeuvres until we figured we could make our exit without looking out of place. We still had a long drive back to Paradise Bend.

Rowan put the top down on the convertible now that I didn't have to worry about messing up my hair, and the breeze washed over us as he set off. I texted Wylder letting him know everything had gone well, sent Anderson's contact info to Gideon, and kicked off my shoes to rub my aching feet. "Stupid heels."

"No more of them for a good long time," Rowan said with a laugh.

"I sure hope not." I glanced over at him. "You were really great tonight, you know. It's no wonder you managed to hook him."

"*We* managed to hook him," Rowan corrected me. "You were amazing too. Getting his attention with the bids was a great warm-up."

I elbowed him lightly. "Obviously we still make a great team."

I turned on the radio and leaned back in the seat, and the hours passed with occasional chatter and a few spurts of singing along when a song we particularly liked came on. The late afternoon darkened into evening and then night. By the time we reached the edge of Paradise Bend, it was totally dark, everything silhouetted by the harsh glow of the streetlamps.

Maybe now was a good time to speak up, while we were high on the victory, our hair wind-blown and our fancy clothes loosened. I looked over at Rowan. The headlights of an oncoming car deepened the brown of his eyes.

"There's something I've been wanting to tell you."

He glanced at me. "Yeah?"

"Yeah. I—"

I didn't get a chance to finish my sentence. The car that'd been coming toward us abruptly veered in front of us, just as two more roared up from behind. There was nowhere for Rowan to turn to avoid them. He hit the brakes, and the car behind us crashed into the back of the convertible.

We jerked to a halt with a screech and the distinct sound of safeties clicking off all around us.

15

Mercy

MY HEAD BANGED AGAINST THE CAR WINDOW. I slapped my hand to my temple at the sudden ache, but there was no chance to do more than that. Doors were flying open on the three cars that'd surrounded us, armed men spilling out.

They had to be the Storm's people. It was only a matter of seconds before they started shooting. There was no way for us to drive away from them when they'd boxed us in like this.

My gaze darted to Rowan, confirming he was okay other than the fear paling his face, and then to the buildings beyond the sidewalk. A scruffy brick structure stood on the other side of a paved parking area patchy with weeds. It was our closest option for shelter.

The second I spotted it, I shoved the car door open. Rowan unsnapped his seatbelt and clambered after me.

We bolted for the building without a word, both understanding the situation, keeping our heads low.

Someone yelled, and footsteps stomped behind us. We veered left and right as bullets whizzed through the air around us. Bits of gravel dug into my bare feet, and I almost missed the heels I'd kicked off. But all that mattered was reaching the shelter of the building in time.

As Rowan kicked the rickety door open, another bang pierced the night, and he flinched. The bullet had sliced across his upper arm, carving a channel in the fabric of his suit and the skin beneath. Gritting his teeth, he pushed me onward into the dark, dusty space.

It was one of the Bend's many abandoned warehouses, mostly one huge room smelling of old plywood and grease. The hulking outlines of various pieces of mechanical equipment showed in the faint streams of city light that drifted in through the high, grimy windows amid scattered wooden shipping crates, some stacked on top of each other, most of them yawning open. Whatever they'd delivered was long gone.

Rowan heaved the nearest crate in front of the door, ducking to avoid another barrage of bullets. The door's wood was already splintering—blocking it wasn't going to keep our attackers out for long. I groped around for anything to defend myself with and realized I'd left my purse with my shoes on the floor of the car. The pretty little gun Anthea had given me was way too far out of reach.

Rowan wasn't armed either, but he was creative. He

snatched up a metal rod that was lying on the ground and wielded it like a sword, testing its weight. His expression had gone taut with tension. Blood was soaking down the sleeve of his suit from where the bullet had grazed his arm.

I grabbed his hand, ignoring the stinging in the soles of my feet. "Come on. Maybe there's a back door." The windows were too high to easily reach, and who knew what the drop on the other side would be like. My parkour skills might be up to it, but Rowan didn't have the same training.

As we darted farther into the building, the door exploded with a hail of bullets, bits of wood flying everywhere. We dove behind a couple of the crates. I spun around and noticed a vicious-looking steel hook dangling from a chain overhead.

If I could get that swinging, I could smash a whole bunch of skulls. I just needed to get to it.

Rowan was tapping out a message on his phone. He shoved it back into his pocket, his grip tight on the metal bar. Our enemies were fanning out through the building, shouting to each other as they searched for us.

"We're too far from the mansion," Rowan said under his breath. "I don't think anyone will be able to get to us in time."

"Then we'll just have to deal with these assholes ourselves," I said, my heart thumping. I could do this. The machine looming next to the crate should mostly block me from view—and bullets.

I dashed over to the machine and scrambled onto a crate partly wedged behind it. The hook was just within reach of my grasping fingers. I spotted a lever I could use to adjust its height on the wall just a few feet away.

But I also spotted a few of the men coming up on Rowan's hiding spot. If only I'd had my fucking gun. Grimacing at myself, I leapt up to grab the hook, meaning to whip myself right into them and kick them all square in the face.

At the same moment, Rowan charged out from behind the crate. He must have seen the guys coming and figured he'd do better with the element of surprise.

And maybe he was right. He caught one guy in the side of the head with a smack of the bar that must have shattered the man's skull from the crunching sound that followed. Rowan whirled and clocked another guy in the gut. I launched myself at them, bracing myself for a flying kick—

And several more men hurtled toward us, bullets exploding from their guns.

Rowan tried to jerk himself out of range, but he didn't have enough time. His body spasmed as if he'd been hit. His legs buckled. He fell to the floor, blood blooming around a wound on his upper chest.

No! The silent protest echoed up my throat. I flung myself onto the edge of the crate just above him, meaning to jump down and grab a gun from one of the fallen men, to try to stop the bleeding while I shot at the pricks who'd ambushed us. But the Storm's force was too overwhelming. I was only just starting my spring when a bullet tore into my flesh this time, ripping through the muscle of my thigh.

My leg shuddered, and the impact threw me

backward. I tumbled onto my back in the bottom of the crate with a thud that sent pain spiking up my spine. Pain streaked through my body from the bullet wound like a bolt of lightning.

As I flailed to try to right myself, packing straw rustling around me, someone slammed the lid of the crate down, shutting out the thin light overhead.

I was alone. I was alone in the dark with the walls pressing in around me and blood smearing the floor beneath me.

A cry caught in my throat. My pulse rattled past my ears, and my lungs seized, my breath coming in ragged spurts. Panic rolled over me and sucked me under.

Not this. Not this again. I tried to focus on the reality around me, but too much of my brain was trapped in the pit in the Katz basement again, listening to my father walk away while I sobbed and scratched in vain.

Some distant part of my brain was aware of voices outside—a brief, hollered discussion about what to do with us, someone making a comment about "won't even be bodies to find." I had no idea what they were talking about. I groped in the darkness, my fingers scraping over the splintery boards so frantically the skin split. My breaths were becoming more choked by the second. My head spun with the lack of oxygen.

Then, with one gasp, a new smell prickled into my lungs. I whimpered and gagged, and recognition clicked.

Gasoline. It smelled like gasoline. Why—

Liquid splashed against the side of my crate, and the smell got thicker. There was a click and a hiss, and then a warbling sound that made my blood run even colder. I banged my fists against the boards wildly. "No, no, let me out. Let me *out*!"

The men just snickered as their footsteps thumped off. A hint of smoke tickled into my nose, and the rising crackle filled my ears. My pulse lurched twice as hard as before.

They'd set the building on fire. They were burning it down around us—leaving *us* to burn in it.

I knew that. I knew I had to get out; I had to get to Rowan; we had to run for it. If we stayed here, we'd die for sure.

But even with the smoke curling through the tiny crevices between the plywood slats and fiery heat starting to waft in with it, I couldn't shake myself free of the panic's hold. The old fear had dug its claws deep into my brain. I kept gasping and sputtering, my heart pounding so fast it dizzied me.

Come on, Mercy, I thought. *Come on, come on.* And in the back of my mind the concrete lid slammed shut over the pit again, just after I'd gotten one last glimpse of Dad's sadistic grin.

Something thumped against the outer wall of the crate. There was a ragged breath and a groan. "Mercy?" Rowan's voice said, weak and wavering.

Tears flooded my eyes. It took me a second before I could work any words out of my constricted throat. "Rowan. Are you—I can't—I don't know—" I couldn't even pull more than three words together into any kind of coherence.

Even as rough as he sounded, he managed to speak

with the same warm assurance he'd always had. "Don't worry about me. You need to get out of there." He paused with a muffled grunt. "You—you can do this. Just focus on me. Focus on my voice. I'm right here with you, and I'm not going anywhere. I'll always be here."

His words sank in through the haze of panic just like they had all those years ago when he'd found me trapped in the cabinet in the museum, the day we'd really become friends. I gulped the smoky air and clung on to the sense of calm he was projecting as hard as I could.

"I'm trying," I said, noticing the pain in my thigh again, my body shuddering with it in the growing heat. "I'm trying."

"You're doing great. You'll get there. Just keep—just keep going, one step at a time, one thought at a time. You're in control. You can handle this."

My heartbeat started to even out, my chest loosening. I squeezed my eyes shut, seeing him slumped against the other side of the crate, giving everything he had to talk me through this moment. Resolve cracked through the rest of the turmoil that'd gripped me.

I *could* handle this, and I wasn't going to die here. I wasn't going to let *him* die. Those bastards weren't going to win.

I heaved myself upright, slamming my shoulder into the lid of the crate. The Storm's men had weighed it down with something, but it creaked at the impact. Ignoring the pain searing through my injured leg, I braced both hands against the scratchy plywood and heaved as hard as I could, up and away from where Rowan was sprawled.

The lid slid to the side with a scraping sound. I shoved again, and it toppled right off. Swallowing a whimper at the agony lancing through my thigh, I hauled myself up over the top and dropped to the floor next to Rowan.

He was lying right where I'd imagined him, his eyes closed other than brief twitches of his eyelids, his face sallow. His breath rattled in his throat. He'd passed out while I was freeing myself from the crate. Blood smeared the floor all around him.

The smoke was congealing thicker around us, my skin prickling with the heat. The flames had engulfed most of the crates around us. The inferno roared so loud my eardrums ached.

I coughed and smacked Rowan's cheeks. "Wake up. Please, Rowan, wake up!"

He didn't stir. Fresh tears stung my eyes.

I couldn't leave him here. No fucking way.

I hobbled around him, hissing every time I put any weight on my bad leg, and curled my arms under his until my elbows locked into his armpits. Clenching my jaw, I heaved us both backward. Again. And again. Dragging him toward the doorway slowly but surely.

More blood oozed out of his wounds. The sight of it and the limpness of his body made me want to lie down and give up. Pain screamed through my body, but the scream of refusal rang out inside me even louder.

I wasn't losing him again. I simply *wasn't*.

That defiance and the adrenaline coursing through

my veins propelled me onward. The flames licked closer, scorching Anthea's lovely dress and singing my hair. I winced at the sting but kept pulling, Rowan's body jerking along in my grasp a couple of feet at a time.

The Storm's men had smashed the crate Rowan had wedged by the door as they'd come in. I was grateful for their destructive inclinations now. I smacked aside the scattered boards, some of them already sizzling, and hauled Rowan out into the cooler night air.

I couldn't stop there on the doorstep. The flames lashed after us, roaring up to the doorway. And Rowan needed help. I heaved him and heaved again, over to where the convertible was parked with its crumpled back end. The Storm people had driven off in their cars. The road was clear again.

"Hang in there," I pleaded. Rowan made no indication he heard me. "Please, stay with me."

A thin moan escaped his mouth as I hauled him into the back seat. I cringed, guilt stabbing through my gut at the thought that I might have hurt him more. "We're going to get you help," I swore, tucking him against the smooth leather as carefully as I could. "You're going to be okay." Oh, please, please, please, let him be okay.

I straightened up and nearly blacked out with the pain that blared through my mind. Somehow, I managed to hold on. With lurching steps, I stumbled around the car and fell into the driver's seat.

The key was still in the ignition. I murmured a ragged prayer under my breath while I turned it.

I'd never heard a more glorious sound than the

engine growling to life. I swiped at the blood and tears coating my face, angled myself so I could set my foot from my uninjured side against the gas pedal, and took us into drive.

The car leapt forward. I gripped the steering wheel so tightly my knuckles were pure white, and trained all my attention on the image of the Bend's hospital in my head. I just had to get there. I just had to get there and let them take care of Rowan, because this was one injury Frank didn't have a hope in hell of fixing.

Mercy

THE DOCTOR FLASHED A BEAM OF LIGHT OVER MY eyes. "Look to one side and then the other," he said.

Irritation rippled through me. "For the umpteenth time, I don't have a concussion. The only place I'm really hurt is my *leg*, not my head."

The doctor looked at me disapprovingly, but to my relief, he finally stepped back. The room, like the rest of the hospital, smelled like disinfectant and bleach. But the stench of smoke that still lingered in my nose overpowered everything else unless I took a particularly deep breath.

"You and your friend came in here pretty battered up," the doctor said warily. "What happened exactly?"

I straightened my spine. They had been trying to crack me and get me to admit to some kind of criminal activity since I'd driven up to the emergency room doors, yelling for help. While they'd rolled Rowan toward surgery, I'd been detained so they could stitch up my leg, check my lungs, and up my fluid intake. Apparently the bullet had slashed across my leg but not sunk right in, but they could still tell it was a bullet wound—and Rowan's had obviously come from gunfire too. Those kind of injuries led to a lot of questions, which was exactly why the Nobles turned to Frank for this kind of treatment when they could.

"I'm sorry, but like I said before, it was official business, and I can't disclose anything," I said, trying to keep my voice neutral. Maybe he'd buy that I might be involved in some kind of work on the right side of the law.

From his expression, that was a no. "Right," he said, eyeing me skeptically. He looked like he was getting ready to pick up the phone and call the cops.

There was a knock at the door. Both of us looked up at the same time to see Wylder there.

Relief rushed through me. If he'd made it this far, that meant that he'd dealt with all the hospital formalities. Before now, all he'd managed to do was pass on a T-shirt and sweatpants for me to change into since Anthea's dress was no longer wearable.

Wylder's mouth pressed into a hard line. "Can I take her?"

The doctor frowned. "She should avoid straining her leg during the initial healing period, and she may have taken some damage to her lungs from smoke inhalation. I personally think she should stay at the hospital for tonight while we run more tests."

"I'm fine," I said. To make a point, I slid off the bed

and stood up. Immediately, a shock of pain jolted from the wound on my thigh up through my chest and down to my foot. I grimaced but quickly covered it with a forced smile.

The doctor wasn't convinced by that performance either. "See, miss—"

"She's fine," Wylder said. It was a statement. Period. "We'll make sure she's well taken care of."

The doctor swallowed hard. When Wylder loomed on him, he took a step back. Either he knew the Noble heir by reputation, or he could tell he was dealing with someone he shouldn't mess with. "Yes, in that case, take her home."

"Thank you, doctor," I said.

Wylder gave me his hand, and I limped out of the room next to him.

As soon as we'd left the doctor behind, he turned to me, peering into my eyes with a storm raging in his. "You sure you're okay, right? Those bastards..."

I squeezed his hand. "I'm fine. Sore, but nothing that won't heal. I want to see Rowan if we can. Do you have any idea how *he's* doing?" He'd been alive when we'd made it to the hospital, but I didn't know by how thin a thread. What if he didn't make it? A lump rose in my throat.

"They're not letting us see him yet," Wylder said with a hard edge to his voice. "We'll wait them out until we can convince them otherwise."

He led me on down the hall toward the seating area where I could see Gideon and Kaige poised opposite each other on the rows of metal chairs, which were bolted to the ground as if the hospital was afraid someone might try to steal them otherwise.

"Did the doctors even say anything?" I asked Wylder. "How did the surgery go?"

Gideon looked up at the sound of my voice. His face was so serious that my heart sank. He got up and gave me a quick, tight hug that was so unlike his typical undemonstrative self that I got even more worried. "It doesn't sound great," he admitted in a low voice.

Kaige had stood up and hastily helped me into a chair with Wylder at my other side. He kept his arm around my shoulders. "They don't want to tell us much of anything," he grumbled. "We had enough trouble even getting them to admit that *you* hadn't taken any life-threatening wounds. I was starting to think I'd have to knock some skulls together."

I gave him a baleful look. "I appreciate your dedication, but let's not take that approach here. We need them putting their heads toward fixing Rowan."

"Fine," he growled. "Then I'll just settle for pummeling every single one of the assholes who did this to the two of you. There's going to be nothing left but a bloody pulp."

Wylder didn't say a word, but I'd never seen him so deathly quiet, not even when he'd found his brother's corpse. Cold fury seemed to engulf him as he stared down stubbornly at the floor.

Before I could say anything to him, a doctor approached us. "You're here for Rowan Finlay?" he said to the guys.

Wylder leapt up. "Yes. Is he all right? Can we see him?"

The doctor looked so solemn I wanted to punch him. As I hefted myself back onto my feet, he motioned to us. "You can, but only briefly. And I'll warn you, his current appearance may upset you. One of the bullets ruptured a major organ—we have him in a medically induced coma while we encourage his body to recover from the trauma. He's going to need at least one more surgery you'll have to sign off on."

My throat closed up. "Do you even know if he's going to make it?" I asked in a thin voice.

The doctor's expression told me he didn't. "We can't make predictions of prognosis in situations like this. We'll do our best for him."

Shit. My hands clenched tight as I walked with the guys down the hall after the doctor. He showed us into a small private room where a limp figure lay on a gurney in a hospital gown. Even though I should have known what to expect, it took me a second to process that the figure was Rowan.

His blond hair was stained with soot and blood. His face was so pale it looked like wax. He had tubes going into his arms and another into his mouth, and bandages protruding here and there all over his limbs and torso. I pressed my hand to my mouth to muffle a gasp. The pain in my leg suddenly seemed miles distant.

"Give us a moment alone with him?" Wylder said. "Then I'll sign your damned forms."

The doctor dipped his head and hustled out as if he couldn't leave fast enough. Wylder stood right by

Rowan's head, gazing down at him. His stance had gone even more rigid. When he finally looked up, pure rage blazed in his bright green eyes.

"I'll tear Xavier limb from limb. He'll pay for every single drop of Rowan's blood that his men spilled. I swear it on my fucking soul."

Kaige smacked his hands together, intense in his agreement. "Oh yes, he will."

"And I'll be right there with you," Gideon said in a flat voice edged with his own anger. "I'll rip the Storm and his people apart every way I possibly can."

Their collective anger couldn't fill the hollow of grief and guilt in my heart. I wanted to see Xavier gutted, sure. But what would the price be?

Rowan had already paid for the war I'd dragged the Nobles into—he might pay with his life. Was this war worth it if it took away one of the people I cared about most? How much else would I lose before it was over?

I glanced between Kaige and Wylder. They looked ready to go after Xavier right this instant, guns blazing. Even Gideon's face was a mask of worry and frustration. How many more people would have to be sacrificed in my crusade to protect my home—a crusade that was seeming more hopeless by the day?

I'd never even gotten to tell Rowan I loved him. What if I'd lost that chance forever?

What was the point in all this fighting if everyone ended up dead anyway?

I closed my eyes against those awful questions and the horrible specter of Rowan's injured body. There was a rustling as the doctor came back in.

"I'm sorry to disturb you, but the operating room is open. The sooner we can get started, the better off he'll be."

"Of course," Wylder said gruffly. A pen scratched across a paper form.

I forced myself to open my eyes. I stared down at Rowan as the attendants wheeled his gurney out of the room. *I love you*, I thought at him, as if that would make a difference now. *I love you. Please come back to me.*

Wylder turned to the rest of us. "It sounds like there won't be any news for a while. We should let them work and get ourselves sorted out. It won't do Rowan any good if he survives only for the Long Night to cut him down in a few days' time."

I wanted to protest, but deep down I knew he was right. For a second, my pain seemed to cut right through the center of my being. Hanging around here was only making it worse. I needed to get away, to think, to figure out where I stood now that my world had been upended in a way I hadn't really been prepared for.

"Can I get a lift?" I asked. "I want to go home."

"You shouldn't even have to ask that," Wylder said.

He and Kaige supported me on either side as I limped out to Wylder's Mustang. Kaige stayed with me in the back seat. The sun had risen for the morning, blazing over the streets with a brightness that made me feel like I was hallucinating. How could it be *daylight* when Rowan was locked in darkness?

Wylder drove straight to the Katz house. He parked out front, nodding to the Claws men stationed on the lawn, who studied me with obvious concern. I was going to have to put on a brave face for them.

"We can come in with you," Wylder said. "Keep you company."

As much as I appreciated his offer, I shook my head. "I think I need to be alone for a little while to collect myself."

Kaige grunted. "Are you sure that's a good idea? Feelings can be quite a bitch."

My lips twitched with a hint of a smile at his blunt statement. "Yes, they can. But I think I'm having a few that I'll work through easier on my own." I touched his cheek. "Thank you. I'll call in an hour or two. Let me know if anything comes up."

I got out, careful of my injured leg, and walked up to the house as steadily as I could. Quinn and a couple of the other guys were hanging out in the living room.

"Hey," Quinn called out. "We hit the jackpot last night. Picked up some cars and cash we can put to good use."

"That's great," I said, my voice coming out stiff. I couldn't summon any enthusiasm.

Put them to use attacking the Storm people some more? Maybe I should tell all the Claws men who'd joined my cause that they should cut their losses and just get out of here before the Long Night rolled in to lay down his brand of the law. How many of them would die in the next few days if I didn't?

I limped on down the hall to the kitchen, not feeling up to handling the stairs. Part of me wanted to go out in the backyard and sit under the big oak tree, as if it would give me answers, but Xavier had ruined my favorite part of my childhood home the other night along with so much else. My teeth set on edge.

I paused at the sound of a high-pitched giggle up ahead and then pushed myself forward. Through the kitchen window, I could see Sarah dashing around in the backyard, letting the wind whip through a pinwheel covered in tassels. She had no sense of that space as dangerous—not yet, anyway. I was relieved to note the guards standing by the fence, keeping watch.

Jenner was leaning against the kitchen counter, gazing through the window too. A soft smile curved his lips. It amazed me that a man ruthless enough to be my dad's former lieutenant could be so loving with his daughter.

Without thinking, I stepped closer to the glass. Sarah stopped playing long enough to wave at me.

"She seems... happy," I ventured. It felt like a foreign concept.

Jenner nodded. "She's pretty good at finding joy in little things. Never made much trouble for me or her mom. It's one of the things I really admire about her." He glanced at me, taking in my off-balance pose and the lump of the bandage on my leg. "How are you?"

I didn't really want to answer that question. And somehow at the same time I had the sense that my answer lay just beyond the window. "I'm fine," I said, concentrating on Sarah.

She deserved all the joys she could find. She deserved to keep her home. What would happen to her if we all had to make a run for it? What would happen to Beckett—would the Long Night kill him too?

I'd wanted to make a better future for all the kids in the Bend, hadn't I? I didn't see how that was going to happen if I let the Long Night take over. I'd seen the cold ruthlessness behind his polite exterior.

Rowan wouldn't have wanted me to give up on my dreams, no matter what happened to him.

The mounting pressure on my shoulders eased. I was doing this for Sarah, and Beckett, and all the other kids. And for little Mercy who'd lost her childhood, and now wanted to make sure that others didn't have to suffer the same fate. Things *would* be better in the future than they were today. They were counting on me to make that happen.

Jenner let me hold my silence for a long stretch. Then he ventured, in a gentle tone, "We're not done yet, are we? What's up next, boss?"

The way he said "boss" set off a weird glow in my chest that burned away a little more of the anguish twisted around my heart.

"We're close," I said. The Storm people had to be scared, or they wouldn't have gone out of their way to track down Rowan and me like that. They'd tried to steal my best friend and my first love from me, but I wouldn't let them back me into a corner.

My resolve bled into my words, turning them firm. "We're close, and we're going to make the Storm pay."

My phone buzzed in the little purse of Anthea's I'd brought in with me. I pulled it out, seeing Gideon's name on the call display.

"Hey," he said when I answered. "Something's just come up with the Storm. I know you just got home. We can handle it if you need to rest—"

"No," I said before he could go on, my chin lifting. "Swing by and get me. I'm still in this fight."

17

Gideon

"WHAT'S GOING ON?" MERCY ASKED, LEANING forward from the backseat. "Why are we headed for the shopping strip?" Kaige was sitting next to her, his face caught in silent fury.

"The Storm's men have launched attacks on several Noble properties throughout the city and the Bend," Wylder said, his gaze intent on the road as he wove in and out of traffic. His irritation was only evident from the tightness of his grip on the wheel.

"Several—all at once?"

I nodded, tracking incoming text reports from Noble men scattered across the county. "It seems to be some sort of divide and conquer strategy. Thankfully with Ezra's permission for us to call on all the Noble forces, I don't think they're going to manage the conquering part."

"At most places," Wylder put in. "Xavier himself and

the largest bunch of men have turned up at the old furniture store where we stashed the rest of the Glory and all the extra weapons we stole from them. He must have figured out it was important after we started giving out Glory to screw over his previous plan. He's trying to turn the tables on us—but no way in hell are we going to let him."

"There were guards already there, weren't there?" Mercy said, her dark eyes flashing with anger.

"There were five on the premises when the attack started," I said, confirming the data on the screen in front of me. "Unfortunately, a couple of them were shot in the initial skirmish—at least one fatally. The other men inside have managed to keep the building secure, but Xavier and his people have surrounded the place. The Nobles may not be able to hold them off much longer."

"We've called in reinforcements, and they'll follow us as soon as they can," Wylder said. "Unfortunately, a lot of them have gotten tied up in the other attacks. But I want to take this prick down myself. We'll give them something to worry about other than their little siege. How many Claws were you able to round up?"

Mercy glanced through the back window at the car following us. "We only had four who could come right away, but I told Jenner to put out a wider call. I'm not sure how far off the others are. How many people does Xavier have with him?"

I grimaced. "I don't have a clear report. The men at the factory haven't had a whole lot of time to chat. It sounds like quite a few."

And there were only eight of us to go up against them so far. Well, seven, really, when you considered that I wasn't going to contribute much other than sorting through the incoming data and filling Wylder in. I didn't even have the benefit of the full computer array in my van, since we hadn't made it back to the Noble mansion before we'd gotten the call about the attacks.

My stomach twisted. Ever since I'd told Wylder I'd be staying with him when he set off to deal with Xavier, there'd been a pang in the back of my head, like the start of a throbbing headache. Images of my last encounter with the psychopath flashed through my mind.

The last time I'd been close to Xavier, he'd nearly killed me. He *could* have killed me—I was just lucky he'd decided to wait and use me as bait. Who knew if I'd survive this time?

But I couldn't let my nerves get the better of me. We were down one man with Rowan in the hospital. Everyone had to pull their weight. I couldn't hide away in my office while my brothers-in-arms and my woman did all the fighting for me. Maybe I'd get the chance to take a shot or two that could help turn the tide.

We turned the corner, and Wylder eased to a stop. My heart sank.

It was a hell of a lot more than twenty men. Cars were parked all over the street from halfway down the block to the next corner, surrounding the old store and cutting off the flow of traffic. The Storm's men were hustling between the vehicles or staked out behind them, some taking shots at the second-floor windows that our men were using as a vantage point. At least one of our people was around at the back too, shooting anyone who tried to get to the back door.

Thankfully, the store's windows had already been boarded up. But the front and back doors wouldn't withstand a steady barrage if Xavier sent enough people in that the guards couldn't pick them all off.

The menace himself was standing on the roof of one of the cars near the back of the horde, apparently unconcerned about the possibility that anyone might shoot *him*. "Just you wait," he was hollering at the Noble men inside. "As soon as we get in there, we're going to chop you up like chicken liver. Why don't you make a run for it now?"

A bunch of men were hauling something out of one of the other vehicles, a large SUV. I squinted at it, and my pulse hiccupped.

"They've got explosives," I said, pointing. "They're going to blast the doors in—maybe bring the whole building down." I wouldn't put it past Xavier to care more about making sure *we* didn't have the drugs and weapons than getting them back for himself.

"Shit." Wylder pushed open his door. "We'd better deal with this fast, then. We can at least cover the front of the building so they can't bring the bombs close enough." He glanced at me. "You stay in the car, but keep the window down in case you pick up on anything you need to give us a shout about."

I tipped my head in acknowledgment, my gut full of a queasy mix of relief... and shame at the fact that I was relieved. But the relief part flooded me even more sharply when Xavier's head swung toward us.

A savage grin stretched across his face. Wylder's hand whipped up with his pistol, but the shot that would have hit Xavier smack in the face missed as the giant leapt down from the car at the same moment. He sauntered closer to us, moving between the cars so he could keep us in view with his body almost entirely shielded.

My heart thumped faster at the sight of him looming closer, some part of me clenching up with the urge to flee, to put as much distance between him and me as I could. I clamped down on that impulse, forcing myself to breathe slowly and evenly like I did when my lungs acted up.

This must be similar to how Mercy felt when she was trapped in a tight space—this irrational panic. Except it wasn't totally irrational, was it? We were both reacting to a reminder of a situation that'd been quite literally life-threatening.

Mercy, Kaige, and the four Claws men who'd joined us had gotten out too. They stuck close to our cars and a couple other vehicles belonging to regular citizens that were parked along this stretch of sidewalk. There was an empty space of maybe thirty feet between the horde of Storm vehicles and ours. I didn't think Xavier would risk trying to cross it, opening himself up to our fire. But we couldn't dash across it to get to the building without getting picked off by his men either.

As I'd expected, Xavier stopped before he passed the last of his vehicles. He leaned his massive arms on the top of the car, still grinning but tensed to duck if anyone aimed their gun at him. Wylder glanced past him and motioned to the Claws men. They opened fire on a few men who'd made a dash for the entrance with the explosives, and the bunch fell back.

"Look who's shown up," Xavier said in a drawl. "Why am I not surprised? The scared little kitten, the second-rate heir, and even the mouse who hides behind his computer screens most of the time." His gaze narrowed in on me, and my heart outright lurched. "I missed getting to snap your neck last time. Wouldn't want to lose the opportunity again."

He was just bullshitting, spewing out crap. He was nowhere near me. I knew that, but adrenaline kept racing through my veins all the same. My hands balled on my lap.

"Fuck you!" I yelled out the window, which actually made me feel a little better, even though Xavier just chuckled. Kaige aimed an approving grin at me.

Then Xavier turned away from us to call out to his men. "Bring one of the trucks right up onto the sidewalk to give us a clear path. These dipshits aren't going to stop us from getting what we want for long."

Damn it. Wylder and the others started firing again, forcing Xavier to jerk out of range, but the truck the Storm's men hurried to was sheltered by other vehicles around it. None of our force managed to pick any of them off. And as soon as they got it in place on the sidewalk, they'd be able to run the explosives right to the front door while it shielded them, nothing we could do about it short of charging at them straight to our deaths.

"In just a few minutes, we'll all be smelling baked Nobles," Xavier announced in a weird singsong voice. The man was totally deranged.

Even as my nerves jittered with that thought, something clicked in my head. Xavier made a terrifying figure, sure, but he shouldn't have been that much of a challenge. He was reckless and savage. All we needed to do was outthink his animalistic brain. How hard could that be?

What did I have around me that I could use?

I scanned the entire street, my physical symptoms of panic fading into the background as I focused on my new goal. My gaze snagged on a building at the far corner, beyond the Storm siege.

A huge poster of a man's slickly smiling face was posted in the window, the sign overhead announcing it was the office for one of the new mayoral candidates. I'd barely even noticed the election campaigning getting started a few months ago, it mattered so little to us. The Nobles lived above the law.

I doubted that dork had been doing much campaigning since war had broken out on the streets of the Bend anyway. But he had a loudspeaker system set up in the building, with speakers mounted all along the front of the structure. They should have some kind of control center that ran them from inside. If I could just get access to that...

"Wylder," I hissed, keeping my voice low enough that Xavier shouldn't be able to hear. "Hold them off as long as you can. I need a few minutes, and then I think we can send them running."

Wylder raised an eyebrow at me, but my best friend trusted me without needing to hear more than that. At his gesture, our men all started shooting again, one of them managing to shatter the back window on the truck. The warmth of his faith in me sped my fingers across the tablet's screen.

Xavier thought he could lord his strength over me, taunt me like I was pathetic. He had no idea what *real* strength looked like—or just how many forms it could come in.

The local network was still running inside the campaign office. I clicked on a device I'd stashed in the glove compartment that boosted my own range and disabled the security protocols in a matter of seconds, peeling them away like tissue paper from a present. A different sort of adrenaline coursed through me now, thrumming with confidence rather than quivering with fear.

I might not get far with a physical confrontation, but this was what I was made for. Xavier couldn't beat me at my kind of game.

He'd noticed I was up to something, though. He leaned against the car he was poised behind and cocked his head. "Look at the poor little geek, scrambling frantically to save his skin."

I let out a laugh, not even needing to fake it. A couple more taps—and there, I was in. I barely needed to look at the screen as I set up the final pieces of my gambit.

"You're the one who's going to be running scared in a moment," I shouted out the window. "You'll get going right now if you know what's good for you."

Xavier snorted. "Big words from a puny little man. Am I supposed to be afraid of this tiny band of resistance."

"Nope," I retorted. "But I don't know how much you'll enjoy dealing with our friends in blue."

I concealed the click of a button on my lap out of his view, and the wail of police sirens sounded as if in the distance. The truth was, it was a recorded sound I was playing through the loudspeakers, keeping the volume low to give the Storm's men the impression that the cars had only just gotten close enough to be heard.

Xavier's head jerked around toward the sound. Then he turned back to me with a sneer. "The cops wouldn't want anything to do with the likes of you."

I shrugged. "We've paid them off to look the other way plenty of times, and now we're paying them to crack down on the mess you're making on our streets. Every cop in a twenty-mile radius is headed this way right now, fully armed and ready to rumble."

A flicker of uncertainty crossed the big man's scarred face. I nudged the volume a little louder as if the sirens were getting closer.

"How would your boss feel about you getting into a massive shoot-out with the local law enforcement?" I asked. "Is that really what he sent you here to do? I'd have thought *he'd* want to get them in his pocket, not have you turn them into enemies. You know how the police feel about cop-killers."

I could tell I'd struck the right chord. Xavier's jaw twitched. A man like the Storm, someone who kept his own hands as clean as possible, didn't care how many fellow criminals Xavier took down, but he wouldn't want to set himself completely at odds with the police before he'd even claimed this territory.

Most of the Storm's men were listening now. Several had lowered their weapons. They looked at Xavier and each other nervously.

I increased the volume even more. It sounded perfect, like a whole swarm of cops about to descend on this street.

Wylder didn't know exactly what I'd done, but he was smart enough to play along. He set his hands on his hips and smirked at Xavier. "I look forward to watching the boys in blue mow you down."

Xavier cursed, but I could tell he was finally convinced. He pulled back, shouting at his men. I pushed the volume higher, as if the sirens were just a few blocks away now. It was almost hilarious watching the Storm men scramble into their vehicles and peel out like they had a pack of demons on their tails.

"Run, baby, run," Kaige hollered after them. Xavier gave us one last ominous look before he leapt into his car. The vehicles scattered into the side-streets, a few of them almost colliding with each other in their haste to get away.

As soon as they'd roared off, Wylder and Mercy waved to our people, and they rushed to the store. "Bring the injured down so we can get them out of here right away," Wylder called to the guards who'd been holding their ground inside. He shot a glance back at me. "That was fucking brilliant, Gideon."

Kaige glanced around. "There aren't any actual cops coming, are there? Because I don't think they see us as friends."

I chuckled. "It's just a sound effect I found online. Go get our guys out of there."

We'd beat Xavier even hugely outnumbered and out-armed. We would beat him again and again. For the first time, I could really believe that we'd take him and the rest of the Storm's forces down for good before our time ran out.

And I'd be right here fighting alongside the rest of the Nobles in my own way.

18

Mercy

I directed Sam and his friend toward the right corner of the room. They were carrying a wooden crate between them. "Put it there with the rest of the boxes."

They did as I asked and heaved the crate to the top of the last of the neatly stacked rows.

Gideon came in after them, carrying his tablet. He ticked something off on the screen. "That's the last one."

Beyond the garage-style door, Kaige waved off the truck we'd used to carry the stash from the old furniture store to a different Noble property where hopefully Xavier wouldn't discover it again. The factory had reinforced windows and doors in case it did face an attack. Wylder had gone to fill his father in and get approval to have a new contingent of guards posted here.

Kaige watched the truck leave and then came inside,

dusting his hands as he walked. "So, that's all wrapped up."

I turned to Sam. "You guys must be tired. Thanks for your help."

He gave me a teasing salute. "Anything for the Queen of the Claws."

I laughed. "I think we're good now. Why don't you go back to the house and relax for however long we get before we have to be on the move again?"

He and his friend nodded, and they headed out.

"Probably won't be very long," Kaige muttered. "After the stunt we pulled off this morning, I'd bet Xavier is pissed. We humiliated him in front of his own men." He glanced at Gideon. "Which was a total genius move. I'm just saying... he won't be happy."

Gideon shrugged with a newfound assurance that I had to admire. "Whatever he throws at us, we'll be ready."

Kaige's gaze roved over the stacked crates—the wooden ones along two of the walls that held the weapons... and the few large plastic ones against another wall that held the remaining Glory. "At least the prick didn't get his hands on all this."

As if drawn by a magnetic pull, he walked up to one of the plastic containers, his expression hardening. Setting his hands on the edges of the crate, he glared at it as if he could incinerate it with the force of his eyes alone.

"Kaige," I said softly, "you can go now too. Gideon and I can finish going through the inventory."

He shook his head and straightened up again with a

grimace. "I'm fine. I just hate that we have to be a part of this twisted system that's hurting so many people. Now *we're* the ones handing out Glory, getting the junkies even more hooked."

"It was the best option we had in the moment," I pointed out.

"Maybe. I wish we could have found some other way, any way except for this." The tendons on his neck flexed as he began to pace the room, his fists clenched at his sides. "You didn't see them that day, Mercy. Willing to break their own city just to get a hit. Those people...they're sick. And instead of helping them, we're only making the situation worse."

I dragged in a breath, my chest tightening. "I don't like it either. And I get why you're upset. Just remember that it's only for a few more days until we've gotten rid of the Storm, and then we can destroy any Glory that's left in the county. We'll support the people already hooked on it any way we can."

"Wylder and Rowan have already been working on that," Gideon piped up. "They were encouraging people to take lower doses than the Storm's men suggested so they'll start to wean off. I mean, we didn't say that's why, but it'll work the same way, and the people just think they're getting to stretch their supply longer. They didn't seem to notice any difference in the effect, so they were happy to go along with it."

"Well, that's something," Kaige grumbled, but he didn't stop pacing. "We should have figured out how to crush Xavier and all the rest of those Storm assholes by now. We only have a few days left. I just want to march right out of here and smash them all to pieces." He took a swing at the empty air.

"You'll get your chance to smash them," I promised, walking over to him. He came to a halt and let me wrap my arms around him, hugging him. As I bobbed up on my toes to embrace him more tightly, the wound on my thigh protested, but the pain was dulled by the medications Frank had sent over.

Their numbing effect didn't do anything to mute the thump of my pulse as Kaige stroked his broad hand down my back. He sighed and leaned into my arms, and an ache filled my chest.

Under his tough shell, Kaige had such a soft heart. He cared about the people not just in the Nobles but all of Paradise City and the Bend, and he wanted to do right by them. Maybe he didn't always show it in the most graceful of ways, but that was just who he was. I wouldn't have asked him to be any different.

I pulled back to look up into his warm brown eyes. His musky scent with its gingery bite engulfed my senses, and I closed my eyes to inhale it deeply.

I'd waited too long to confess my feelings to Rowan, and maybe I'd never get to now. I didn't want to lose my chance with Kaige too.

"What?" he asked in his sexy baritone voice, as if he sensed I was working up to something. His hands slid down to the small of my back, his palms rubbing soft circles there.

There was no backing down now, not from our war and not from the feelings I'd never expected to grip me so powerfully.

"I love you, Kaige," I said.

Kaige's eyes widened, shock rippling through him. I winced inwardly with a pinch of regret. I'd said it totally out of the blue, and it probably wasn't at all what he wanted to be thinking about right now. More words tumbled out of me as his grip on me loosened. "You don't have to say anything right away. I don't expect you to—"

"I love you too," he said.

I stopped talking, not sure I'd heard him correctly. "You what?"

He grinned. "I love you, Mercy. Would have said it a lot sooner if I hadn't been worried you'd sock me in the face."

A giddy feeling rose in my stomach, and I couldn't hold back a giggle. "Really?"

"You mean it hasn't been obvious?"

I swatted him. "As far as I can tell, you go around charming the pants off all the ladies you meet. How was I supposed to know I'm so special?"

He pointed at himself. "What can I say? This thing, it's a total machine. You can never turn it off." Then he sobered a little. "It's always been different with you. Felt like more with you from the very beginning. I'm all yours now, Mercy. Anyone else who wanted a piece of me is shit out of luck."

I beamed back at him. "Mittens might have a few things to say about that."

"Any other woman," he amended with a wink. "Cats are another story."

Kaige was back to his former flirty self. I was glad

that I'd at least momentarily managed to distract him from his darker thoughts.

His hands circled my waist, and I looped my arms around his shoulders. As soon as I did, he jerked me to him so that the length of our bodies fused together. I could feel him harden almost instantaneously against my belly. "Now that we've gotten that all straightened out, maybe we should celebrate. We're finally alone."

He swiveled his hips, and I swallowed a gasp at the press of his cock. My eyes flicked to Gideon, who was standing near the door, tablet clutched in his hands, looking uncertain but not uncomfortable.

"We're not *completely* alone," I pointed out.

Kaige followed my gaze. He paused for a second as if debating with himself and then shot a grin at his friend. "Is that a problem? It wasn't before." Heat flared in his eyes, and I knew he was thinking back to when all five of us had collided in spectacular fashion in the back of Gideon's van. "Besides I think it's a lot more fun for you with extra company, isn't it, Mercy? The more the merrier?"

I couldn't deny that. I wet my lips automatically as I nodded. "You won't find me complaining."

Kaige leaned over and caught my bottom lip with his mouth. He sucked on it for a second before pulling me into an open-mouthed kiss. It was messy and hot and made my panties dampen in an instant. His insistent cock resting against my hip only urged on the desire surging through me.

Kaige eased back an inch and raised his eyebrows at Gideon. "Care to join us?"

Gideon shifted on his feet, and then a sly smile crossed his lips. The same kind of spark came into his cool eyes as when he'd been hit by one of his brilliant inspirations. Without a word, he yanked the garage door closed, set his tablet down on the nearest crate and walked over to us. He slid his fingers along my jaw and tugged my face around so he could claim a kiss.

Kaige swore under his breath, sounding so turned on it only made me wetter. I kissed Gideon hard, drawing his tongue into my mouth, swaying as Kaige's hands traveled over my body. Gideon caressed me too, cupping one hand over my breast and squeezing with just the right force to bring a moan to my lips.

Maybe we'd all needed this—a moment to let go, to get caught up in emotions we hadn't been able to spare much time for in the past few days. To celebrate the joys we had.

When Gideon released my mouth, Kaige dove in again. His tongue tangled with mine. He grasped my hips and hefted me into the air, and all of a sudden I was flying—until he set me on top of one of the crates.

I hooked my knees around his thighs instinctively, grateful to have my weight off my wounded leg. He leaned even closer, capturing my lips again. As he fucked my mouth with his tongue, Gideon clambered onto the crate and sank down behind me. He teased his hands around my chest to play with both of my breasts, pinching and tugging the hardening nubs until I whimpered with need. The heat from both men's bodies engulfed me with a heady sensation.

I trailed one hand down Gideon's arm encouragingly while I tilted my head into Kaige's kiss. Gideon nudged the hair away from my shoulder and pressed small kisses to my neck along the line of my shirt collar. His lip ring brushed my skin. I broke from Kaige's mouth to tip my head against the man behind me, sinking into his skillful touch.

Kaige took the opportunity to unzip my jeans and yank them off my legs, careful around the bandage. I groped for his shirt and tugged it up, and he tossed it aside without a second's hesitation. His eyes devoured me and Gideon's hands on me. "So fucking sexy."

Gideon took that remark as his cue to peel my shirt off me. Kaige moved in to make short work of my bra. He ducked his head and lapped my nipple into his scorching mouth, and I growled in encouragement as I arched to meet him.

We continued to make out like that, me pressed between their taut bodies, their hands and mouths roaming over every inch of my uncovered skin. Finally, Kaige's fingers slipped between my thighs. He rubbed up and down my sopping wet slit before flicking his finger against the overly sensitive nub above it.

At my back, Gideon continued to explore my body, laying kisses where he knew I liked it the most. He sucked on the curve of my neck and squeezed my breasts before gliding his fingers down to spread my thighs to accommodate Kaige. His own rigid cock bumped against my back.

Kaige watched us while stroking his cock, which seemed to grow impossibly harder. While Gideon slipped his finger inside my pussy, Kaige tore open a foil packet and rolled the condom over him.

Gideon didn't move away. Instead, he opened my pussy lips wide for Kaige who in turn started to rub his cock up and down the length of my slit. I moaned at the feel of him.

"Take my cock, Mercy," he groaned, and buried himself inside me in one quick jerk. My eyes widened, and I had to grip his shoulder tight so I didn't slip off the crate. My body felt like putty.

Kaige adjusted my legs around him before he slipped out, and then thrust right back in, his strokes shallow and fast at first. I cried out at the overwhelming surge of pleasure and sagged heavily against Gideon, who was panting at my ear. He and Kaige worked together with their fingers and cock respectively, stroking every ounce of pleasure my body was capable of out of me. I closed my eyes as the wave of bliss rose.

It wasn't quite enough. I groped behind me and curled my hand around Gideon's cock through his slacks. It twitched at the contact. He fumbled open his fly, and I delved inside his boxers to grip him skin to skin. As I ran my fingers along his stiff length, he groaned.

Kaige let out an animalistic grunt, his thrusts becoming erratic. I bit my lip as he hit a spot so good that my eyes almost rolled inside my head.

I stroked Gideon faster, determined to bring him with us, rubbing the sensitive tip of his cock before sliding all the way to the base and squeezing his balls. My breasts bounced in front of me as Kaige fucked me harder. Gideon reached around and kneaded them roughly, his breath ragged against my neck.

I crested the peak in one swift surge and moaned as my pussy walls began to convulse around Kaige's cock. A cry broke from my mouth, and at the same time Gideon's cum shot across my arm. Kaige came with a shout.

Kaige wrapped his arms around me while I settled into Gideon's lap. I trailed my fingers down his face and over Gideon's arm, spent and sated. We shared a private smile between the three of us.

I wanted to believe that no matter how many enemies we faced, no one could take this amazing connection away from us. But even with the afterglow rippling through me, my mind tripped back to the vision of Rowan in the hospital bed. The thought of losing Kaige, Gideon, or Wylder as well sent a dagger into my chest.

And we were running out of time before all our lives were forfeit.

19

Mercy

"And that's how I tripped down the roof and survived the fall," Kaige said. The dining room burst into laughter. I stood leaning against the door frame as I watched the Noble and Claws men bond and talk. The guys had swung by the Katz house this morning to discuss strategy, and somehow it'd turned into storytelling time while Jenner had whipped up a big breakfast for everybody.

"Yo, that's sick, man," Sam said with a shake of his head. "Was that part of your initiation?"

"Yep," Kaige said. "We all had to go through the trials. They don't make any exceptions, not even for Rowan. He saved Wylder's life when we were in school —took a knife to his chest and everything."

My smile faded. We still hadn't gotten any news from the hospital other than they were continuing to monitor Rowan's situation. He hadn't woken up yet.

The waiting was killing me.

"He was always loyal," Gideon said quietly, catching my eye.

"And he always will be," I said. "Until the end, which hasn't happened yet."

Wylder's phone pinged with an alert. He checked his phone and tensed up, springing to his feet. "We've got to go."

I stood up too. "What's wrong?"

"Beckett just reached out. He says he found out his father's men are going after the waterfront property—they're planning on ruining the construction that's happened so far. They're already on their way."

"Shit." Even I knew how much that waterfront development mattered to Ezra. If the Storm's people succeeded in tearing down all the progress he'd made there...

I motioned to the Claws men around me as Kaige and Gideon leapt up. "We're going to need everyone who isn't on guard duty or injured with us to take them down. Are you with me?"

Jenner nodded without hesitation. "We've got your back. Come on, men."

"Grab all the weapons you can get your hands on," I ordered. "We won't have much time to strategize once we get there, but our primary objective will be to hold them off the property."

I didn't wait for them, hurrying ahead to catch up with Wylder, who'd already gotten Ezra on the line.

"Dad," he said as he yanked the front door open,

putting the phone on speaker so he had more use of his hands. "We need our men in the Bend."

"What's going on?" Ezra said almost testily on the other side.

"Xavier and his men are gunning for the waterfront property. They want to blow it all up."

Ezra swore under his breath. His previous apathy disappeared, replaced by urgency. "I'm sending all the men not already needed in the city over. You'll have the full Noble force at your disposal."

Wylder smiled tightly. "I appreciate that."

"I want the property secured," Ezra said. "Nothing less."

"Of course, Dad," Wylder said in a taut voice. "You don't have to worry about it."

"And I intend to monitor everything that is happening there. Give the phone to Gideon."

Wylder seemed to debate on his decision before he turned off the speaker and handed his phone to Gideon, who looked surprised.

"Yes, Ezra?" Gideon said as we hustled toward the car that was parked outside the house. While Wylder took the driver seat, I slid in next to him, with Gideon and Kaige jumping into the back. Behind us, the rest of the Claws were already making their way out of the house, hollering and shouting, pumping themselves up for the big fight.

Wylder pulled away from the curb and tore off toward the river. My stomach tied itself into a knot. We'd been planning on getting in another hit against the Storm this morning as soon as we'd finished breakfast, hitting them while they were down. Our men had been out tackling any smaller groups they came across all night. Xavier must have rallied even faster than we'd counted on. Did he have any idea about the timeline we were up against?

Gideon made agreeable noises a couple of times while Ezra must have spoken. By the time the call ended, he was frowning.

"What did he want?" Wylder said, checking from the rearview mirror.

"He asked me to see if I can remotely fix the CCTV connection on the property. It went down when the cops marched in there the other day, and with everything else going on, no one got around to fixing it."

"Can you?" Kaige asked.

Gideon shrugged. "I mean, I can try, and maybe it'd be a good thing. Ezra needs to see first-hand how bad things are out here."

Wylder snorted loudly. "He doesn't care about that —or us, for that matter. He'll lose a ton of money if the existing construction is demolished, and it'll look bad to the investors. The only things Ezra Noble protects are his wealth and his reputation. He probably just wants to ensure that his development doesn't come to any harm."

"Yeah, no wonder he's sending in the entire Noble troop," I said, making a face. "He seemed awfully obliging all of a sudden."

"Exactly." Wylder's grip on the steering wheel tightened. "Because God forbid anything happens to his *property*."

I stayed silent. Wylder was right. Ezra cared more about the condos he was building than his own son's well-being.

"We need to turn this around," Wylder added. "Maybe with a whole army of Nobles and the Claws, we can come down on the Storm so hard he'll roll over. I want to see that Xavier psycho dead, whatever we do."

I nodded, my body buzzing with anticipation. We had to strike some kind of fatal blow, and soon. We had less than two days left.

I spotted the looming tower of the half-constructed project and the metal bars of the crane poised next to it. The rising sun blazed through the steel girders. The waterfront project was easily the tallest building in all of the Bend, surrounded by tall construction walls that the Nobles had reinforced after the Storm's people had broken in before to frame them for dealing Glory.

We weren't alone. Up ahead, engines roared closer as the Noble forces Ezra had called on converged with us. The Claws men behind us honked their horns.

But as we came around the last corner, a swarm of other cars racing our way came into view down the road. "Fuck," Wylder said, stomping on the gas. "They're practically here already."

He ripped across the asphalt and screeched to a halt outside the gates to the construction site. The other vehicles with us, Nobles and Claws alike, parked haphazardly around us. But our men had only just started pouring out of the vehicles, more still arriving, when the Storm force sped to meet us from the other direction.

A swarm of Storm men streamed out, already taking shots at us. We ducked behind the cars. I pulled my pistol from the back of my jeans and curled my fingers around the grip and the trigger.

Bullets were flying freely on both sides, making the air thunder and my eardrums ring. I eased up in time to fire at a few Storm men who'd made a run for the gate. They probably figured that once they'd gotten inside, they could pick us off from over the fence.

One of my shots caught a guy in the shoulder. Wylder took another down with a bullet in the side of his head. There was no time to think, only to react.

More men on the Storm side fell, but I saw a few of the Nobles and Claws men stagger and slump too. Anguish squeezed around my heart. We were fighting and some of us dying to protect the only home we'd ever had. What fucking right did the Storm have to come in and try to wrench it away from us? Wasn't his empire big enough already?

"Head around the back," Wylder shouted to a new contingent of Noble men who couldn't reach us through the fray. "Make sure they don't sneak around that way!"

A few cars tore off around the side of the development. Others parked with the men leaping out, guns already in their hands. They blasted away at the Storm forces.

The front line of the Storm's men pulled back to a farther row of cars. We were starting to drive them off. Triumph surged up inside me.

They'd underestimated us yet again. We were so

much stronger than that rich bastard in his mansion had ever imagined.

But the Storm's people had other tricks up their sleeve. I spotted Xavier poised in the back of a pick-up truck, wavering and hollering at the men around him. I couldn't make out what he was saying amid the rattle of gunfire, but his intention became clear soon enough.

"They've got fucking TNT," Kaige bellowed, his lips pulling back in a snarl. "They're going to try to blast right through the wall—or us—like they were going to at the store yesterday."

"Don't let them get close to the wall!" I cried out, hoping that enough of our people would hear me. I shot at the men carrying the explosives, catching one in the chest. He collapsed. Another dashed in to pick up his cargo, but a renewed hail of bullets from our side caught him too.

"That's right!" Wylder shouted. "Push them back! Push them right out of our county."

Just as hope started to unfurl in my chest, at least a dozen more cars roared into view to join the Storm's forces. I swore under my breath and reloaded my gun. "We've got even more to deal with."

Wylder's face hardened, but he kept his jaw firm. "We've still got enough manpower to hold them off. We're taking down more of them than they are of us."

That wasn't necessarily going to be true for long. With the new men joining the Storm's crowd, a different sort of gunfire reverberated in the street. A few of them held machine guns. They pelted our front lines, and several more figures on our side crumpled with blood spurting from their wounds.

"Take cover but keep shooting as much as you can," Wylder ordered, pitching his voice to carry through the chaos. "Keep protecting the wall!"

The air had gotten thick with the stink of hot metal and spilled blood. My gut churned. My ears must have been numbing with the constant barrage of noise, because it didn't sound so loud anymore. I shifted my weight to get a better angle to aim from and hissed as pain lanced through my wounded thigh.

These fuckers were responsible for that too. We'd come here to win, and that was what we'd do.

I managed to drop another man hauling explosives before he got close to the fence. Kaige was yelling something I couldn't even make out and shooting wildly. The Storm's people weren't pulling back any farther, but they hadn't made any progress pushing *us* back either. We were holding them off, by however small a margin.

All of a sudden, a strange movement caught my attention from the corner of my eye. My head jerked around in time to see a bunch of the Noble men who'd been fighting with us hurrying to the cars farthest from the fight.

"Where the fuck are you going?" Wylder yelled after them, his eyes furious. "You're needed here!"

Gideon jabbed at his tablet where he'd crouched next to the car, his gun beside him. "I can't see anything that could explain it."

The men didn't answer Wylder, didn't even look back. They dove into the cars, and five vehicles peeled away from the fray, leaving us that much more outnumbered. A chill washed through me. What the hell was going on? Why would they just *leave*?

I didn't have time to wonder for very long. Xavier let out a triumphant roar, and the Storm's men pressed in on us. I glanced at Wylder and saw the same flash of panic in his eyes that I was feeling.

We were absolutely fucked.

Mercy

Xavier watched the retreating cars and threw back his head with a raucous laugh that echoed through the streets. "Sniveling cowards," he roared, and swept his arm to urge his men onward in the battle. "Kill them all except the girl. She's mine."

"Not if I have anything to say about that," Kervos announced from behind the car next to ours. He raised his gun just as another wave of gunfire swept over us— and a bullet caught him between the eyes. He collapsed on the ground with a red blotch expanding over his forehead.

My mind froze, my thoughts seeming to stutter. Kervos's eyes stared at the sky, his body totally limp. Just like that, he was gone.

The first man who'd really supported my bid to lead the Claws was dead.

And not just him. Even as we fired back as well as

we could, Nobles and Claws were dropping all through the maze of cars. I saw Sam's friend who'd helped us move yesterday's cargo fall, and then one of the men who'd been laughing at Kaige's story in the dining room just an hour ago. My vision swam, my body wobbling with a momentary dizziness.

Wylder yanked me down below the level of the car just as a bullet whizzed by where the top of my head had been. "What the hell are you doing?" he said, but he sounded more panicked than angry. "You're going to get killed."

Like everyone else was. I shook myself, willing my mind to focus. Forcing my gaze away from Kervos's lifeless body.

Too many men were dead—good men. And I didn't even have time to mourn them.

I had to make sure the ones still living stayed that way. That was my job as their queen. I hadn't come here to embark on a suicide mission.

The words stuck in my throat before I could propel them out. This wasn't how I'd wanted the battle to end. "We'll be slaughtered if we keep fighting," I said. "We have to get out of here, regroup, or the war ends here. With the Storm winning."

Wylder's jaw tightened, but after a moment, he nodded. "Damn it," he spat out, and then waved to the nearest men. "Pass on the word. We're cutting our losses and moving out. Get to whatever cars aren't boxed in and head back to the mansion—or Claws to their own headquarters. Keep firing at the Storm's forces to cover each other, but getting out of here alive is all that matters now."

"Are you sure, Mercy?" Jenner called over from a few cars away, but I saw his gaze catch on Kervos's body. Horror flashed across his face.

"We have to live to fight again another day," I said.

We took off through the maze of cars, bobbing up just long enough to fire at the Storm's men as well as we could. They were pushing toward the wall now. I didn't realize they'd already gotten some of their explosives there until the first *boom* echoed through the air.

The impact of the explosion shook the ground beneath our feet and threw me forward. I tried to twist myself into a flip to land more steadily, but my wounded thigh gave out. Instead I crashed to the ground, scraping my chin on the rough concrete.

Kaige grabbed my shoulder, hefting me up. "I'm fine, I'm fine," I insisted, but he stayed right beside me as we took off running again, Wylder close at my other side, Gideon right behind us.

I didn't even bother trying to shoot anymore. All that mattered was getting to the cars at the edge of the mess. My legs pumped under me, my teeth gritting at the pain searing from my wound. That doctor would have been *really* pissed if he'd known he was releasing me to get into this kind of trouble right after.

The Claws and Nobles who'd already been near the fringes made it to the outer cars first. A few tore off down the street in the vehicles they managed to grab. Others fell under the next barrage of bullets. We paused, panting, just a few car lengths from a Ford we could grab—as long as the driver had left the keys in it.

Just as we braced to make a final run for it, a furious bellow split through the air from behind us. The gunfire went momentarily quiet. I craned my neck around to see Xavier still poised on the pickup truck, his face now ruddy with rage as if *he* had any reason to be upset with how the tide had turned.

"You fucking cowards," he bellowed after us, spit flying from his mouth so wildly I could see it even at a distance. "Playing stupid fucking tricks. You'll find out what thieves get. I'm going to make you pay even more than I was already planning. No one will even be able to recognize you when we're through."

"What is he talking about?" I whispered to Wylder, who shook his head, looking totally bewildered.

We couldn't exactly ask the lunatic. At his urging, the Storm men charged straight at the rest of us, firing off whatever shots they could take as they closed in on our remaining forces. A couple of them leapt onto the hood of a car and mowed down three Nobles who'd just reached an accessible car.

Wylder grimaced and shot both of the assholes down with a few squeezes of his trigger. More cars were peeling away from the mass. We sprinted toward the Ford, my breath rasping in my throat. Gideon was starting to wheeze.

Just as we came up on the car, Jenner leaned over the back of the one next to it and spewed bullets from a rifle at the advancing Storm men. He bought us just enough time to dive into the vehicle, Kaige taking the wheel. He twisted the key that'd been left there, its original driver probably having fallen nearby assuming he'd be coming right back to it, and rammed his foot down on the gas.

I stayed crouched in the back seat next to Gideon as the car swung around and raced away from the waterfront property. I squeezed his arm in a soothing rhythm, and his breaths started to even out. He raised his head, meeting my eyes with a haunted look in his. "We lost too many men out there."

I choked up abruptly. "I know." I couldn't even say yet how many we'd lost, how many the Storm's people had killed that I hadn't even seen.

I sat up slowly, brushing shards of glass and bits of gravel from my clothes. My heart was still thundering, but we'd left the horrific scene behind. The street we were racing down now looked almost peaceful in the mid-morning light. I sputtered out something halfway between a laugh and a sob.

Gideon eased upright too, his gaze dropping to my leg. He sucked in a breath. "Mercy, you're bleeding."

I glanced down. Blood was seeping through my jeans from where I must have reopened the wound on my thigh. That was no surprise, considering the hell I'd just put it through.

"We need to rebandage Mercy's leg," Gideon insisted.

"Let's get the fuck away from those maniacs first," Kaige retorted. "Or we're going to need a lot more bandages."

I grimaced. "I'll be all right. I've already survived this wound once. I just—I need to put pressure on it."

I fumbled for something to use to staunch the bleeding, and Gideon whipped his shirt off as quickly as if he gave it up for use as a bandage every day. I offered him a grateful smile and balled it in my hand before pressing it hard against the wound.

"I don't suppose any of you have a clue what Xavier was ranting about?" Wylder said. "What trick did he think we played? How were we being thieves?"

I bit my lip. "I mean, obviously we've stolen Glory and weapons from the Storm in the past. But he seemed to get upset all of a sudden, not like he was still fuming about stuff that'd happened before."

"Maybe he was pissed off that we were... stealing his opportunity to take the waterfront property without a big mess?" Kaige said doubtfully.

Gideon shot the big guy a baleful look. "Somehow I don't think it's that. He sounded *very* upset. I saw one of his men talking on a phone and then passing a message on to him right before he started ranting."

He squirmed around, and I realized he'd managed to drag his tablet all the way to the car with him. It figured. "Let me see if I can find out anything," he muttered, waking up the screen with a tap.

An uncomfortable sensation coiled around my gut. "You don't think his outburst has anything to do with the Nobles who up and left out of the blue, do you? We don't know what was going on with them either."

Wylder frowned. "They're definitely going to be

taken to task for fleeing their duty, you can count on that."

My voice hardened. "People *died* because of them." Images of the crumpled bodies rose up in my mind, Kervos at the forefront. I swallowed hard. I'd pulled him and the other Claws into this war, and I hadn't been able to get them through it. I hadn't even been able to salvage his body. Guilt snaked around my lungs, making it hard to breathe.

Wylder leaned past the passenger seat. "Mercy, you can't blame yourself. If anything, you should blame me. It was my men who screwed us over. And you've got to know that every man who was out there today was aware of the danger of the situation—of this whole life. They wouldn't have been in it if they hadn't come to terms with that."

"Still..."

Gideon cleared his throat, his hands tightening where he was gripping the tablet. He glanced at Wylder. "It isn't your fault either."

Wylder's eyebrows drew together. "What do you mean?"

"I think I know what happened. I'm seeing a new report from our typical communication channels that the Nobles captured a major storage facility in the Bend, one that belonged to the Storm—one of the places we were considering attacking earlier. It's where they've been keeping their supply of Glory once it's transported into the county."

Kaige's head jerked around, and he nearly drove us into a mailbox. "Say *what*?"

"I have to guess that's where the Nobles who took off on us went," Gideon said. "There wouldn't have been enough men available to take down the guards protecting it otherwise."

"Why would they up and do that of their own..." I trailed off before I finished the question, because I already knew the answer. The mission hadn't been of their own accord. My stomach twisted.

"My dad ordered them to," Wylder said before I had to, his gaze darkening even more than before. "That's got to be it. They wouldn't have listened to anyone but him after I'd already given *my* orders. *Fuck.*" He slammed his fist into the dashboard. "No wonder he sent all our troops to the Bend. He probably never intended to help us. He wanted us as bait against Xavier to distract him and most of the Storm's people while he took what he wanted."

"That's why he told me to make sure the cameras were set up. He wanted eyes on each one of us, Xavier included, so he knew just exactly when they would have to leave." Gideon worried at his lip ring. "Everything makes sense now."

"But why the hell would Ezra want to take the Glory?" Kaige demanded, his voice raw. "What the fuck was he thinking?"

"It could be just to stop the Storm from continuing to use it," I said tentatively.

Wylder met my gaze. "Do you really think he'd go to all that trouble and sacrifice the waterfront property if he didn't believe he was getting his hands on an even bigger prize? He's seen the power that drug has over people, how much they're willing to do for a hit of it."

A shiver ran through me. Yes, that did sound exactly like Ezra. For Wylder's sake, I had to say, "We won't know for sure until we talk to him."

Wylder sank back into his seat. His voice came out flat. "We do know one thing: He fucked us over by not informing us about his second, secret mission. He never intended to save the waterfront property. It—we—were only a decoy. He purposefully sabotaged us and left us for dead."

21

Wylder

I BURST THROUGH THE FRONT DOORS OF MY HOUSE. A couple of guards stared, uneasiness flickering across their faces, as I strode through the foyer with Mercy, Kaige, and Gideon at my heels.

I didn't say a word to the Noble underlings, just stalked up the stairs and onward into the hall that led to Dad's office. I hadn't paused for even a second since Kaige had parked outside the mansion. Fury burned in my chest and unfurled through my limbs, making my hands flex and clench with the urge to find something to punch.

The sight of the study door up ahead cooled my rage just a little. I had to get my temper under control to have this conversation, or Dad would just brush me off. I needed to be clear and incisive, not ranting and raving.

He wasn't getting away with his betrayal.

I stopped and dragged air into my lungs. Then I

glanced back at my woman and my friends. "I think I'd better talk to my father alone."

Mercy frowned. "Are you sure that's a good idea? We know what he's capable of."

Kaige nodded, cracking his knuckles. "We'll back you up every step of the way."

I shook my head. "I'll get the most honest answers out of him if it's just family. I don't want him focused on anything but what I'm saying to him. You don't need to worry—I can handle it."

"We'll be right outside," Gideon said, quiet but unshakeable. He wasn't going to question my competence by outright saying it, but the implication was clear: if I *did* happen to need them, all I'd have to do was shout.

If this situation came to that... I didn't even want to think about it. I wished I didn't have to wrap my head around the things my father had already done in the past few hours.

Keeping an iron grip on my temper, I walked the rest of the way to the study and grasped the doorknob. I half-expected it to be locked, but it twisted easily in my hand. I marched in without preamble and kicked it shut behind me.

Dad was sitting behind his desk, his expression its typical impenetrable mask. "I expect a knock rather than you barging right in," he said, as if this was the time to be chiding me like a toddler.

I bit back half a dozen snarky retorts that leapt to my tongue and strode up to the opposite side of his desk. I braced my hands against the top, leaning slightly forward, and met Dad's eyes with a gaze I kept as firm and steady as my voice.

"You undermined our operation at the waterfront property. You ordered a bunch of the men who were supposed to be supporting us in defending it to leave— so they could steal the Storm's supply of Glory while his men were distracted."

Dad gazed back at me, looking so unruffled—almost bored—that it took all my self-control not to lunge right across the desk and sock him in the nose. "I'm glad that you were able to put the pieces together so quickly," he said. "Maybe that mind of yours hasn't gotten so soft after all. It was a perfect plan, as evidenced by the fact that it went off without a hitch."

A perfect plan? I couldn't stop a little venom from creeping into my tone. "Do you have any idea how many of our men *died* because of that plan? We were holding the Storm's forces off until we lost so much support. We could *all* have been slaughtered."

Had Dad hoped that even more of us would die? The thought struck me with a chill that cut through my anger. Maybe he'd wanted Xavier to mow me down like so many of the Noble and Claws men who'd fallen today. One disobedient heir off his plate.

Dad simply shrugged. "Our men know the risks of our line of work. Sacrifices must be made for the greater good."

Funny how those sacrifices had all been by the men he hadn't trusted enough to call on for his secret operation—the ones he must have known would be more inclined to stick with me. He'd played a move that would secure his goals and also eliminate underlings he thought could become a future problem without getting his own hands the slightest bit dirty.

But I still didn't understand what those goals were. I gritted my teeth. "The greater good? What about the waterfront property you've invested so much money and time in? We had to pull back—we were going to lose it anyway. Lord only knows what Xavier and the others have done to the site now."

Dad chuckled, a low humorous sound. "Well, I, for one, hope they took as much aggression as they pleased out on it. It'll be easier to claim insurance if I can easily prove that the damage was maliciously caused by an outside source."

I still couldn't wrap my head around what he was saying. "You had all these plans for it—you put so much effort into getting the contract—"

Dad waved aside my protest. "Plans change. We have to think on our feet and adapt to changing circumstances. Ever since the drug distribution incident, that property has become too much of a hassle to deal with. It's much more to our benefit to cut our losses and focus on a new business venture."

I stared at the face of the man I had once thought held absolute power in Paradise Bend. I knew that wasn't the truth anymore. He knew it too, and maybe that was why he was going off the rails like this.

"A new business venture," I repeated slowly. Something that to him was worth even more than the waterfront property. All the unpleasant suspicions that'd entered my head when Gideon had announced what he'd discovered came rushing back to the front of my mind. "Tell me you're not going to start selling Glory."

Dad gave me a thin smile. "Why shouldn't I? You've seen how avidly the people of the county are responding to it. We certainly couldn't leave it in the Storm's hands with the power it was giving his people."

"One warehouse full isn't going to last all that long."

"Which is why it's a good thing my men were also able to find information about the Storm's suppliers in that warehouse. We can set up our own distribution channels and take over the entire market. Even expand it farther abroad."

My mouth tasted as if it was full of ash. Images flashed through my mind of the desperate junkies smashing storefronts along the edge of the city, of the addicts wandering in a daze around the waterfront property when the Storm's men had been handing out samples there.

Dad wanted to keep those people in that fucked-up state? To make a whole county full of druggies who'd do anything for their next hit?

Come to think of it, that outcome might suit his power fantasies just fine. Junkies were easy to control, which was exactly why Xavier must have taken that route. But my father used to care about more than just holding all the cards. Staring at him with a pit opening in the bottom of my stomach, I thought I might have an inkling how Beckett felt about *his* dad.

The kid believed it might not be too late to get the Storm back on the right track. I wasn't so sure with

Ezra Noble, considering how far gone he already appeared to be.

"This doesn't make any sense," I said. "Didn't you want to branch out into more legitimate business opportunities, not ones that are totally illegal? You've always said it's better not to get too involved in the drug trade specifically because of how messy it is. And yeah, I've seen the effect Glory has—it's fucking messy, all right."

An unsettling glint came into Dad's eyes. "I avoided this type of business because I hadn't found a drug that made it worthwhile. Amphetamines, meth, and the rest, they don't hold a candle to where Glory could take us."

He got up from behind his desk and walked over to the window, gazing out it over the lawn. "The world is a boundless well of possibilities, Wylder. I let my faith in that fact get shaken for a little while, but now I'm taking hold of the future of the Nobles with both hands. The Storm has barely gotten started with Glory, from what I understand. The distribution here was only a test run. I can take it to the heights it deserves and show *everyone* what the Nobles are capable of."

"This is crazy," I burst out, unable to hold in my frustration. "We've still got a war on our hands. We won't be around to sell even a gram of Glory to anyone if we don't focus on tackling the Storm. If you'd actually backed me up today, maybe we'd have turned the tables on them and ended this. Now we're down dozens of men and running out of time and options."

Dad swiveled on his heel, his tone going icy. "I think you're forgetting that I'm still in charge, *son*." He stressed the last word, but it sounded hollow to me. "You follow my orders, not the other way around. I'll handle my business as I see fit, and you can work on seeing through the agreement *you* made with this Long Night person. If you can't manage that—if you can't accept that I know what's best for our organization— then perhaps I'll have to do some clearing of the slate myself."

Those last words came out razor-sharp. The threat was so clear I had to restrain a wince.

This was what our simmering feud had come to. He was outright stating that he'd kill me if I kept disagreeing with him—definitely if I got in his way. While he got our men massacred and ignored the most pressing problem looming over us as if it'd go away if he pretended it out of existence hard enough with his dreams of future triumphs.

He was going to get all of us killed, even himself, and there was nothing I could say that would accomplish anything other than earning me a bullet in my heart. So I'd better get back to the real work rather than wasting my remaining hours here.

"Thank you for your time, Dad," I said. Without another word, I simply walked out of the office.

Mercy straightened up from where she'd been leaning against the wall. Gideon and Kaige raised their heads too, all waiting for me like they'd promised. Their gazes asked a question I didn't know how to answer.

If I was ever going to become the leader the Nobles needed, I was going to have to go through Dad. He couldn't have made it clearer that he was never going to step aside of his own accord.

I hadn't wanted to come to blows with him, but if that was the only way to set things right... I'd do what I had to do to maintain the Nobles' legacy and the security of Paradise Bend.

But for now, before I could even think about that problem any deeper, we had a deal to fulfill and a psychotic maniac to crush.

"Let's go to my office," I said. "We've got a war to win."

Mercy

WHEN WYLDER HAD FINISHED FILLING US IN ON HIS conversation with his father, we all sat for a moment in shocked silence. Beyond the window, evening was rapidly falling, turning the sky an ominous shade of red.

Anthea, who'd joined us on our way over to Gideon's office, shook her head, her mouth twisting. "I'm sorry. I wish I could have helped, but I had no idea what my brother was planning."

"It's not your fault," I said. "Ezra was obviously keeping the whole thing as quiet as possible."

Wylder grimaced. "The fact is that Dad screwed us over, and he feels zero guilt about it. In fact, he's practically gloating about his new plans."

Kaige was scowling. "His new plans are shit. I thought the Nobles had a policy to keep a ten feet pole between us and drug dealing."

"We did," Wylder said. "And I'd have kept to that

policy if it were up to me. But as long as he's still around, Dad's the one calling the shots."

"Fuck." Kaige slammed his fist into his other palm hard enough to leave a red mark on the skin. "This isn't what I signed up for. I don't want anything to do with spreading that crap around the city."

Wylder's voice turned deadly firm, his face hardening like I hadn't seen it since he first came out of his father's study. "You won't have to. I'm not going to let it come to that. But we've barely got a day left in our deal with the Long Night. We can't think about anything except tackling the Storm for the next twenty-four hours."

Anthea touched his shoulder lightly, regret still marked on her face. Her voice came out quiet but firm. "If I don't get another chance to say it before it matters —just know that I understand that you'll have to do whatever you have to do."

Wylder glanced at his aunt and nodded, a tiny bit of the tension seeping out of his stance. The coolness of her tone sent an uneasy quiver down the center of me. I didn't want to examine what she might mean too closely.

The Noble heir was right. We had to focus on the Storm for now.

"Could Ezra's takeover of the Glory distribution work in our favor there?" I asked. "That's how the Storm was funding a lot of his operations, wasn't it? Grabbing it out from under him has to be a major blow. Xavier was obviously furious about it." The thought of his raging face sent a shiver down my spine. I'd seen him purposefully menacing and hostile, but I wasn't sure I'd ever witnessed so much uncontrolled fury from the psycho.

"Not enough to get him to leave town," Anthea said. "We've been getting reports of the Storm's men still roaming all over. I'm not sure they're even finished demolishing the waterfront property yet." Her nose wrinkled as if she found all this overt aggression distasteful.

"We lost so many people out there," Kaige said. "He's got to know we're having problems too, right?"

Wylder sighed. "It doesn't really matter. Our time is up tomorrow night. We have to assume that the Long Night is prepared to rally his forces and set them on us as soon as the sun goes down. We need to move fast and figure out some final move that'll give us the best possible chance at driving the Storm's people out of Paradise Bend." He turned to Gideon. "I don't suppose there's anything in your surveillance of the city that's given you any brilliant brainstorms?"

Gideon rubbed his mouth, but his hand didn't hide his frown. "I think Xavier is the key. He's the Storm's figurehead here, and if we took him down, then the Storm would have to step up himself—which it sounds like he doesn't want to do—or admit defeat. The trouble is making that happen."

Kaige smacked his hands together. "Let me at him, and I'll take care of it."

Gideon shot his friend a bemused look. "It'd be hard to do that when we can't even be sure of where he is. He left the waterfront development not long after we did.

The Storm's men who didn't stay there to work on demolishing it have scattered throughout the city and the Bend, and I'm seeing them constantly on the move. If we can't corner him anywhere, we wouldn't have a hope in hell."

I worried at my lower lip. "He *was* really pissed off about losing the drug stash, so maybe we could use that as bait somehow? Lure him over there thinking he'll have a chance to take it back?"

Wylder shook his head. "I wouldn't be surprised if Dad's given the men he's stationed out there orders to shoot anyone who tries to interfere, even if it's me. He thinks the Glory is his key to taking back the power he thought he already had in the world."

Gideon leaned back in his chair, his forehead furrowing. "It'd be a long-shot, but it's possible we could—"

A knock on the door interrupted him. Wylder sprang up as if he expected it to be his dad, arriving to announce more horrible plans, but he opened it to find one of the Noble underlings who'd stuck with us in the fray earlier today standing outside.

"Mr. Noble," he said with a dip of his head. "That kid who came around the other day is here again—he says he needs to talk to you right away..."

I leapt to my feet too. "Beckett? Of course."

I paused, because technically I wasn't in any position to give orders here in the Noble mansion, but Wylder glanced at me with a small smile and nodded to the guy. "Bring him up. And... don't let word get to my dad about this, if that's possible."

A shadow crossed the guy's expression, and I wondered if he was thinking of how we'd been betrayed by the Nobles loyal to Ezra just hours ago. He inclined his head and hurried off.

Less than a minute later, he returned, ushering Beckett to the doorway. At the sight of the teenager, my heart lurched.

"Are you okay?" I asked automatically.

Beckett stepped into the room with his shoulders slightly slouched. His face had turned paler since we'd last seen him, other than the dark circles under his eyes that suggested he hadn't slept well in days. He was wearing posh clothes like last time, but he hadn't seemed to notice that the collar of his shirt had gone askew. His gaze darted around the room as if he thought we might lunge at him rather than welcome him.

"I—not exactly," he said in a raw voice.

Gideon looked him over and reached for one of his spare mugs. "Coffee?"

The kid couldn't have known how rare it was for the tech genius to offer up his precious brew, but he managed a hesitant smile. "Yeah, that might be good."

Wylder motioned him to the chair the Noble heir had gotten out of and stood over him while Gideon poured the coffee. Kaige studied the Storm's son too. "You look terrible."

"Kaige," I chided.

"It's okay," Beckett muttered, a little of his usual spirit coming back. "Tell it like it is." He accepted the mug from Gideon and chugged about half the liquid in one go, not even wincing at the bitter flavor I could smell from a few feet away.

"Has something else happened at home?" I asked carefully. "It was a big risk coming all the way out here to see us in person, wasn't it?"

"I didn't know—it's hard to tell what's a risk and what's not even in the house these days." He took another gulp and stared morosely into the mug. "Things have gotten worse in all kinds of ways. Dad's on edge— he's freaking out over the trouble he's facing here and looking for people to blame. I don't really feel safe there anymore."

My heart squeezed. He *was* still a kid, really. It wasn't fair that he'd had to grow up so quickly.

Then Beckett raised his head, and I saw the man being forged beneath all the fear and uncertainty he was facing. He wasn't beaten yet.

"I think I know how you can force him to back down. For good. That's why I came here. I want this to finally be over."

Wylder perked up. "You have a plan?"

Beckett nodded, but I could see the hesitation on his face. "You have to really trust me on this one."

Gideon gave him a penetrating look. "More than we did before? What's so special about this time?"

The kid dragged in a breath. "You'd have to confront my dad face to face."

Wylder laughed for a second before it became clear to all of us that Beckett was serious. Wylder's eyes narrowed. "How do you expect that to work? We know how powerful your dad is. We've been having a hard enough time dealing with his underlings here on our home turf. It's not as if he's going to sit down for a negotiation with us."

The corner of Beckett's mouth twitched with a hint of a wry smile. "That isn't exactly how I'm picturing it. I can make it work—I'm your inside edge. I can get you to him in a way that'll put you at an advantage. You just have to promise you won't kill *him*. If you do things my way, he'll listen. It'll work; I'm sure of it."

Hope rang through his voice, but my stomach had clenched. The same resistance showed on the expressions all around me. We'd already come face to face with one member of the Devil's Dozen, and it hadn't been a reassuring encounter. If we followed Beckett's advice, we'd be putting our lives very literally in his hands.

"We need to talk about it," Wylder said. "Just us. This is too big for us to jump right in without a full discussion."

"I understand," Beckett said. "You don't trust me."

"It isn't just about trust. We're the only line between our men and their total destruction. We have to think this through." Wylder turned to his aunt. "Anthea, will you escort him outside? There were leftovers from dinner—Beckett looks like he might be hungry."

Beckett's mouth opened but closed again without a sound. His head drooping, he followed Anthea out into the hall.

As soon as the door shut behind them, Kaige whirled on us. "What the hell is he on? Going right up against the Storm head to head?"

"I don't think he's lying about believing this is our best chance at ending the conflict quickly," Gideon said. "I *hope* he isn't lying, because we need that."

Wylder nodded. "His heart seems to be in the right place, but I don't know how well he's thought through the possible fallout. And what if he's misjudged the situation? If we go into this confrontation, there might be no way to pull out before it's way too late to save ourselves."

"And we're going to be relying on his inside intel to guide us." Gideon made a face at his computer array. "I won't be able to confirm everything he says to be sure the details add up."

"We should at least hear the whole plan, shouldn't we?" I put in. "We can't make any definite decisions until we know exactly what he has in mind. We do need to do *something*, and fast."

Kaige let out a huff. "But what if he's setting us up to get assassinated? That'd be a quick way to end the fighting too."

Wylder raised an eyebrow at him. "Not really, considering it'd only take out us and not my dad, who's proven he's got a stake in this war now too. All the information Beckett has given us so far seems to have been legit. I can't imagine he'd have let us blow up his dad's secret base and undermine his real estate business just to set us up for this. The only person who's actually screwed us so far is Ezra Noble." A hint of bitterness crept into his tone.

"That just proves my point," Kaige said. "You can't

trust anybody. How do we know the kid didn't set up the attack on Rowan and Mercy?"

Every part of me balked at that suggestion. I didn't know if Beckett's plan was solid, but I couldn't believe he was trying to get us killed.

"That doesn't make any sense," I said. "We weren't attacked until we got back to the Bend—which is where Xavier's been watching for us and attacking us all along, since before Beckett was ever in the picture. If going to that gala was a setup, then Beckett would have arranged for the ambush to happen before we got a chance to talk to Anderson and mess up the Storm's business arrangements."

Gideon gestured to me. "I agree with Mercy on that point. And from what I've seen in the street cam footage, the ambush appears to have been a spur-of-the-moment attack that was launched because several Storm men happened to be nearby when you were coming into the city. My best guess is that a sentry spotted your car and called them in just a few minutes ahead of time. That doesn't fit with a larger conspiracy."

"Fine," Kaige grumbled. "That still doesn't mean we should go along with some kid's plan."

"Do you have a better one?" Wylder asked dryly. When Kaige just glowered at him, the Noble heir exhaled roughly and looked at me. "I think that unless we hear something in his plan that sounds off, we should give it a shot. It's better for us to go down fighting until the end than to wait around to get slaughtered by the Long Night's people. The question is, are you and the Claws going to join us?"

I hesitated. Was I going to stake both my life and those of my men on this kid? Maybe I was being swayed by my instinctive sympathy because of his age, and he really did have malicious intentions.

I closed my eyes, and the flames in the old warehouse flickered up in my mind. I could still feel how helpless Rowan's body had felt in my arms as I'd dragged him to safety. See how broken he'd looked lying on that hospital bed. He hadn't come out of his coma yet. We didn't know if he ever would.

But he'd trusted Beckett. He'd been the first of us to speak up for the kid, recognizing something in him that he related to himself.

And I wanted to trust the kid too. I could see some of *myself* in Beckett: the rebellious teenager who'd spied on the Claws' moves and stored up my resentment of my father's treatment while wishing I could have earned his respect. Back then, before Dad and Colt had totally beaten any idealistic sense of hope out of me, I'd been able to imagine a future where conflicts could be solved by making deals and negotiating rather than through bloodshed.

What if I hadn't been wrong? What if we could make that teenage idealism real after all? Wasn't it worth trying?

"I'm in," I said. "I meant to set a different course for the Claws than the men who came before me did, and I'm going to start on that right now. I'm choosing trust over paranoia. The kid's been here for us the whole time, he's risked his life more than once to help us, and now we're going to be there for him."

Wylder smiled, and even Kaige's stern expression relaxed a little. Gideon stood up, brandishing his tablet. "Let's go hear this plan, then."

We found Beckett in the kitchen, scarfing down teriyaki chicken from the plate in front of him while he chatted with Anthea. She caught my eye with a sly glint in hers as we came in, and I had no doubt that she'd managed to find out a few more things about him without Beckett even realizing. Nothing that bothered her, though, because she simply tipped her head in acknowledgement.

"All right, Beckett," I said, tugging back a stool to sit next to him. "Tell us about your plan."

Beckett's face brightened. He set down his fork and looked around the island at all of us. "I know you're putting a lot of faith in me, and I'm not going to let you down. We're going to set up a meeting early tomorrow morning."

"First things first," Wylder cut in. "Everything else apart, what guarantee do we have that the Storm will leave Paradise Bend alone after this, even if the meeting goes in our favor? What's to stop him from changing his mind after a few days of peace and attacking us again once our guard is down?"

Beckett gave him a pained smile. "You don't have to worry. I know exactly how to take care of that."

Mercy

Walking into the lion's den felt exactly as it should. My heart thundered in my ears, and my mouth had turned to sandpaper. We'd driven two hours to reach a city I'd never visited before, and I felt totally out of my element.

As soon as we stepped into the small boutique mall, the air conditioning hit me at full force. The space was dark and empty, only our wavering reflections showing on the polished marble tiles. The mall didn't normally open for another hour anyway, but we'd ensured we'd have it to ourselves. Beckett had managed to send around a strategic message to all the businesses inside using his father's contact info, telling them that emergency work was being done today.

In a way, it was even true.

Our footsteps clacked against the floor as we walked down the cavernous main hall past the shuttered storefronts. At the far end, the ceiling lifted even higher into a huge dome with a honeycomb of skylights that loomed over the upscale food court. Gleaming tables with attached seating stood at wide intervals in the glow of the early morning sunlight. A broad terrace with more shops ran around the second floor overhead, their shuttered entrances visible through the gaps in the railing.

Kaige looked around and shuddered like he'd seen a ghost. "Seems like a weird place to have a business meeting."

"My dad and Anderson worked on this place together," Beckett said. "From what I've been able to gather, they often met in the buildings they invested in, so he won't think it's too strange." He motioned to a set of stairs that led to the second-floor terrace. "You'll want to have your men waiting up there. I picked this spot specifically so you'll have as much high ground as possible."

"We appreciate that," Wylder said in a dry tone, and motioned to the Noble men he'd trusted enough to bring along. I nodded to Jenner, Sam, and the handful of Claws who were with us too. Altogether, a dozen men tramped up the stairs to position themselves just out of sight around the terrace, their guns at the ready.

"What about us?" Gideon asked. "You suggested it was best for us to face him on equal ground."

Beckett pointed to a couple of thick, regal columns that stood at the far end of the food court. "We can wait behind those until your men have... subdued any opposition." He paused and looked at me and then

Wylder sharply. "You did make it clear that they're not to hurt my dad?"

In that moment, hearing the fierceness of the question and knowing that he'd set this whole operation up to ultimately protect his father and their empire, I wouldn't have gone up against Beckett for any money in the world. If we made an enemy out of him, we might be screwed in the long run regardless. He obviously wasn't the type to forgive and forget.

"They have their orders," I said.

Wylder nodded. "The only way anyone's shooting at him is if he makes a move to shoot us. I assume you'll accept that as a reasonable exception?"

Beckett grimaced, but he tipped his head. "I don't think it'll come to that. He isn't stupid—and he'll want to get out of here alive if he can. But I won't blame you if you need to defend yourselves."

The five of us gathered behind the columns, Beckett with me and Wylder, Kaige and Gideon behind the other. Gideon was monitoring street cams on his tablet. "He's on his way. I'd estimate his time of arrival to be five minutes from now."

"Very punctual," Wylder muttered.

That was the whole reason we'd used a supposed meeting with Evan Anderson as bait. We were counting on the Storm being particularly eager to re-establish ties with his real estate associate after their recent dispute. Little did he know that Anderson had just reached out to us last night wanting to talk more about the proposal we'd sent.

It'd been hard to get excited about his interest when

the man most instrumental in earning it was still unconscious in a hospital room. At least we had some hope of letting Rowan wake up to a world where death wasn't lurking right at our doorstep.

Wylder adjusted his earpiece. We'd agreed that he'd give the signal to all of the men above, both Nobles and Claws, to ensure they were fully coordinated. "Just a few more minutes," he said into the mic. "Stay alert."

I couldn't make out any of the figures through the railing. They were keeping well out of view like we'd discussed. My heart thumped even harder as the seconds slipped past us.

There was a distant squeak of hinges and then a soft rasp of several sets of footsteps heading our way. My back stiffened. I held myself rigidly still as the Storm and his usual contingent of bodyguards marched toward the food court. I had no idea what the man who'd rained so much terror down on the Bend even looked like, and in my mind's eye, I saw a shadowy figure like the dark god tattooed on Gideon's chest slinking through the grand hall.

"Planning on being fashionably late as usual, I suppose," a low, gravelly voice said at the far end of the atrium. I dared to peek from our shadowed position beneath the terrace.

The man who was just walking into the food court was nowhere near as intimidating as the supernatural figure I'd imagined, but the solid frame encased in his expensive gray suit had an imposing air all the same. He looked to be in his late forties, with thinning hair that was flecked with gray. I could have mistaken him for a regular, if powerful, businessman if I hadn't known better.

That was how the Devil's Dozen blended into society, I guessed.

He was flanked by eight bodyguards in darker suits. As they strode deeper into the food court, they fanned out a little amid the tables. Wylder was watching their progress now too. As the last of them came into the open area beneath the skylights, my fingers curled into my palms.

"Now!" Wylder whispered into his mic.

On cue, the men on the terrace leapt forward and opened fire. They took down most of the bodyguards in the space of a second, the men crumpling to the floor before they even had a chance to reach for their guns. The sound of the shots blared through the atrium and rang in my ears.

When the Storm and his two remaining protectors moved to make a run for the hall they'd come out of, our men fired several warning shots into the floor around them, as they'd been instructed.

"We don't want to hurt the rest of you," Wylder said, stepping out into view. "Stay where you are, and we can talk like civilized people." I followed him at a slower pace so that the limp from my leg injury wouldn't show. Gideon and Kaige joined us, leaving Beckett still hidden behind the column.

The Storm stared at us and then at the corpses around him, his face taut with horror. One of the remaining bodyguards made a grab for his weapon, and

Wylder raised his own pistol to shoot him in the shoulder. "Next time it'll be your head," he warned.

In that moment, standing in front of the man who'd caused so much pain and bloodshed in my home, I wanted to put a bullet of my own between his eyes. My hand itched to leap to the gun tucked into the waist of my jeans. The only thing that held me back was the thought of Beckett and his pleas that we let his father leave here alive.

We'd trusted Beckett, and he'd delivered on his promise. Now we had to show we'd been worthy of *his* trust. We'd never have gotten this opportunity without his help.

"W-what is this?" the Storm demanded, his voice getting firmer with each syllable. He drew his substantial frame taller. "Who the hell are you, and what do you think you're doing here?"

I exchanged a glance with Wylder. The man didn't recognize us at all. He knew so little about the county he'd invested so much in taking over that he wasn't familiar with his main opponents. Somehow that both pissed me off and took the wind out of the sails of my earlier desire for revenge.

We were just pieces on a gameboard to the Storm, not actual people he'd been fighting like we were to Xavier. That must make it awfully easy not to think about the blood being shed—until it was trickling across the pretty marble floor all around him.

"We're the people whose territory you're trying to steal," I said, coming to a stop right beside Wylder. "Mercy Katz, leader of the Claws of Paradise Bend."

"Wylder Noble, heir to the Nobles of Paradise Bend," Wylder said, with a motion to his friends. "And my close associates. We're here to see if we can't come to some arrangement that involves *you* getting your men the hell out of our home."

A starker fear flickered in the man's eyes. He knew what was at stake for us now—and he'd already seen how far we'd gone to secure what was ours. "You won't get away with this," he snarled, but his bravado was obviously only for show.

"We already have," I said. "We got you here, didn't we? Ironically enough, you're now at our mercy."

Kaige snickered at my remark.

Wylder stepped a little closer to the Storm, leaving plenty of room in case one of our men overhead needed to take a shot. "Exactly. We've just proven that we have the means to overpower you. You could make a run for it and let the rest of your guards take the bullets, and *maybe* you'd make it out alive—though I doubt it—but then you'll be on your own again. And we're only getting stronger."

"We've damaged your operations in multiple ways," I said, picking up the thread, and folded my arms over my chest. "Ways you never expected we'd be able to, I'll bet. You thought your men could roll into Paradise Bend and crush us with a snap of their fingers, but it hasn't been anywhere near that easy, has it?"

The Storm's lips pulled back from his teeth. "Perhaps you've given me a little more trouble than I counted on, but you have no idea what you're up against, how much force I can bring down on you if I choose to."

"But should you choose to?" Wylder said with a quizzical air. "Do you even really want to? Is that tiny place that you'd never even heard of until, what, a few months ago worth so much to you that you'd refuse to cut your losses and move on?"

"Just how much do you want to lose while you keep fighting us?" I added.

"I couldn't possibly lose as much as you will," he snapped.

"We'll see about that." I motioned to the fallen bodyguards. "Looks like today the sacrifice was all on your side. *You* have no idea what else we might be capable of." Never mind that if we didn't succeed today, both sides would be wiped out. I wasn't going to tip him off to the Long Night's involvement. If he knew how closely his competitor was watching his movements here, his ego might balk even more at giving up.

Wylder shrugged. "Maybe it's not even your decision anymore, and you just don't want to admit it."

The Storm's eyes narrowed. "What are you talking about?"

"Xavier," Wylder said. "It seems to me that he's the one who's been in charge for a while now. He pushed for you to move on Paradise Bend in the first place, didn't he? And he's been badgering you into letting him take more and more control over operations there. I'd say at this point he's gone right off the leash."

"Bullshit. Xavier acts on my behalf—what he captures will be mine."

"Really? Or is that just what you want to believe?" I said. "Maybe your pride won't let you face the truth that you're no longer in charge. He's made himself the boss, and you know it, but you're too *scared* to stand up to him, no matter how much this war of his is costing you."

My taunt made the Storm bristle, but I caught a hint of doubt in his expression. His anger was starting to fade. At the end of the day, maybe he was simply a businessman at heart—finally realizing just how much of a liability one of his supposed assets had become.

"Nonsense," he said. "I can call him off anytime I want. I simply don't want to."

Wylder hummed. "It's hard to believe that when we've all seen him out there carrying out his own personal vendettas. What's in it for you anymore? I'm sure you've already made a fortune selling Glory. If you don't get out now, the losses are going to keep piling up. I can't see a man as smart as you risking so much unless he was frightened of the consequences of taking charge."

The Storm sneered at him, but he'd deflated a little more. "Of course I'm in charge. Maybe your little territory simply wasn't at the top of my list of concerns."

"Well, it should be right at the top now," I said brightly.

His gaze snapped to me. "You people have festered like an infected wound, refusing to leave."

"The feeling's mutual," Wylder said. He spun his

pistol in his hand. "And we can finish this here, but only if you have the guts to do it."

The Storm stayed silent for a long moment. "And I'm supposed to believe that if we put an end to this war now, you'll let me leave here alive?"

I motioned toward the entrance to the food court. "Make the call to bring your men out of Paradise Bend, and you can waltz right out of here. We just want our home back. We can live and let live as long as you're doing the same."

The wheels appeared to be turning behind the Storm's dark eyes. I couldn't tell how much he was coming to terms with the situation and how much coming up with some new scheme. Whatever the case was, he raised his chin as if he still held the authority here.

"Now that I've given the matter more thought, I believe your pathetic county is far more trouble than it's worth. I have bigger prizes to pursue anyway."

He pulled his phone out of his pocket and dialed a number. As he held the phone to his ear, his stance tensed.

I didn't think our jabs about his fear of Xavier had been so far off the mark.

My breath caught in my throat as he started to speak. "Xavier. Yes. No, I don't want to hear about that. You listen to me." He swiveled, turning his back to us. "I want the entire operation in Paradise Bend scrapped. We're done there. Pull all the men out, and we'll discuss the next job I'll have for you tomorrow."

Whatever Xavier said in response, the Storm didn't

quite contain a flinch. "I don't want any argument about it," he retorted. "Get your asses out of there *now* or I'll be having them served to me on a platter. Do you understand?"

His tone was cold enough to chill me to the bone. Just like that, I could imagine him sitting at the same table as the Long Night and their other menacing colleagues in the Devil's Dozen.

The two men talked back and forth a little longer, and then the Storm asked to speak to a couple more of his people who must have been high up in the operation. Finally, he hung up and turned to face us again.

"It's done," he said. "They're already packing up. Are we finished here?"

I might have trusted Beckett, but I sure as hell didn't trust this prick to keep his word. "And they won't be back? We expect to be left alone from here forward."

"Of course," the Storm said, way too easily.

Wylder cleared his throat. "Naturally, to ensure your cooperation, we're going to be holding onto a little something as collateral." He motioned toward the back of the room.

As Beckett stepped out from behind the column and walked over to join us, the Storm's expression shifted from haughty confusion to tight bewilderment. It took him a moment to speak. "Beckett?" His gaze shot to me and then Wylder. "What the fuck is my son doing here? Why did you drag him into this?"

"They didn't drag me into it, Dad," Beckett said with impressive calm. "You did."

The Storm sputtered. "What?"

"Beckett will be our collateral," I said, setting my hand briefly on the kid's shoulder. "As long as your son and only heir stays with us, that should be enough incentive for you to stay away."

"Fuck you," the Storm said.

"You have no choice," Wylder said. "Beckett walks out with us."

"Beckett," the Storm said, directly addressing his son. "I'll get you out of this. I'll—"

"I'm sorry, Dad." Despite his best efforts, Beckett's voice cracked. "But this is the only way. I *want* to go with them so I know you'll keep the peace and get back to focusing on what's really important. Just think of it as me doing my bit for the business."

Right then, I saw the father behind the hardened criminal—a look of the kind of anguish my father had never felt over my fate. "Please," the Storm said.

"If you want us to trust you to keep your word, then you should trust us to take good care of your son," Wylder said. "It's his decision anyway."

"Goodbye, Dad," Beckett said. "I'll still call. And maybe when things are back on track, I'll be ready to come home."

The Storm shifted on his feet. Wylder waved him off. "You wanted to leave here safely. Now go, before we change our mind about that part."

The Storm gave his son one last wretched look. Then he dragged himself away, trudging with his two bodyguards toward the hall. We waited until we'd heard the far doors bang shut behind them before we called our men down and headed out the back entrance.

Beside me, Beckett's posture was totally rigid. "Are you okay?" I asked him.

He nodded. "I didn't think it'd be easy, but... I didn't think it'd be quite that hard, either."

"He loves you," I said quietly. "I could see it. He'll keep the peace for you."

The kid gave me a tight but genuine smile. "I hope you're right."

So did I. I should have felt triumphant as we made our way out onto the sun-lit street, but tension stayed coiled tight inside me.

Gideon was checking his tablet. As we reached the cars and got in, he smiled. "I'm already seeing the Storm men driving off. They're not wasting any time now that the big boss has laid down the law."

Somehow that didn't relieve me as much as I would have expected it to either. "All of them?" I asked.

"I mean, some of them must have things to sort out first, but it's a good sign that any of them are already getting out of town."

Beckett stared out the window. After several minutes of silence, he let out a rough chuckle. "I'm starving."

Wylder laughed and relaxed into the driver's seat. "Let's put a little distance between us and your dad and then see if we can't—"

Gideon's curse cut him off. Wylder's head jerked around, and my pulse lurched. "What?" I asked.

Gideon looked up at us, his mouth tightening. "The

Storm's men are continuing to head out of the county... but not Xavier. I've just caught him on a street cam. He's going totally crazy—rampaging through Paradise City, taking shots all along Main Street. The rest of the Storm's people might be willing to listen to orders, but it looks like he's a different story."

My heart sank. The war wasn't over yet.

Mercy

Gideon turned his tablet toward me with some of the footage playing. It was even worse than I'd expected after what he'd said. Xavier was walking down the normally busy city street with a large semi-automatic rifle in his hands. Most of the pedestrians must have already scattered, but he took random shots at people who were still dashing for shelter, at the windows of the stores on either side of the road, and at the cars parked along the street.

My stomach churned. I found myself grateful that the street cam feed didn't come with sound so I didn't need to hear the booming of the gun and the panicked shrieks that must have been splitting the air. Hearing them in my imagination was bad enough.

Sitting between me and Kaige in the back, Beckett sucked a breath through his teeth. I felt a quiver go through his body where his arm brushed mine. "Fuck. I knew he was a loose cannon but—*fuck.*"

"The Storm screwed us over," Kaige said, his voice harsh with anger. "He pretended he'd gone along with our deal—"

Gideon was already shaking his head. "I don't think the Storm ordered this. Most of his men are on their way out of the city as he promised. The kid told us that Xavier's been chafing against his leash. Seems like he's snapped it and gone totally rogue."

And yet the psychopath was walking almost casually down the street, as if he had all the time in the world to wait for what he really wanted. A chill ran over my skin. I knew exactly what that was—or rather, *who.*

"How is this going to affect our—" I cut myself off before I mentioned the deal with the Long Night, remembering that we hadn't told Beckett about that part. Maybe we should fill him in now that he'd proven his commitment to us, but I wasn't going to make that decision on my own. "We needed the war to be over," I said instead. "Everyone out."

"I don't know how this will factor in," Wylder said darkly, hitting the gas hard as the highway came into sight up ahead. "One thing is for sure—we've got to get back to the county quickly. It's time to put this rabid dog down."

He must have broken a dozen traffic laws zooming along the highway toward Paradise Bend, but thankfully there weren't many other cars taking this route at this time of day to get in our way. Gideon monitored the situation via the street cams the whole time, his frown pulling deeper and deeper.

"Almost all of the Storm men and vehicles I was aware of have left the county," he reported as Paradise City's skyscrapers came into view. "A few stragglers seem to have joined up with Xavier for whatever insane reason. Maybe just enjoying the rush of power. They've cleared the street completely, everyone keeping out of their way. They even took down a couple of cops who tried to intervene. It looks like the police are hanging back while they try to figure out a workable strategy... or maybe just hoping they can wait until he tires out."

"Useless as usual," I muttered. "That means it's up to us."

Wylder drummed his hands on the steering wheel and veered to pass another, slower car. "We'll head straight there and take the lay of the land. There's got to be something we can do. We haven't got any legal restrictions holding us back from taking him down, whatever it takes."

I glanced at Beckett, who'd shrunk in on himself with each glimpse of the street cam footage. "We shouldn't let him see you with us. He's already pissed off enough—I don't want to put you in danger like that. I'll get one of my men to take you back to..." I paused, not sure where the safest place was. But as long as Xavier was rampaging through Paradise City and I was there trying to deal with him, I didn't think he'd suddenly head to my house. "You can stay in the Claws headquarters in the Bend until we sort things out."

Beckett nodded with obvious relief. "Thanks. I—I wish I had some idea how you could stop him, but even my dad didn't seem to know how to keep him in line."

"Obviously," Kaige muttered, and let out a growl of frustration. "We can't let him ruin everything."

"We won't," Wylder said firmly. "This is our city, and we're taking it back whether he fucking likes it or not."

I texted the Claws who'd come with us for the ambush to confirm that they were sticking close by and then called some of the men at the house for additional backup and someone to pick up Beckett. Gideon had been coordinating with our Noble allies too. By the time we parked a few blocks from where Xavier was currently wreaking havoc, an occasional gunshot reaching our ears, we had five other cars joining us.

One of the Claws guys motioned Beckett over to him. I gave the kid a wave before they drove off. Then Wylder and I looked around at the assembled men.

"We need to try to kill Xavier before he can do any more damage," I said. "If you get a shot, take it. Same with any of the other Storm people still attacking the city. They've made their choice, and now we have to show them the consequences before they tear our home completely apart."

Wylder's mouth curved into a crooked grin. "You heard her, boys. Let's go prove to them what the true rulers of Paradise Bend are made of."

We hustled through the streets until Xavier's voice reached my ears. He was alternately mumbling and yelling. I could only make out the yelling parts, which were things like, "You're all going to pay!" and "Fucking coward!" I wondered if even he knew who he was talking to.

We got into position along some parked cars that could act as shields. A couple of the vehicles had already had their windows shattered by bullets.

Xavier was strolling down the middle of the road, almost carelessly. The other Storm men were sticking closer to the storefronts, smashing windows and shooting out door handles. As I watched, they burst into one building and ended up on the second floor, where they tossed furniture out onto the street just because they could.

My blood ran cold. What if they broke into a place that still had people inside? I hoped anyone who was still in the stores or apartments overhead had a back door they could escape through.

Xavier was too far off and weaving back and forth too randomly for anyone to get a good shot. A few of the guys darted closer along the line of cars, but even with his back turned, the monstrous man heard them. He spun around and shot at them before they could even start firing. As they ducked low, he sprang behind a van with the swiftness that'd startled me before.

Our men took a few shots at the Storm guys emerging from the building they'd broken into and had better luck there. One crumpled, clutching his wounded knee, and the next bullet caught him in the skull. His companion dashed farther down the street, aiming a couple of shots over his shoulder at us.

I pulled out my gun and flicked off the safety. My gaze traveled from the van where Xavier had disappeared to the other figures roaming the street. It caught on the sprawled bodies of pedestrians who hadn't gotten out of the way in time. Blood stained the asphalt beneath them.

A weight sank into my stomach. I was responsible for this carnage; I was the reason the city bled now. Xavier was never going to stop until he had me. He was always going to be one step ahead of us, destroying and killing everything and everyone in his path.

My legs wobbled abruptly, and not because of the healing wound. I sank down behind the car, willing my breaths to even out.

Kaige dropped down next to me, his gaze concerned. He grasped my shoulder. "Are you okay?"

"He's here because of me," I said. Another wave of gunfire nearly drowned out my voice. I couldn't tell how much was ours and how much from the Storm's men.

Kaige's brow furrowed. "What are you talking about?"

"Xavier. He came here because he wanted revenge on me and my dad. He won't leave because he hasn't gotten it, and that's all he cares about. I'm responsible for this mess."

"That's not true."

"He loved my mother, and my dad killed her." I shook my head. "That was the beginning of the end, even if I had no idea at the time."

Kaige's grip on me tightened. "Do you see what Xavier's doing now? This isn't about you—it's about him being fucking insane. Besides, you're not responsible for what your father did. You can't blame yourself."

"Maybe I should have figured things out sooner. Maybe I could have made a difference then."

"You still can." He gave me a little shake. When I looked up at him, his brown eyes were unusually serious. "Your dad is the only one to blame for his own actions, and the same with Xavier. Any way they try to pin this shit on you is just them looking for an excuse for what they want to do anyway. If what Xavier is doing was about love, it wouldn't end with all this violence. I know *that* much about love. I would move worlds to be with you, but if you asked me, I would let you go."

Something about Kaige's words sank into the place where my chest had started to constrict. My lungs loosened, letting in more air again.

I wasn't trapped by Xavier or anyone else, not if I didn't let myself be. I could still stop this horror—without losing my life in the process.

"We always have your back. *Always*," Kaige added.

"I know," I murmured, squeezing his hand. Then I pushed myself up, filled with a renewed sense of determination. I wasn't the one to start the war, but I would end it.

Our men had been spreading out along the street, trying to get closer to Xavier while he continued to take shots at them. The other Storm men were still firing away too. I added my own bullets to the fray—and then I saw one of the Storm's men take off down the street with a bundle of what looked like dynamite in his arms.

Shit. Did they have more explosives? How much else would they destroy if they got their way?

I didn't think any more than that—my legs were already in motion. Ignoring the throbbing of my wound, I threw myself after the man.

I shot at him as well as I could, but it was even harder with both of us in motion. One bullet dinged off a lamppost, and another embedded itself in a wall.

The man scrambled down an alley on the other side of the street, and I ran after him, gritting my teeth. The pain in my leg was slowing me down. As I hustled after him, a limp came into my gait. But I had to get to him before he blew up somebody's house and livelihood— and maybe a whole lot of people too.

The alley connected to a lane that ran down the length of the block between the streets. I veered around the corner and spotted the Storm lackey several buildings ahead of me. I took another shot and raced after him as fast as I could push my legs to go.

I was just passing one of the side alleys when an immense figure charged out of it, straight at me.

I was flinging myself backward out of the way before I even registered Xavier's face. My body instinctively hurled me toward the nearest passage—but when I spun around to make a real dash for safety, my heart plummeted.

The alley I'd stumbled into was a dead end, boxed in by buildings on either side that met several feet beyond where I stood, leaving no gap between them. And Xavier's hulking form filled the only exit.

I raised my pistol and pulled the trigger, but all I got

was a hollow clicking sound. I'd used up all my bullets. My mind leapt to the tiny gun Anthea had gifted me, but that was in the purse I'd yet again left in the car. That little handbag wasn't the kind of thing it was easy to carry with you on tense missions.

Xavier gave me a sharp-edged smile. "Here we are again, little kitty. I think you've finally used up the last of your nine lives." He took a menacing step toward me.

I tossed the useless pistol aside—Wylder could get me another when I needed it, and right now I wanted both my hands free. My gaze darted over the brick walls around me. "Killing these people isn't going to bring Josey back. They've got nothing to do with it, Xavier. *I've* got nothing to do with it. It's not like I asked to be born."

"Oh, but you were," Xavier said, his smirk stretching wider. "And now you'll die."

"You're sick," I spat, backing up a couple of steps. "You didn't need to involve all these people. You want to pick a fight with me, then fight with *me*."

"I intend to." He raised his gun. "I think I'll start by blasting away those tricksy feet of yours so you can't run off again, and then I'll take the rest of you apart with my bare hands."

I took another frantic glance around me and spotted an open window on the side of the building two floors up. But I had to buy enough time to get to it first. I groped at my pockets, as if I might have brought a knife and just forgotten about it—and my fingers brushed the slight protrusion of my childhood bracelet.

My pulse hiccupped. I reached into my pocket and

yanked out the silver chain. When I held it up to the streaks of sunlight that penetrated the alley, Xavier paused, frowning.

Every nerve in my body screamed at me to squeeze the bracelet tight and tuck it away where he'd never find it. I'd clung to this last concrete memento of my mother for fifteen years. But I didn't need it to remember her. I understood the full sacrifice she'd made for me now. And I knew with absolute certainty that Mom would have cared less about me holding onto it than about protecting me any way she could like she hadn't managed to before.

I wasn't really an angel anyway, little or otherwise.

"This is the last piece of my mother I have left," I said, closing my fingers around it. "If you want her so badly, you'd better go get it."

Xavier's eyes fixed on my hand with a sudden flare of longing. The next second, I hurled the bracelet into the strewn debris along the edge of the alley.

Xavier dove after it, nearly dropping his gun in his haste. I sprang at the wall. Using the uneven texture of the bricks to brace my shoes, I spun and launched toward the wall kitty-corner, bouncing back and forth between the sides on a diagonal. Sweat beaded on my forehead at the pain in my thigh I was ignoring.

Xavier let out a cry of triumph—and I flung myself in one final leap to grab the sill of the open window.

A roar echoed up from behind me. I didn't look back, only hurled myself through the window. Gunfire sputtered in my wake, chipping the ledge. I sprawled on the floor in a vacant apartment and shoved myself to my feet.

"This isn't over!" Xavier bellowed after me. "You're going to realize eventually that it's going to come down to you or me."

————

I met up with the guys by the base of the hill that led to the Noble mansion, my feet and my thigh aching. I fought the urge to sink down on the sidewalk. The somber expression on all their faces only made my spirits sink more.

"You couldn't stop him," I said.

Wylder blew out a frustrated breath. "We couldn't get close enough. The cops came by again and totally failed too. He's too smart and too fast."

"And has too much ammunition," Kaige grumbled.

"We'll regroup," Gideon said. "It's barely noon. We've got the rest of the afternoon to come up with the right approach—and we don't even know that the Long Night won't consider the deal fulfilled already."

I was pretty sure he wouldn't, but I couldn't bring myself to say that. "All right," I said, and limped over to the car.

I'd only just made it to the doors when my phone buzzed. I didn't see how it could be good news, but I pulled it out anyway. I didn't recognize the number.

"Hello?" I said.

"Is this Mercy Katz?" said the voice at the other end.

I hesitated. "Yeah. What's this about?"

"I'm calling from the Paradise Bend County Hospital. We have some good news for you. You're the contact for Rowan Finlay? He's just woken up."

25

Rowan

My chest felt as if it were being stabbed by tiny pins and needles, and everything around me seemed hazy. Somebody hovered to my side. "Mercy?" I said softly.

"No, dear." My vision cleared a little, and the nurse's face came into view. She was in her late forties and definitely not the woman I was looking for.

"Over here," came a voice from near the curtain. I whipped my head around so fast that the dull pain at the back spread into a pounding headache.

I winced and fell back against the pillows. Bandages were wrapped around my arms and torso. An IV drip was pushed into a vein on my right wrist, and monitoring equipment next to me gave off a quiet but persistent beep.

"Easy, dear," the nurse cooed. "You don't want to strain yourself."

Mercy hurried into view, her eyes wide with worry and her forehead furrowed. "Rowan, are you okay?" There was a smudge of grit on her cheek, a healing scrape on her chin, and strands of hair had come loose from her ponytail. She looked as if she'd walked through hell to get here.

"I've felt better," I managed. My voice came out creaky.

"Be glad you're feeling anything at all," the nurse announced. "You've been off in your own little world for almost three days."

Three days? I stared at her as she stepped aside to detach my IV, but my attention was caught by Wylder, Gideon, and Kaige coming up beside Mercy to circle my bed. I didn't mind. They made for a welcome sight, one that sent a rush of relief through me.

"*You're* all still okay," I rasped, my voice getting a little stronger and my mind a little less dazed as I regained my focus. "How is— Is everything—?" I didn't know how to ask the questions I wanted to with the nurse here in the room.

Mercy squeezed my hand. "We're still working on it, but we're almost there. You don't need to worry about that right now." She blinked hard. "I'm just glad to hear your voice."

Seeing her fighting tears, I knew without her saying it that she'd been afraid I was going to die. I had a vague memory of thinking the same thing myself when I'd been slumped in the warehouse with flames rising around me and pain radiating from the places where the bullets had hit me.

But somehow I was still here. That was some kind of miracle, wasn't it?

"How *do* you feel?" Gideon asked.

"Like a truck ran over me," I said. "Or maybe two."

"Wow, Rowan is cracking jokes," Kaige teased. "I think you should check for a concussion, nurse."

The nurse frowned at him, but Kaige only chuckled.

"Don't mind him," Mercy said. "That's just how we are."

That was right. We were a team.

Which brought to mind another question. "How—how did we get out of the fire?"

Mercy smiled bright but tightly. "You talked me through my panic, and I dragged you out of the building."

"But you—you were shot too." I remembered that clearly: the jolt of panic that'd struck *me* when I'd watched her fall.

"One way or another, we were both getting out of there," Mercy said stubbornly, and I caught a glimpse of the girl I'd seen that night. She was my fierce angel, my savior. "Besides you're the one who saved me first."

"You both got out, and that's all I could have asked for," Wylder said with typical assurance, but his gaze held mine for a few beats longer than usual. "I expect you to put as much effort into healing up as you give to all your other work."

My lips twitched with a smile. "Aye, aye, boss."

The nurse motioned to the bunch of them. "You've said your hellos. You can't all stay in here at once. The patient needs room to breathe."

"Right, right," Kaige said. He gently tapped his knuckles to my shoulder. "You're tougher than me now, Finlay. No more showing off, all right."

I snorted, and he grinned before following the nurse out of the room.

Gideon dipped his head to me. "We've ensured, thanks to the Nobles' accounts, that you have the best room available in the hospital."

"Thanks," I said. "I appreciate that."

"Come on," Wylder said to the other guy, cuffing him lightly. "I think we should give these two a little time to 'catch up'." He winked at Mercy. "I'll make sure no one interrupts you for a good long while."

Mercy rolled her eyes at him and waved him off. They headed out, the door closing with a click behind them. Then it was just her and me in the small but private white-walled room.

Despite Mercy's reaction to Wylder's innuendo, I still wanted her as close to me as I could have her. With a wince I suppressed, I scooted over on the bed to make room for her to climb up beside me.

Mercy took the unspoken invitation and nestled against me. I wrapped my arm around her and kissed her forehead. Tension I hadn't realized she was holding in loosened as her body relaxed against me.

"What did you mean, we're almost there?" I asked quietly. "Today's the last day, isn't it? What's going on?"

"I really don't want you thinking about that," Mercy said, tucking her head next to mine. "You need to focus on getting better."

"I'm going to have trouble doing that if I have no idea what you all are facing out there."

She sighed and hugged me tighter but still carefully. "The Storm pulled his men out. Most of them have left. So we won in that way. But Xavier is rampaging around Paradise City, and we haven't figured out how to stop him yet." She nuzzled my cheek. "But that's *really* not for you to worry about right now. We'll figure it out."

I could hear the anxiety in her voice, and I didn't want to add to it. "I know you will," I said. "You and the guys have gotten through an awful lot."

"And so have you." Her breath grazed the side of my face, warm and sweet. "I'm so glad you're back with us."

"Me too."

I turned my head and found her lips bare inches from mine. Nudging closer, I brushed my mouth to hers. She was too damn magnetic for me to resist, and I'd been without her touch for way too long.

Mercy kissed me slowly at first, almost leisurely. Her hand came up to caress my cheek. I teased my fingers into her hair as I kissed her back. It felt even better than the day when we'd finally come back to each other after so long apart and so much turmoil and misunderstanding. I knew exactly how much we meant to each other, how far I'd go for her and she for me.

For several minutes, we didn't do more than kiss, until the press of her warm body against mine became too irresistible. With my cock hardening behind the hospital-issue gown, I skimmed my fingers down the side of her body. When I reached Mercy's ass, I couldn't help tugging her closer and kneading those taut curves. A pleased murmur escaped her.

When I tried to sit up more to catch her mouth at a deeper angle, Mercy pushed me back down on the bed. "Relax. Let me take care of you."

I might have protested if her next move hadn't been to peel off her T-shirt and her bra. My gaze drank in the creamy mounds of her breasts with unrestrained eagerness. Any pain I'd still been feeling had faded away.

This was my girl. My *woman*. The queen of the Bend. And even if she was trying to make this easy for me, I intended to show her just how glad I was to be back with her in every way she'd let me.

She leaned over me, and I reached up to cup her breasts. Her nipples pebbled at the swipe of my thumbs. My mouth watered, and my cock turned even harder. I hoped Wylder had done a good job of barricading this room, because once we got going, I didn't know if I'd be able to stop, even if a doctor marched into the room. I needed her too damn much.

Mercy leaned even closer so one nipple hovered right over my mouth. I latched my mouth on it and sucked hard. A perfect little gasp escaped her lips. Her palm flattened against the wall for support as she kept most of the weight of her body off me, but she rocked with the movements of my tongue. The brush of her thigh against my hard cock brought me to even stiffer attention.

I meant to make good on my silent promise to give as much as I took, though. I sucked and pinched, alternating my attention between the two soft mounds. Above me, Mercy started to moan. With my free hand, I inched closer to her pussy and fumbled with the fly of her jeans. As soon as they were unzipped, I tucked my fingers right inside. I caressed her slit, moving my finger up and down the length of it before curling my forefinger against her clit.

She moaned again, louder this time. I spanked her ass. "Shh, be quiet. We don't want anybody to hear us."

She whimpered in answer. A wicked idea took over me. I moved the flat of my palm over the soft curve of her ass before slapping on it again. Mercy's body jerked with a gush of wetness from her pussy. I spanked her lightly, careful not to be loud enough for the sound to echo around us while I continued to work at her pussy.

"Please," she said as she sat back down, adjusting her legs on either side of my thighs. "I need you."

I nodded, my own breath ragged with desire. She eased up the hospital gown and slid off her panties before bracing herself right over my throbbing cock. I gripped her hips, pulling her down over me.

Her slickness closing around me was absolute heaven. As she took me fully inside her, both of us groaned together. Mercy raised herself, squeezing my balls slightly as she went, before her greedy cunt swallowed my cock again.

She clutched my shoulders in an almost vice-like grip as she continued to pump over me, rotating her hips around my hard dick. "Fuck," I whispered, and her eyes rolled up in her head in answer. Suddenly an impulse gripped me that had nothing to do with lust.

"Look at me," I said softly.

Mercy lowered her gaze, her eyes dark with so much longing I almost came just seeing it. My cock pulsed with need, but I reined that urge in for now. I brushed her hair back from her forehead so I could have a better look at her, and said the words I'd said so many times before, but not recently enough. "I love you, Mercy."

The way she beamed at me told me it'd been exactly the right time. She leaned in, kissing me hard, and then spoke with her cheek resting against mine. "I love you too, Rowan. I don't think I ever completely stopped. I'm sorry I didn't tell you sooner."

At the choked quality to her voice, I hugged her to me. "Don't be sorry. I'm lucky enough to be able to say it after I almost lost you."

"I'm lucky to have you too. I'm so glad we found our way back to each other."

We held each other for a little longer, and then Mercy began to move over me again, taking my dick deeper inside her. She felt so hot and wet and perfect. I tugged at her hips to encourage her to go faster, knowing I could take it. Knowing she'd like it best that way too. An ache had woken up in the wound in my side despite the painkillers, but it was worth it to have this moment of connection with her.

Mercy gasped, following my guidance. She rocked against me, lifting and slamming down so I pounded into her. It only took a few more times before her pussy clenched around me, setting off a sharper flare of pleasure all through my veins.

Before I came inside her, she slipped off and eased

down the bed to wrap her lips around me. With a few passionate swipes of her tongue, she brought me right over the edge, spurting into her mouth.

Smiling slyly, Mercy snuggled next to me. We stayed there in each other's arms until our breaths evened out.

"I did love you back in high school, Mercy," I said, feeling the need to clarify. "But I love you just as much the way you are now too—fierce and unstoppable."

"I'm not unstoppable," she said, her face falling.

"Yes, you are. No one gets between you and what you want. Your dad treated you horribly, but you've come out of it stronger. I couldn't be prouder to stand by your side, and I'll keep telling you that until I know you're just as proud of who you've become."

Mercy swallowed audibly and pressed a tender kiss to my lips. "Thank you." After a few more minutes, she sighed. "I want to stay here with you for the rest of the day."

"But you need to go deal with Xavier. I understand." I grimaced. "I just wish I could come with you to help instead of being stuck in here."

She slowly pulled on her clothes. "I'm sure you'll hear all about it afterward. And I did bring some things to distract you."

My curiosity stirred. "What do you mean?"

She fished into the tote bag she'd carried in with her. "I figured you might get bored, so I brought you drawing supplies." She placed my pencil case and a sketchpad on the table beside me.

I glanced around the room and let my tone go wry. "So much inspiration to draw on in here."

Mercy swatted me. "I guess you'll just have to use your imagination then, huh." She paused, and something about her expression made my heart skip a beat. She looked at me cautiously. "And your mom called."

My pulse outright lurched. "What?"

"I answered the call but then I didn't know what to tell her." She bit her lip. "She wanted you to call her back when you could. I brought her number in case you didn't have it programmed in, and here's your phone, even though I don't think you're supposed to have it in the hospital room." She slipped the phone under the sketch pad. "It's totally up to you, but if you ask me, you really should give her a call. She's never going to stop being your mom."

Mercy gave me one more lingering kiss before she left. I settled into the pillows, grappling with my emotions. The aches of my body were asserting themselves again, and part of me wanted nothing more than to close my eyes and let exhaustion drag me into sleep.

My hand went to the phone instead. I weighed it in my fingers for several minutes. Then I dialed Mom's number, my mouth going dry.

Mom picked up on the third ring. "Hello?" she said. When I didn't answer, she said, "Rowan, is that you?"

"Hey, Mom," I said slowly. "How are you?"

"I'm good. Just glad to hear from you after all this time. I know that's a mom thing to say, but... well, it's true."

Carina's voice carried from farther away. "Is that Rowan? He finally called?"

My lips twitched with amusement at her impertinent voice. "Sounds like someone else has been waiting to hear from me too. You can put Carina on— we'll talk more after she has a chance."

"All right," Mom said, sounding bemused, and handed the phone over.

"I missed you at my birthday," Carina announced first thing. "The present was nice, but I really wanted to see *you*."

Homesickness for the family I'd once had squeezed around my heart. "I want to see you too, kiddo," I said, using the old nickname that I knew made her grimace now. "I just..."

What excuse did I have, really? Life had dealt a hard blow to me, and the blows had kept coming. But after each one of them, I had come out stronger, just like Mercy had.

An unexpected sense of hope unfurled in my chest. I'd convinced myself that the life I was living made me toxic to the family I had left. But talking to Mom and Carina now without resisting their concern, I didn't feel like poison to them.

Maybe I could be both Rowan Finlay, one of the Noble elite, and I could be a good son and a brother at the same time. If they ever needed it, I could even protect them better from my position of power.

"You know what?" I said. "Never mind excuses. How about I catch a flight over there in a couple of weeks, and I'll make it up to you then."

Mercy

WHEN I REJOINED THE GUYS IN THE HOSPITAL waiting room, their grim expressions swept away any lingering peace from my interlude with Rowan. "What?" I said, hurrying the rest of the way to them.

They were already getting up from their chairs. "We've received another report from the men who've been tracking Xavier's movements," Gideon said, keeping his voice low so the people around us wouldn't overhear. "He and the Storm's lackeys who've stuck with him have set up explosives around a building where there are a couple of families and some other civilians hiding out in the upstairs apartments. He's threatening to blow them all up if anyone comes close to him."

My pulse stuttered. Somehow I didn't think Xavier would hold back on the blowing up part no matter what anyone else did, if he got testy enough. He'd probably wanted this news to get to me so I'd feel even more horrible about running away.

But could I really believe that he'd stop his rampage even if I gave myself up? No, not for a second. He was reveling in the destruction, using his anger as an excuse, just like Kaige had said. Once he'd killed me, he'd start blaming all of Paradise Bend for stealing Josey too, and the Bend would be without a queen to defend it.

Wylder looked as if he'd gone through the same thought process. "You can't give in, no matter what he demands. We'll find a way to take him out that doesn't end with him getting his hands on you."

I inhaled deeply. "I'm all for that. But we're going to need help. Should we call together all our men—the ones we can count on, anyway—and see what we're working with?"

Wylder nodded. He turned to Gideon. "Contact all the Noble underlings who stuck with us at the waterfront property and survived. I don't trust anyone who's in tight with my dad to have our backs. Tell them to gather on the front lawn at the mansion—we need room for a larger group—and we'll be there in half an hour." He glanced at me. "If you're okay with bringing the Claws to my house, that is. I think it's best if we talk to them all at once."

"Agreed." I took out my phone. "I'll have Jenner assemble everyone."

"Tell him to bring the kid too. I'm not sending Beckett in to fight, but he's been instrumental in bringing down the Storm. He might know something about Xavier that'll help."

I added that note to my text message and sent it off as we hustled out of the hospital to the car.

We reached the Noble mansion just ahead of the Claws forces. A couple dozen men were already milling around on the lawn, Anthea in their midst looking like she'd had a hand in corralling them, but the atmosphere was tense. She caught my eye as we passed with a tight smile that was closer to a grimace.

As we wove through them to the front steps, Wylder catching people's eyes and nodding here and there, I picked up a few snippets of hushed conversation, things like: "bomb" and "psycho." It seemed that word about Xavier's current gambit had spread widely already.

Several of the men didn't quite meet Wylder's gaze. Apprehension prickled down my spine. When we reached the steps, we stopped at the base and looked over the crowd, including the few cars of Claws men that were just arriving to join the bunch. The men stirred restlessly on their feet, looking like they wanted to be someplace else.

"What the hell's wrong with them?" Kaige muttered.

"They're probably nervous," Wylder said. "Xavier's acting like a maniac, and they've got my dad breathing down their necks in a not-much-better state too." His jaw clenched. "But Nobles don't back down, not when our city is on the line. We'll get them sorted out."

I grasped his hand, tugging him a little apart from the others for a second, closer to the house. "You know you're twice the leader your dad is, right?" I said quietly, searching his eyes. "Ten times, even."

The slightest hint of a smile curled the corner of Wylder's mouth, even though his eyes stayed dark. "If you say so, then it must be true. Now we've just got to get them to believe it."

I glanced at the unsettled men who'd nonetheless turned up to hear what the Noble heir had to say. "I think they already do. You just need to remind them of why."

Wylder didn't say anything for a moment. His fingers tightened around mine. Abruptly, he leaned in to kiss me. I swayed into his touch, his intoxicating musk washing over me. Then he pulled back to meet my eyes again. "How do you do it?"

I raised my eyebrows. "Do what?"

"Always make sure I see reason while keeping me on my toes."

I tapped his chest teasingly. "I'm your queen, remember."

"You're my equal in every possible way. Maybe my better in a few, but we won't talk about that in front of company." He managed a small grin, looking a little more relaxed than before, and tugged my arm. "Are you ready?"

"As I'll ever be."

He dropped my hand as we climbed onto the front steps together, but we stood shoulder to shoulder— equals, like he'd said. Wylder clapped his hands, and the uneasy murmurs died down. Everyone turned to face us.

"I think you know why you're here," Wylder said, slipping effortlessly into his role as leader. His commanding presence had been impossible to ignore even when I'd first staggered into the Noble mansion months ago, and now he wore it with total assurance. Watching him stoked the flames of my love for him. "The menace that calls himself Xavier is tearing up our city's streets and threatening our people, and it's time we dealt with him once and for all."

"How the hell are we going to do that without *us* getting blown up?" someone asked from the crowd.

"That's what we're here to figure out," I said. "He's lost most of his allies. With all of us working together, we should be able to end his reign of terror."

"He's out of control," another guy said from the edges of the group. "There's no way to predict what he'll do next. We already lost a ton of people at the waterfront property, and now he's even crazier than before."

"Yeah," a third man piped up. "Let the cops deal with him for once. They can take the hits this time."

I didn't like the approving hum that spread through the gathering. Wylder scowled at them all. "Really? That's your answer—wait for the police to finally step up? Chances are that dozens more people will be dead before that happens, and if we don't act now, their blood will be on our hands. The last time Xavier got the better of us, it was because we were abandoned by those who should have been fighting with us. But we have the strength in numbers this time."

"He can't hold us all off at once," I added. "Once we're coordinated, we can find an opportunity to pick him off, and this war will all be over just like that."

The expressions in the crowd still looked doubtful. I

spotted Jenner, Sam, Quinn, and several other Claws hanging back by the edges with Beckett standing among them. An impulse gripped me. I caught Beckett's eye and motioned for him to come join us.

The kid skirted the crowd and walked over to the steps a little hesitantly, but his shoulders pulled back and his chin rose as he came to stand next to me. He peered out over the gathered men as if daring them to challenge his right to be there. "What do you need?" he asked me under his breath.

"Just for you to be yourself." I smiled and set my hand on his back, pitching my voice to carry farther. "This is Beckett. Take a good look at him. How old are you, Beckett?"

"Sixteen," Beckett said, his shoulders stiffening even more.

Someone in the crowd snickered, and Kaige took a step toward the guy with an intimidating pose. After all his skepticism about Beckett, he'd obviously come around.

"This sixteen-year-old," I said, "is the reason we were able to take down the man behind Xavier and most of his forces. You've noticed that most of the men who worked with Xavier have already left town? It's thanks to Beckett that we were able to force the Storm to back down."

Wylder folded his arms over his chest, picking up my thread. "If one sixteen-year-old kid can make all the difference in tackling a huge crime lord, then the bunch of you should be able to manage one psychopath, don't you think? Beckett wasn't afraid to take action when he needed to, and we can't let ourselves cower either. We're Nobles, and Nobles fight for what's theirs."

Anthea nodded approvingly. The gathered men stared at Beckett. I saw flickers of shame and then resolve cross their faces. They stirred again, but this time the energy was more aggressive than uneasy.

"Right!" Jenner shouted. "The Claws are going to fight. We're going to put this asshole down like the mad dog he is."

"I'm going to be there going at him," Kaige said, flexing his arms.

Gideon gave a tight smile. "And me."

"Who else?" Wylder called out. "I only want people who are ready to go all in, who'll stick with us and not turn their backs when the going gets tough. I *thought* that was what you were all made of. If that's what you want the Nobles to be, then stand with us now."

The murmurs that rose up now thrummed with eager determination. "Hell yeah!"

"I'm in."

"Let's take that bastard down and show him who the real boss is around here."

"Wylder'll make him pay!"

I glanced at the Noble heir, knowing what an important moment this was for him. The Nobles were throwing their lot in with him, with no guidance from his father and even against what they might have suspected Ezra would prefer. Wylder had just proven that he was stronger than his father, with solid principles and a desire to protect everyone within this city, not just those who kissed his feet.

It might not be just Xavier we conquered today.

But we did still have to conquer the psycho. We waved everyone closer.

"We head out now," Wylder said. "We have the numbers to surround Xavier and his lackeys on all sides. Stay where you have some cover but get as close as you can without provoking him into setting off his explosives. When we have every possible angle, one of us will get an opening soon enough. Be ready to take it if it's you. I don't care how you do it—if you can kill him, make it happen."

The men let out a whoop and started streaming toward the cars. I didn't know if that plan would be enough to get us all the way there, but it was a solid start. We couldn't be sure exactly what we'd need to do until we faced Xavier on the turf he'd tried to claim as his own.

"Thanks," I said to Beckett, and sent him off to the Claws so Jenner could arrange transport back to the house for him while the rest of us headed downtown.

Anthea had ambled over. "I'll see about getting more weapons and ammo sent over there so you can handle a long stand-off."

"Perfect," Wylder said with a tip of his head.

"We'll have to set a specific boundary," Gideon started saying as we walked away from the house, but my attention was drawn away from the conversation by a movement at one of the front windows.

Ezra was standing in the living room, half hidden by one of the curtains, watching us. His lips were pursed and his eyes narrowed. When he realized I'd noticed him, he stepped back, fading into the shadows.

A chill pooled in my gut. Xavier definitely wasn't our only enemy.

But he was the one we had to tackle first. I yanked my gaze away and hurried over to join my men.

Kaige

THE STREET WAS SO EMPTY IT WAS EERIE. USUALLY AT this time on a late summer afternoon, music would have been spilling from restaurant doorways and masses of shoppers would have been ambling past the storefronts. Now it was all still and silent, as if frozen in time.

A pretty awful time. Several of the windows had been shot out, shards of glass glinting in the fading sunlight. A dead body sprawled across the sidewalk nearby, and I spotted another near a car down the street. Xavier had continued to leave a path of carnage in his wake.

But there were some signs of living humanity left. A few faces peered out of the windows on higher floors, pale with fear.

"He's been shooting anyone desperate enough to try to make a run for it," Gideon reported. "Hard to say whether they're safer taking that chance or staying put."

Mercy peered down the street. We could see Xavier and the two Storm men still with him a few blocks away, pacing by a small delivery truck they'd stalled in the middle of the road. As I watched, Xavier took another shot, shattering a second-floor window. Someone yelped, whether in pain or just fear I couldn't tell.

"Where's the building he's set up the explosives around?" Mercy asked.

Gideon gestured toward the distant figures. "It's that coffee shop on the corner. The upper floors are divided into three apartments, and several of the shop's customers ended up fleeing upstairs when the shooting started. Xavier's set up the explosives all along the front of the building with a trigger switch he hasn't moved more than ten feet from since he placed it. The Storm's men barricaded the back door so no one can escape that way."

"Who's going to try me now?" Xavier hollered, still pacing like a caged lion. He slammed his fist right into a store window, making it burst apart. "You want a piece of me? I'll tear *you* to pieces."

The guy was fucking insane. Not that I'd had much doubt about that fact before, but he'd somehow pushed the title of maniac to a completely new level.

A familiar burn of rage spread from my gut up through my chest. My teeth set on edge. This asshole had destroyed enough already. He'd tormented the woman I loved, smashed up the city I called home, and tried to kill the guys I considered family too many times to count. It'd gone on for too long. I was going to end the motherfucker and protect what was mine before he could do any more damage.

"Let's go," Wylder called to our troops. "Remember, keep low and don't make yourselves an easy target. Surround him as close as you can safely get and pick off him and his men as soon as you have an opening."

A few of the Claws men pumped their hands in the air. "For the Claws!"

"For the Claws!" Mercy echoed. "And the Nobles, and freeing Paradise Bend together!"

With a rush of energy, the men dispersed, some hustling along the sidewalks where the parked cars offered some shelter, some jumping back in their own cars to drive around and come up on Xavier from the other side.

The four of us stuck close together, moving down the street with our eyes fixed on Xavier and our guns ready. My free hand balled into a fist. I wanted so badly to charge right up to him and pummel his face into a pulp, but I wasn't reckless enough to give in to that urge, which would probably end with me dead before I got within half a block of him.

It was a good thing I didn't go dashing off into the open, because we'd only closed the distance by one block when bullets sprayed down at us from above. We leapt back against the nearest buildings, but one of the Noble men hadn't been fast enough. He slumped with the back of his head blown out.

"There's someone on the roof," I yelled out.

Wylder motioned everyone in view as close to the buildings as we could get, where the shooter wouldn't be able to take proper aim. The anger inside me churned even more furiously. Our job had just gotten twice as hard.

Xavier had taken notice of the activity at our end of the street. He let out a roar that sounded as enraged as it did triumphant and smashed another window with his fist. Blood was trickling over his knuckles, but I saw no sign in his wild expression that he cared. Then he let loose his own hail of bullets from his rifle, forcing us to drop low to the ground. Gunfire battered the sides of the cars and set off a couple of alarms.

But a few of our men had made it farther down the street to come at Xavier and his accomplices from the other side. With a *bang*, one of the Storm men next to Xavier crumpled. Xavier growled and jerked back closer to the safety of the truck, shooting indiscriminately all around him. We couldn't move any closer, not without walking into the path of a bullet from one direction or another.

"If we could just kill *him*, the other men would take off," Wylder muttered. "They've only stuck around because they've got him on their side."

"But how do we get close enough?" I asked. "Do you think the other Nobles—"

Before I could even finish the question, more of our men opened fire farther down. The other Storm lackey went down with a splat of torn guts, but Xavier had stayed out of range. Then he grabbed something he'd stashed under the truck and hurled it toward the combined Noble and Claws forces.

"Watch out!" Mercy cried.

I couldn't tell how many of the men managed to dash far enough for safety before the device Xavier had thrown exploded with an earth-shattering force. Two cars flipped right onto their sides with the impact. When the dust cleared, I thought I spotted a few limbs lying on the street with no body attached to them.

My stomach clenched with nausea, and my rage burned hotter. We couldn't let Xavier keep at this.

I aimed my gun around the side of the nearest car and shot at his head as well as I could, but it was too far. The bullet just dinged the truck's side mirror five feet to Xavier's left.

I glared at the buildings around Xavier as if it was their fault for not simply jumping off their foundations and burying him in rubble, and my gaze caught on the electrical wires running from post to post along the street. I grimaced. "Too bad we can't just shoot one of the wires and electrocute the fucker."

To my surprise, Gideon perked up. "I don't think it'd work that way, but the basic idea might have something to it."

I let out a startled chuckle. "I guess I can be smart every now and then, huh? Who'd have thought?"

Gideon studied the buildings, his face hardening with intense thought. I swore you could see the gears turning in his head when he got like this. "He hasn't smashed up that shoe store over there yet. I might be able to use it. But we'd need to get him to come over and make contact with some part of the building when I'm ready. I don't know if we can be sure—"

Mercy straightened up. "I'll do it."

My spirits plummeted. "No. You're not getting anywhere near that bastard." Gideon looked equally unnerved.

Mercy shook her head. "Xavier's here because he wants revenge. He wants it most of all from me. You're not going to get any better bait than that. I'm fast, even with my leg hurt. I won't get too close to him. But I can get him over to the store. You just have to make sure you don't electrocute me too."

"Here." Wylder handed her his headset and nodded to Gideon. "Stay in contact with each other, follow each other's cues. I know you've got this... but be careful."

"There's got to be another way," I said desperately, but even as I spoke, I knew Mercy had a point.

She motioned in Xavier's direction just as he sent another volley of bullets over the street. "Look at him. He doesn't care if he walks out of here alive so long as he takes everybody out with him. He hates me more than anything else, and that makes me his greatest weakness."

She was right. There was no other way. But it didn't mean I had to be happy about it. I pulled her in for a hug while I laid a kiss on top of her head. "Good luck."

She nodded and stepped away.

"I'll need someone to get me to the back of the building," Gideon said.

"I'll do that," I volunteered. "It was my idea—I should go with you."

Mercy set off down the sidewalk, walking slowly but steadily toward Xavier, braced to duck if she needed to. I stared after her until Gideon tugged on my arm.

"Come on. I know you're worried about her—I am too —but Mercy can handle herself. We have to do our part."

"Right." I forced myself to follow him down a narrow lane between two of the stores and into the back alley that ran the length of several blocks. We had to reach the shoe store and get everything set up in time.

As soon as we were in the alley, we set off at a jog. Gideon's breath started to rasp within seconds, but he didn't let up his pace.

Just as we came up on the street between us and the next section of alley, a Storm man we hadn't spotted earlier stepped out to confront us, his gun pointed right at me.

I didn't think, just sprang at him, bringing my full weight to bear. The gun went off, the bullet ricocheting off the pavement. I slammed my elbow into his forearm, hearing the bone crack, and heaved him down onto the ground. With a swift punch, I crushed his windpipe. He sputtered and sagged, the life going out of him.

"And that's why I'm glad I brought back-up," Gideon remarked, sounding just a little shaken. "Let's go before Xavier catches on to what we're doing."

We rushed the last short distance to the back of the shoe store. Gideon had me bash the lock on the back door and then, once we were inside, punch holes in the walls here and there so he could get at the wiring. When he was satisfied, I left him fiddling with the wires and mumbling to himself as he worked out how to adjust the connections and lay his trap.

I peered out through the big display window at the front of the store. The awning outside shaded it, and with the interior lights off, you would've needed to come right up to the glass to make us out inside. For now, I kept well back just in case, but Xavier didn't appear to have noticed us. I could see him ranting and waving his gun around just a little farther down the street.

Then Mercy came into view. She'd crouched down as she got closer, staying hidden behind the cars. She had her gun in her hand, but I knew as well as she did that Xavier was moving around too fast and erratically for her to get a good shot in. Still...

"Tell Mercy to try to shoot him first," I said to Gideon. "Even if she misses, it'll be a good way to get his attention and get him pissed off. And maybe she won't miss."

"I'm trying to concentrate here," Gideon muttered, but he passed on my suggestion into his mic, following it with, "But keep laying low for another minute or two. I've almost got it..."

Xavier strode a little to the left and then a little to the right, taking more shots at the Nobles who were holding their ground farther away after the earlier blast. Then he went around the truck to where he was keeping the explosives. The hairs on the back of my neck stood on end.

"Hurry!" I snapped.

"I'm doing my best," Gideon hissed back. "If you don't want to end up electrocuted too, chill out for five seconds."

I might have been annoyed, except it seemed like it really was only five seconds later when Gideon moved to the hole I'd made closest to the window and snipped a wire there. Holding it by the insulated covering, he pressed the frayed end to the metal window frame. It stayed in place when he moved back.

"Okay," he said to Mercy. "All he needs to do is touch the window frame, and he'll get a good shock. The glass and the sidewalk should be safe. Just avoid anything metal."

Mercy murmured something and nodded in return. She cocked her gun, bobbed up, and fired off a shot.

As I'd expected, Xavier wove to the side just as she pulled the trigger. At the sound of the gun firing, he lurched even farther out of the way and spun around.

Her body rigid, Mercy stood up to show herself. Her voice carried through the glass. "Hey asshole. I'm the one you want, aren't I? So why don't you come and get me?"

In answer, Xavier snarled and spewed bullets at her from his rifle. Mercy leapt down with her well-honed reflexes, rolling to the far side of the store. Xavier marched forward, his expression getting fiercer as he came.

Our plan was working, but I hated it now. He was getting way too close to her. My muscles strained all through my arms. I could dash out there and punch the lights out of him...

Except I wouldn't get very far while he was still armed and totally aware.

"Missed me," Mercy taunted. "What's taking you so long?"

Xavier let out a wordless bellow and rushed at the car. Instead of hurtling around it, he leapt right onto the hood. Mercy dove underneath it, out of the range of his next spray of bullets. I winced at the thought of her limbs getting scraped on the asphalt.

"You're stuck now, pathetic little kitty," Xavier snapped, and jumped onto the sidewalk right outside the store.

The second his feet hit the ground, Mercy struck. She was fucking amazing, and in that moment, I couldn't believe I was lucky enough to call this woman my own. She whipped her legs out from under the car and slammed both of her heels into Xavier's calves with all the strength she had in her.

Xavier stumbled and teetered to the side. His heavy form crashed into the window. The glass shattered around him. As he twisted to the side to avoid the jagged shards, his shoulder smacked into the edge of the frame.

It wouldn't have mattered if we hadn't set everything up. He'd probably have bounced right back around, barely bruised. But Gideon had been fucking amazing too.

The second Xavier's shoulder hit the frame, a crackling sound hummed through the air. Xavier's entire body jerked and spasmed, his muscles jiggling like Jell-O.

He managed to break away from the frame, but he

was reeling so badly he nearly tripped over his own feet. And that was my cue to jump in.

I fired off all the shots left in my gun as I ran at him through the broken window. At least two caught him in the chest. He swiveled around, staggering, and I sprang over the window frame so my own body didn't catch so much as a spark of the live electricity. Then I was on him.

I rammed into Xavier, shoving him to the ground. My fists connected with his jaw, then his nose, drawing a spurt of blood that added color to his scarred face. He twitched underneath me, and I pummeled him even harder, smacking his head back against the sidewalk, my vision hazing red.

This was for all the horrible "gifts" he'd left that'd freaked out Mercy. *This* was for every injury he'd ever given her. *This* was for killing our men, kidnapping Gideon, and siccing his lackeys on Rowan. *This* was for passing out Glory like candy and getting all those people hooked. *This* was for encouraging the Storm to set his sights on our home in the first place.

"Kaige. Kaige!" Mercy's voice reached me through my furor.

My mind started to clear. My hands slowed and then fell to my sides. I stared down at the ruin of Xavier's face, his features battered beyond recognition other than a few shreds of the scars clinging to what was left of his cheeks. His skull had broken open like a cracked egg leaking brains and blood onto the concrete. His body lay totally limp beneath me.

Mercy's arms wrapped around my shoulders. "He's dead. Xavier's dead. You did it."

I had. I blinked a few times, and something released inside me. Pushing myself off of the mutilated body, I turned and grabbed Mercy in the tightest hug I had in me.

She squeezed me back just as hard, a bit of a sob coming into her next breath. The other Nobles and Claws gathered around us, Wylder and Gideon pushing through the crowd to reach us. Someone let out a low whistle.

I forced myself to look at Xavier again and then down at my raw, bloodied knuckles.

I'd done that. I'd beaten the man into a pulp. It'd been brutal and horrific, but also so fucking necessary. He'd already hurt so many people. I'd just spared who knew how many more the same pain.

"The guy on the roof made a run for it when he saw you take Xavier down," Wylder said, clapping me on the back. "We managed to take him out before he got very far. They're all gone."

"It's over," Mercy said with an air of wonder.

A smile stretched across my face. Hell, yeah, it was. And I'd seen it through to the end, with my best friends and my woman with me every step of the way.

Mercy

MY HEART WAS STILL POUNDING DOUBLE-TIME. Xavier was dead. My worst enemy was *dead.* I felt laughter bubble in my chest, but no sound came out of my throat.

"You're bleeding," Wylder said, pushing closer, and it was only then that I registered the stinging on my arm. I'd scraped the skin raw on my elbow when I'd hurled myself under the car to escape Xavier.

"I'll be okay," I said, taking one deep breath and then another. A smile started to curve my lips. "I'll be just fine." And it felt like I was stating a fact this time, not just a hope that the words would be true.

Gideon finished fiddling with the wires to cut off the electrical current in the store and hurried over. He brushed the loose strands of hair back from my cheek and looked me over. "I knew you could handle him, but I was pretty worried for a few minutes there."

The laugh finally tumbled out. "So was I," I admitted.

I glanced down at the broken body lying near my feet. Kaige had battered Xavier's head so badly that his skull had literally split open. The gore made my stomach churn, but a sense of victory gripped me at the same time.

This was the only fate that monster had deserved after the way he'd terrorized our city.

Wylder slipped his arm around me. "Come on. Let's get you home. Or to my home first. You played a huge role in taking down Xavier—you should be with us when we tell my dad the good news."

I nodded, exhaustion trickling through me. I'd been so keyed up for the entire week, and now it was over. The sun was only just sinking below the level of the buildings, streaks of pink and purple touching the sky.

We'd met the deadline. The Storm's presence in Paradise Bend was at an end. The whole future stretched out ahead of us, and it had to be better than what we'd just gone through.

I walked a little slowly, the wound on my thigh still closed but aching from the strain I'd put on my body. As we headed back to the car, I noticed a few people who were peeking out of the buildings giving us curious looks. None of them would know exactly what had happened on the streets today or who had saved them, and maybe that was for the best.

After I congratulated the Claws and thanked them for their help, I returned to find Wylder talking to Gideon. I didn't catch what he'd said, but Gideon tapped away at his phone texting while Wylder drove. I picked up the little purse that Anthea had lent me off the floor by my feet where it'd spent so much time in the past few days and tucked it onto my lap instead. The gun in the back of my jeans felt uncomfortably heavy, but I didn't want to set that aside until we were safe within four walls again.

Kaige noticed the purse and grinned. "Are you going to get all ladylike on us now?"

I snorted. "Not likely. It's Anthea's. I should probably give it back to her at some point."

"Can you even fit anything in there?"

I thought of the tiny gun tucked inside next to the lipstick tube and packet of tissues. "You bet."

I understood what Wylder had instructed Gideon to do when we walked into the Noble mansion and found Frank waiting for us in the foyer. "I'm fine," I protested again as he dabbed an antiseptic wipe against the scrape on my elbow and taped a bandage there. Then he gave Kaige's blood-splattered shirt a nervous look.

Kaige's grin widened. "Don't worry, this isn't *my* blood."

"Is my dad around?" Wylder asked Frank.

The older man shrugged. "I haven't spoken with him lately, but I didn't see him leave either."

There was no sign of Anthea either. I shot her a quick text, and she replied that she was tying up some loose ends as far as cleaning up the various bodies we'd left behind, but she'd be back at the mansion within the hour. She finished the message with a *Congrats!*

surrounded by celebratory emojis that had me smothering an unexpected giggle.

Wylder motioned to us, and the four of us climbed the stairs and strode down the hall to Ezra's study. But the doorknob jarred when he tried to turn it, and no one answered his knock. Frowning, he led us to a few other spots he seemed to think his father might have been hanging out—one of the sitting rooms, the dining room, the living room—but we didn't find him anywhere.

"I guess he'll turn up eventually," Wylder said when we came to a stop near the bottom of the staircase, but his brow stayed knit.

Kaige stretched his arms over his head. "Oh well, I need a shower anyway. This dude really stinks."

"I should check up on a few things in my office," Gideon said. He already had his tablet out and was scrolling through some document on it.

I glanced toward the lounge room that held the big mahogany bar. "Why don't I mix up one of my custom drinks for us all to celebrate? I think I've got plenty of inspiration. You guys can meet us there when you're done."

Kaige's eyes brightened. "Yeah, we should totally celebrate! We deserve it after everything." His expression sobered momentarily, and I suspected he was rewinding the brutal events of today. I couldn't believe that in less than twenty-four hours we'd managed to both convince the Storm to back off and take down Xavier.

I was ready to nap for a thousand years.

"Are you sure you're up for it?" Gideon asked, his eyes scanning me.

"I'm okay, really. Besides, Frank didn't look concerned." It was barely evening, and I was still too wound up to think I'd actually be able to sleep. A euphoric sense of freedom was rising through me with the knowledge of Xavier's death. I had a few good hours before exhaustion eventually got the better of me. "Better sneak a little celebration in while we can."

Gideon and Kaige headed upstairs, and Wylder came with me into the lounge room. The gun at my back, the new pistol he'd given me after I'd had to throw away my other one earlier today, chafed at my skin. I set it on one of the stools, put Anthea's purse down on the counter, and went around behind the counter to eye the bottles lined up there.

"Any preferences?" I asked.

"Hmm?" Wylder said distractedly, dropping into the next stool over.

I leaned across the bar to poke his arm. "The booze? Remember?"

"Something that makes me buzzed," he said, finally snapping out of whatever thoughts he had been caught up in. "That'll do."

"Vodka then," I said. "With a little rum to even it out, and a few splashes of this and that." I started setting glasses out on the counter.

Wylder smirked. "It would be better if I got to taste it off of you."

I rolled my eyes. "Since when do you speak Kaige?"

Wylder just kept smiling. "You've changed me in

more ways than you think." He paused, his gaze traveling over the glasses. I'd put out five. "Are we expecting Anthea?"

I paused before looking up at him. "I guess we could be. She said she'd be back soon. But I was thinking of Rowan, actually."

I started to put the fifth glass away, but Wylder stopped me. "No, pour one for him too. I know he's not here to celebrate, but he was equally responsible for our win—and for saving you."

"He has made a habit of rescuing people." I picked out the best brand of vodka on offer and poured a dollop into each glass, including the last one. "For Rowan."

Before I could move on to the other ingredients, Ezra sauntered in through the doorway. I stiffened at the sight of him. He was dangling a bottle of whiskey from his hand. When his gaze caught on us, he stopped in his tracks. The frown on his face deepened. "What are you doing in here?"

Wylder turned to face his father. "Celebrating. Want to join us?"

Ezra didn't look like he was in a festive mood. His eyes were clear enough, but his face was flushed and his mouth set at a sour angle. I suspected he was at least a little drunk. He took a couple of steps toward us, his gaze sliding between me and his son. "What the hell should we be celebrating for?"

"We took out Xavier for good and ran the Storm out of town," Wylder said. "Paradise Bend is ours again with no challengers."

Ezra took a long swig of the amber liquid. "Mine. Paradise Bend belongs to *me*. I'm still in charge."

"Yes, of course," Wylder said.

"Don't you dare use that tone with me," Ezra said. In a split second, he'd reached to his concealed holster and brought out a gun. He kept it pointed at the floor, but my nerves set immediately on edge. "I see what you're trying to do."

"Dad, put that away," Wylder said, calmly but firmly.

"You think I'm so gullible that I don't see what you're trying to pull?" Ezra hissed. I saw him note my gun where I'd left it on the stool on the other side of the counter, too far away for me to reach. My fingers itched for it. He shot me a cold smile and then focused on Wylder again. "You figure you can steal my empire from under my nose while I sit back and do nothing? Well, you can forget about that, son."

My heart lurched in my chest. I had the feeling that it'd only take one wrong move, and he wouldn't hesitate to shoot us.

"Dad," Wylder said, getting up carefully from his seat. "You've got it all wrong. I wasn't doing it for me. It was for all of us—for the Nobles. I was doing my duty as your son and heir, protecting our empire."

"My son is dead," Ezra said. Wylder flinched at his words. "You've undermined me at every turn. Even today, you gathered my men and tried to antagonize them against me."

I would have guffawed at the absurdity of that accusation if Ezra hadn't been in such an unstable mood. *He* was the one who'd constantly undermined

Wylder and worked his underlings against us. Wylder hadn't said a word about his father when he'd rallied the Nobles to fight Xavier.

I eased closer to the counter and set my hand on its polished surface next to Anthea's purse. There was no way Ezra would suspect I had a gun in there, it was so small. I tucked my fingers through the opening, brushing the pistol's surface and sliding it into my grasp. Just in case.

"I was doing what needed to be done," Wylder said, an edge creeping into his voice as he no doubt had some of the same thoughts I'd had. "Someone needed to go up against Xavier—someone had to get everyone organized to defend the city. It isn't my fault that you decided that was all my job and washed your hands of it."

"It was all your fault to begin with," Ezra snarled. "Getting in with this slut and then allying with the Claws as if they could hold a candle to our power. But that was all part of your plan, wasn't it? Leverage as many men as you could against me and then with me out of the way, and you thought you would have the throne. Well, who's holding the gun now? Do you think if I was weak I could do this?" He brandished the pistol at us.

Wylder didn't reach for his own gun. His jaw clenched as he stared at his Dad, his hands raised in a placating gesture. If he pulled a gun on his father, it would come down to two choices—kill him or be killed instead.

I couldn't blame him if he was having trouble

crossing the point of no return. My heart ached for him. Why had it needed to come to this? I knew what it meant to have your father as your worst enemy, and I wouldn't have wished it on anyone.

"Dad." Wylder took a step toward Ezra. He was still trying to deescalate the situation.

"Don't," Ezra warned, clicking the safety off. My fingers curled around the trigger of my tiny pistol as I glanced between the two men. Was there any way all three of us could walk out of this confrontation alive? The wildness in Ezra's face and voice reminded me of Xavier in the middle of his rampage.

"We can talk about it, Dad. Keep the bottle and put the gun away."

"Don't tell me what to do." Ezra's eyes hardened as if he had come to a decision. "*I* know what to do. It's time to start over, to build my empire from the ground up again. But first I need to get rid of the snake in our midst."

"You already have what you wanted," Wylder said. "Open your eyes, Dad. I'm the person you raised me to be."

"You're a fucking traitor," Ezra snarled. Then his gaze snapped to me. "But you're the real problem. You're the reason I lost my son. You spun your web around him, seduced him, warped his mind, and took him away from me. So you die first."

My pulse thundered in my ears. Ezra jerked his gun hand toward me, his grip tensing around it, and there was nothing else I could do. I yanked my hand out of the purse and pulled the trigger on the tiny pistol.

Wylder's hand shot up at the same instant, having snatched his own gun. Two bangs split the air simultaneously. I flinched, half-expecting to feel an impact as a bullet tore through my flesh. But no pain came.

Ezra fell, his grasp going limp and his gun tumbling to the floor next to him, unfired.

With my heart in my throat, I stepped around the counter. Wylder came up beside me. We stared down at his father. Ezra sprawled on his back, his eyes gazing at the ceiling unblinking. Blood streamed from two bullet holes side by side in his forehead. We'd shot him together.

We'd killed him together.

The knowledge took its time sinking in. I kept bracing for Ezra to blink, to sit up and start ranting at us again. But his body didn't so much as twitch.

He was really gone. No more snarky remarks about me and the Claws. No more belittling Wylder's contributions. No more insane power grabs that undermined his own people.

In a way, this was the moment we were finally free.

Wylder dropped his gaze, his mouth tightening. I gripped his shoulder. "I'm sorry. I know you didn't want it to end like this."

He sighed and leaned into my touch just a little. "I didn't, but I knew it was coming. It needed to happen. He was always going to force my hand, from the moment I started questioning his judgment. I just—" He shook his head, cutting himself off. "Maybe it shouldn't have been hard after everything he's done, but it still was."

"I think that just makes you human," I said softly. "But you're going to be okay. You've got Kaige, and Gideon, and Rowan—and me. I'll be right here with you as we rule Paradise Bend together. We'll tell a different story this time. We'll fix our fathers' mistakes, as many of them as we can. I give you my word."

Wylder tugged me to him and bowed his head, his forehead brushing mine. "And I give you mine," he said, and kissed me like he never meant to stop.

29

Two months later

Mercy

"We caught some guys poking around the former Glory supply house," Sam reported, standing on the other side of what was now my desk in my father's old study. "They said some shit about how they were going to pick up the trade if we and the Nobles didn't want it."

I leaned back in the leather chair and rolled my eyes. "There's nothing in there to trade." After Ezra's death—which as far as anyone outside his inner circle knew had been an accident, no matter how they might speculate with the body going unseen—one of Wylder's first decisions had been to dispose of every bit of Glory in the Nobles' possession. Kaige had gleefully joined in the destruction. "I hope you told them Glory is off-limits in the county and that we're going to crack down on anyone who tries to bring it in."

Sam nodded with a sly grin. "I put it to them very clearly." He waggled his fingers toward his gun. "They were hardly more than kids. I think they were bluffing anyway."

"Like so many others," I said with a bemused grimace. Since the Storm had pulled out of the county and the Nobles and Claws re-established ourselves as rulers of Paradise Bend, random small-time crooks kept coming out of the woodwork, trying to figure out if there were any scraps they could snatch for their own. I didn't mind them picking up a little business here and there where we'd left gaps, but Glory was a total no-go.

Quinn had just come in, waiting by the door for his chance to speak. Now he piped up. "There are rumors going around to the Steel Knights revival now. A few guys were spotted at the skateboard park wearing their old bandanas." He snorted.

I waved off that news. "Let them be. They weren't villains—they just ended up under the control of one. If anyone gets it into his head to come at us, we'll crush them then."

I wasn't concerned about this new development. I didn't need to be. The smaller street gangs were already lining up to swear fealty to me, and the Claws were getting new recruits every day. In just the past month, we'd doubled in size.

And most of them specifically wanted to work for *me*. People knew who the new Queen of the Bend was.

They knew who had killed Colt and taken out Xavier. They were afraid, and they believed that I could show them how to conquer the things they feared.

For the first time in my life, I could be the woman my whole life had been preparing me for, whether Dad had wanted to accept the role I could play or not.

"Anything else?" I asked.

As the two men shook their heads, Beckett peeked into the room. "Just finished up my patrol."

I smiled at him, getting to my feet. The kid had been settling in here pretty well, although Anthea kept talking about how maybe she should bring him out to New York City and put him to work there. We hadn't quite figured out what the best position for him would be, and so far I'd just had him running what amounted to errands.

He hadn't shown any sign of minding, though. I got the impression he kind of liked getting to be a regular gang member out on the street, kicking butt and taking names, after all his years keeping up appearances by his father's side.

"All's well?" I asked.

Beckett shrugged, a glint of amusement dancing in his eyes. "I ran into some punk who was claiming that Wylder Noble is the only real power in the Bend and you just follow his orders. So I kicked his ass and informed him that those were my orders from you."

The other two guys cracked up, Sam clapping Beckett on the shoulder. "Good work, kid."

I tipped my head. "If anyone does more than just

shoot their mouth off, let me know and maybe I'll make a personal visit to set a few things straight."

Beckett laughed. "I don't think it'll come to that."

The guys headed out. I checked the time and followed them. It was getting late, but I had one more thing to take care of before I turned to my other business of the night. I had a task ahead of me that'd been a long time coming.

Stopping in my bedroom, I picked up one of the urns I'd finally been able to collect from the coroner's office. I'd already scattered the other ashes in my relatives' favorite spots, saying a private good-bye. This final one, I carried downstairs.

Jenner met me in the hall. "Everything's ready."

"Good." As we tramped down to the basement, I glanced over at him. "How's Sarah doing?" After the chaos had died down, he'd brought her with him to his old house, since her mom had never turned back up. I wasn't sure he'd have handed Sarah over to her mother anyway after the way the woman had abandoned her.

"Oh, she's great," he said with a chuckle. "Loving this year's teacher. I swear she's excited to go to school —definitely doesn't get that from me."

As we came into the basement, his expression turned more serious. A couple of other Claws men were already there next to a huge tub of mixed cement. Jenner walked over and gave it a careful stir.

"Are you sure about this?" he asked me. "You're tying him to this house forever."

"That's fine," I said, shifting the urn in my arms.

"The house is at least as much his as it is mine. But this is definitely the most fitting part of it to bury him in."

At my gesture, the other men heaved open the concrete slab that covered the pit where I'd spent so many tormented hours. I didn't shy away from the sight of the stains of blood and other bodily fluids that marked its base. A flicker of the old panic rose up in my chest, but I breathed through it.

Dad was gone. He would never shut me away in there again, and neither would anyone else. No one in the Claws would use that kind of torture under my rule —or ever again, if I had my way.

I opened the urn's lid and shook the gray dust of my father's ashes into the base of the pit. Then I helped Jenner heave the tub closer. Together, we poured the cement into the hollow. The gray sludge swallowed up my father's last remains and crept up the sides of the pit.

We had a little more than enough to fill it to the lip where the slab would sit. The other men shoved the slab back into place where it would bind with the new cement. Then Jenner sealed the edges with the last few dribbles from the tub. He smoothed the stuff out with a scraper, and just like that, the floor looked seamless, as if there'd never been anything cut out of it.

In the back of my mind, the distant echoes of a child screaming for help faded away. Both my father and the horrors of the past were truly buried.

"Thank you," I said to Jenner and the other men, and turned my back on my worst memories.

As I drove into Paradise City, my eyes caught on the distant spire of the waterfront development. Construction had started up again a few weeks ago, and they'd been making quick progress with the new plans, approved of and invested in by Evan Anderson. From the moment he'd left the hospital, Rowan had gotten to work coordinating with the real estate guru, and more modern office complexes and condo buildings were in the works on Noble-owned property throughout Paradise Bend and where Ezra had started to expand throughout the state.

If the Storm was pissed off that we'd nabbed one of his business associates as well as his son, he hadn't dared to complain.

Anderson wasn't the only new alliance we'd formed. We'd heard from the Long Night a couple of times since the Storm's departure, once to congratulate us and assure us of his continued support of our leadership, and once to connect us with a construction company looking for new contracts that he'd thought might be a good fit. I still wasn't sure exactly how he took his cut of the profits we brought in, but I was resigned to not knowing.

As long as he didn't mess with Paradise Bend, I could live and let live.

When I reached the Noble mansion, instead of pulling into the front drive, I parked the car a little way down the street and scaled the side wall. No one would have stopped me from walking in the front door, but arriving this way was more fun.

I sneaked between the trees to avoid detection, clambered up to the lowest level of the fire escape using a window ledge and a decorative ridge for help, and climbed the rest of the way up the metal structure to the room that was now my honorary guest bedroom in the house.

I slipped through the window to find I wasn't alone.

"You're late," Kaige declared, getting up from where he'd been lounging on the massive bed.

I rolled my eyes. "I wasn't supposed to be here in the first place."

Kaige smiled impishly. "But I was hoping you'd show up tonight." He hooked a finger around the loop of my jeans and pulled me closer. I put my arms around him and grinned.

The door opened, and Gideon came in, just putting his phone in his pocket. He tsked his tongue at me. "No matter how stealthy you get, that alarm is still going to go off."

"Who says I want to avoid it?" I said, leaning over to invite a kiss from him. "It told you I was here, and that's exactly what I wanted."

Gideon caught my mouth with his in answer. The flick of his tongue and the cool pressure of his lip ring combined with Kaige's solid arms around me had me wet in an instant.

"You've been busy," Gideon said when he stepped back. "Still keeping everyone in line down in the Bend?"

"There's always something going on, but I find ways

of dealing with whatever comes up. And I can always squeeze in some time to drop in on my favorite boys."

As if summoned by those words, Wylder and Rowan stepped into the room, Wylder locking the door behind them. My heart still fluttered seeing Rowan walking so steadily, the crutch he'd needed for a few weeks after his hospital stay long gone.

"Glad you stopped by," Wylder said with a smirk. "I had to get in touch anyway. Rowan and I are just working out the details of a deal with Anderson. We're having dinner with him tomorrow, and he wants you to be there too."

I flopped down on the silky comforter draped across the bed. "I think I can fit that into my schedule. What are we building this time?"

"Some kind of entertainment center," Rowan said. "Movies, games, the whole shebang. I think it'll be really good for the county."

I laughed. "The more we can keep people entertained with things that don't involve guns or drugs, the better."

"I absolutely agree," Kaige put in.

Wylder came over, and the brawny guy let his boss tug me out of his embrace. Wylder brought one hand to my cheek and the other to my waist, dipping his head to capture my mouth.

He kissed me only at the edge of my lips, teasing me. Impatiently, I turned to face him fully and deepened the kiss. His tongue caressed my lips before coaxing its way inside.

I murmured encouragingly and slid my hands up his

chest to loop them around his shoulders. Wylder pulled me over closer so our bodies were flush against each other. I could feel the others' eyes on us as their boss devoured my mouth, but there was no jealousy in any of those gazes, only a growing heat.

Wylder ground his hips into me insistently, his rapidly hardening cock pressing against my core. A groan escaped me at the promise of pleasure in that motion. Our kiss turned open-mouthed, our tongues tangling together, sloppy and glorious.

The others didn't stand back for long. Rowan's hands skimmed my back and kneaded my ass. He stepped in so I was sandwiched between the two of them. When he teased his fingers along my jaw, I broke my kiss with Wylder to turn toward him.

Lust hazed his dark blue eyes. He closed them before leaning in to steal a kiss of his own.

As our mouths crashed together, Wylder didn't let go of me. His fingers pinched my nipples through my shirt, making me gasp against Rowan's lips. If my panties hadn't been soaked before, they definitely were now.

As I kissed Rowan harder, Wylder continued to work over my breasts until my nipples were hard nubs, sparking with every touch. Then he bent down to suck them through the thin cotton of my shirt.

Gideon and Kaige came up on either side of me. Gideon slipped his hand between me and Wylder to undo the fly of my jeans. Kaige took it upon himself to tug up my shirt. The other guys eased back for just long enough for him to pull the tee right off me.

Gideon eased down my jeans, and Rowan took the opportunity to unclasp my bra. I let that drop to the floor too, standing before my men in nothing but my panties. Their eager gazes roamed over my naked skin, trailing heat in their wake without even touching me.

"You're a goddess, Mercy," Kaige murmured. The men surrounded me, and I relaxed into their combined embrace. They could do whatever they wanted to, and I'd enjoy being along for the ride.

I slipped my hands into Kaige's thick hair and kissed him, my naked breasts grazing his chest. Kaige put his arms around me and pulled me tight against him. My hands slipped down his muscular frame until I could squeeze his cock through his jeans. He groaned, his hands stroking over me even more urgently. His fingers slipped into my panties, and he curled a finger along the length of my slit.

I closed my eyes, resting my head on his shoulder as his finger continued to fuck me. The other three watched us in rapt attention. Wylder was stroking his cock through his jeans as he took in the sight.

Gideon and Rowan unzipped their slacks in unison, wicked smiles curling their lips. The idea couldn't be clearer. I eased back, letting Kaige step out of the confines of his pants. The rest did too, the sound of heavy breathing and zippers coming undone raising the tingle of anticipation in the air.

I knelt on the ground while the boys circled me, slowly peeling their underwear off until four beautiful and hard cocks sprang out of their respective confines. My mouth watered at the sight.

I reached for Gideon's first, wrapping my tongue around the base and tasting his precum before sliding up. I kept my eyes on him while my mouth greedily engulfed his cock. His hands rested on my shoulders, but he didn't move, letting me work on his shaft. I bobbed my head as I swallowed his length whole before letting it slip out of my mouth. The others pressed close with eager impatience.

Kaige wasn't as sweet as Gideon. As soon as I wrapped my tongue around his cock, he put his hands at the back of my head and rolled his hips so that my mouth was stuffed with his cock. I moaned in the back of my throat as I swallowed him down, squeezing his balls at the same time.

When Kaige's grip on me loosened, I moved to Wylder next. I teased him a little, flicking my tongue around the piercing at the head of his cock before sucking it into my mouth. Not to leave Rowan out of the fun, I grabbed for him too, alternating between sucking their cocks.

Drool trickled down my chin, but I didn't care, licking their shafts and swirling my tongue around them. All of them were panting now, the smell of arousal heavy in the air. My pussy was outright gushing.

I pulled back and gave them all a satisfied smirk. Kaige growled, and before I knew what was happening, he swung me up over his shoulder and carried me to the bed.

I landed with a thump on it. I pushed myself toward the headboard as I watched the boys divest themselves of their shirts. Their glorious tattoos came into view on their chests and arms. I had the urge to lick every single stroke of art.

Kaige crawled toward me and spread my legs wide. Before I could react, he dove into my sopping wet cunt. His tongue licked up and down the length of my slit before flicking around my clit. My back almost arched off the bed at the waves of bliss rushing through me.

The others climbed onto the bed with us. Wylder leaned in and brought his mouth to my breast, suckling it hard while Rowan took the other. Their teeth grazed the sensitive skin of my nipples.

Gideon climbed up near my mouth and kissed me. The sensation of being pleasured at all the sensitive areas of my body overwhelmed me. My eyes rolled back, my hips swaying to meet Kaige's skillful tongue.

The heat of their bodies consumed me like a furnace. I whimpered and keened, letting these wicked men ravage me.

Kaige continued to lick and suckle my clit. The force of an orgasm blazed through me faster than lightning. I screamed as my body bowed upward. My pussy continued throbbing as Kaige pulled away, and the unmistaken sound of foil being ripped open reached my ears.

Before I could recover from my orgasm, Rowan flipped me on my stomach and dragged me toward him. Sometimes he was still the gentle boy-next-door with me, but he knew I liked him fierce just as much. Pulling me up on my knees, he knelt behind me and thrust into me from behind.

I gasped at the feel of his hard cock stretching my

walls. The remains of my earlier orgasm made my pussy even more sensitive, pleasure shooting through me as Rowan continued to stroke in and out of me. He rocked his hips into me before pulling out and slamming home.

Rowan groaned, and I moaned right alongside him. My pussy clenched around his cock almost viciously and before long, I felt him jerk inside me. My body shook as my second orgasm of the night tore through me.

Wylder replaced Rowan in seconds. He turned me onto my back again. I watched him, my eyes at half-mast as he nudged my thighs apart and rubbed the head of his cock over my entrance. The slide of his piercing against my clit made my hips twitch and propelled another moan from my throat.

My legs lifted, embracing his hips to bring him closer. He braced himself over me, his hands bracketing my face as he stroked his way inside. Our bodies jerked together as he stroked in and out of me. Wylder's eyes closed as he continued to fuck me, hard and fast before switching to shallow but slower strokes.

Kaige watched us, lust scorching in his eyes as he stroked his cock. "Let me have my fun now."

Wylder didn't move right away but gave enough space for Kaige to come up beside me. Kaige's fingers skimmed over my heaving tits and swirled down to my stomach before he pressed his palm against my sensitive clit.

Wylder pulled back to give Kaige a turn. The bigger man settled between my thighs and drove his thick cock into me. My wet pussy welcomed his girth with barely any resistance.

Kaige knew just how to pound me to my next peak, gripping my hips and finding just the right angle. He was already almost there too. The second I squeezed around him with another earth-shattering orgasm, he followed me over the edge with a little shout.

Wylder pulled me back to him, rolling over so I was straddling him. As I happily sank down over his cock, his gaze slid past me to Gideon. "Aren't you going to get in here? Haven't you been doing all that 'research' on ideal positions for sharing?"

A hint of a blush colored the tech genius's cheeks. He was always the most adorable when he got awkward. "I *have* found some interesting options. And I made sure to be prepared." He opened the drawer on the bedside table and drew out a small tube. "This lubricant has a warming effect."

I grinned at him. "I think I'm pretty warmed up already."

"Not everywhere." With Wylder's cock still buried inside me, Gideon teased his fingers down my spine to my ass, letting them graze my other opening. "I'd like to take you from behind this time. Both of us, together."

A giddy giggle tumbled out of me. "What are you waiting for, then?"

Gideon's gaze heated. He squeezed some of the lube onto his fingers and massaged it over the pucker of my asshole, his finger occasionally slipping right inside. True to his promise, a pleasantly hot sensation spread over my skin, relaxing my muscles faster than ever before.

I rocked over Wylder, taking him deeper inside my

cunt and swaying into Gideon's touch. Gideon knelt behind me and rubbed his cock over my ass. When I shook my butt side to side, he slapped me. "Steady," he warned.

Somehow, the bossy tone of his voice turned me on even more. I waited with bated breath as he slid inside of me, slowly at first before pulling out. The feeling of being doubly filled was as intoxicating as ever. Gideon pushed into me again, going halfway. On the next try, he was almost completely in.

I held in a breath as I felt his length invade me alongside Wylder's. Rowan bent his head to lap the tip of my breast into his mouth, and Kaige stole a kiss, and just like that, I was completely surrounded in the headiest of pleasures.

"What do you want Mercy?" Wylder murmured in the most seductive tone I'd ever heard.

"I want you both to fuck me," I managed to get out.

Both men obliged by bucking into me. They gradually picked up their pace as they matched each other's rhythm. I whimpered as the pleasure unfurled through me, wrapping all the way around my bones.

Gideon's breath came in short rasps behind me, his sweat-slick chest smacking against my back. Wylder rocked up to meet me, his gaze holding mine with nothing but desire and love in it.

"Our woman," he said in a raw voice. "So fucking amazing."

"Damn right, she is," Kaige said, watching us with avid eyes.

Gideon came first, arching over me with a sputtered

groan. With the last slowing pumps of his cock inside me, Wylder thrust into me even harder, and I shattered all over again. My body sagged over him, and he spent himself inside me with a hitch of his chest.

I settled onto the bedspread on my back, and my men tucked themselves around me, all of us perfectly sated. Our sweaty limbs tangled with each other until I was completely cocooned between them. The smell of sex still hung thickly in the air.

I let out a yawn, cuddling closer to them as sleep crept up over me. Being queen was pretty fucking sweet, if I did say so myself. My father might even have been proud of me if he'd gotten to see how well I'd taken charge of the Claws and the powerful alliance I'd made with the Nobles, both in bed and out.

Well, no, he probably wouldn't have been proud, because I still wouldn't have been what he'd wanted— but he *should* have been proud. It didn't matter to me anyway. *I* was proud of both myself and my men, and that was all I needed.

We'd fought for the lives we wanted and won, and no ghosts of the past could steal away the brilliant future we were making for ourselves.

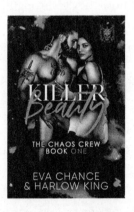

Killer Beauty (The Chaos Crew #1)

I'm the girl you'll never see coming.

Blink and you're dead, another target checked off my list.

But one night everything in my carefully ordered existence falls apart. A bloodbath and a car crash later, I find myself in the grasp of four gorgeous, intimidating men.

Are my captors cops like they claim or something far more sinister? They sure know how to bend the law. And seeing how skillfully they handle a gun or a knife, I can't help wondering what their hands would feel like all over me.

But I have vengeance to wreak, and no man, no matter how powerful, is going to keep me caged for long.

They think they've caught a wounded little mouse. How could they know they've brought a killer into their home?

I'll bide my time, learn all I can, and when I'm ready to strike...

They'll never know what hit them.

Killer Beauty is the first in a new gritty contemporary romance series from bestselling author Eva Chase (writing as Eva Chance) and Harlow King. No major triggers, just hot murderously-inclined men, a deadly heroine out for revenge, and an enemies-to-lovers romance where the girl gets all the guys. Prepare for total bloody chaos!

ABOUT THE AUTHORS

Eva Chance is a pen name for contemporary romance written by Amazon top 100 bestselling author Eva Chase. If you love gritty romance, dominant men, and fierce women who never have to choose, look no further.

Eva lives in Canada with her family. She loves stories both swoony and supernatural, and strong women and the men who appreciate them.

Connect with Eva online:
www.evachase.com
eva@evachase.com

Harlow King is a long-time fan of all things dark, edgy, and steamy. She can't wait to share her contemporary reverse harem stories.

Printed in Great Britain
by Amazon

34067952R00185